LIE IN THE TIDE

Also by Holly Danvers

The Lakeside Library mysteries

MURDER AT THE LAKESIDE LIBRARY
LONG OVERDUE AT THE LAKESIDE LIBRARY
READ TO DEATH AT THE LAKESIDE LIBRARY

The Handcrafted mysteries (written as Holly Quinn)

A CRAFTER KNITS A CLUE
A CRAFTER HOOKS A KILLER
A CRAFTER QUILTS A CRIME

The Mainely Murder mysteries (written as Sherry Lynn)

DIGGING UP DAISY
MURDER UNDER THE MISTLETOE

LIE IN THE TIDE

Holly Danvers

SEVERN HOUSE

First world edition published in Great Britain and the USA in 2025
by Severn House, an imprint of Canongate Books Ltd,
14 High Street, Edinburgh EH1 1TE.

severnhouse.com

Copyright © Sherry Rummler, 2025

Cover and jacket design by Jem Butcher Design

All rights reserved including the right of reproduction in whole or in part in any form. The right of Sherry Rummler to be identified as the author of this work has been assertedin accordance with the Copyright, Designs & Patents Act 1988.

British Library Cataloguing-in-Publication Data

A CIP catalogue record for this title is available from the British Library.

ISBN-13: 978-1-4483-1598-7 (cased)
ISBN-13: 978-1-4483-1668-7 (e-book)

This is a work of fiction. Names, characters, places and incidents are either the product of the author's imagination or are used fictitiously. Except where actual historical events and characters are being described for the storyline of this novel, all situations in this publication are fictitious and any resemblance to actual persons, living or dead, business establishments, events or locales is purely coincidental.

No part of this book may be used or reproduced in any manner for the purpose of training artificial intelligence technologies or systems. This work is reserved from text and data mining (Article 4(3) Directive (EU) 2019/790).

All Severn House titles are printed on acid-free paper.

Typeset by Palimpsest Book Production Ltd.,
Falkirk, Stirlingshire, Scotland.
Printed and bound in Great Britain by
TJ Books, Padstow, Cornwall.

The manufacturer's authorised representative in the EU for product safety is Authorised Rep Compliance Ltd, 71 Lower Baggot Street, Dublin D02 P593 Ireland (arccompliance.com)

Praise for Holly Danvers

"With perfectly drawn characters and edge-of-your-seat suspense, *Lie in the Tide* will sweep you away. Don't miss this one!"
Paige Shelton, *New York Times* bestselling author

"Perfect for fans of Agatha Christie, Lucy Foley, and Liane Moriarty, *Lie in the Tide* weaves together flawed, relatable characters and escalating suspense . . . Holly Danvers has crafted a clever, compelling page turner that will keep you guessing until the final pages. My favorite book this year!"
Edgar Award finalist and award-winning author, Tracy Gardner

"*Lie in the Tide* is a wild ride that kept me guessing right until the very end. Secrets, lies, and old friendships combine for a juicy read with a supremely satisfying conclusion"
Liz Alterman, author of *The House on Cold Creek Lane*

"Plot twists, warm relationships . . . and the vividly described setting all distinguish this satisfying cozy"
Booklist on *Murder at the Lakeside Library*

"The perfect start to a new cozy series . . . Well-paced and plotted"
Fresh Fiction on *Murder at the Lakeside Library*

"*Murder at the Lakeside Library* has delightful touches and twists with a nimble plot that will keep you turning the pages until the very end"
Denise Swanson, *New York Times* bestselling author

"Danvers' writing is good; she brings the reader right into the story through her description and use of tension"
New York Journal of Books on *Long Overdue at the Lakeside Library*

"A fast-paced, enjoyable read"
Seattle Book Review on *Long Overdue at the Lakeside Library*

About the author

Holly Danvers grew up devouring every mystery novel on the shelf of her local library. Previously, she has penned multiple cozy mystery series under numerous pseudonyms. *Lie in the Tide* is her first thriller.

www.authorhollydanvers.com

To Sandy, for believing in me and taking a chance.

They found her motionless. Her nose smothered in the sand. Her right eye was as vacant as frosted sea glass. Her skin translucent, akin to a jellyfish. The surf had tangled her hair like a mass of unwanted kelp in which the ocean had rudely regurgitated. Despite the sun burning overhead, she was frozen to the touch, her lips as dark as the Atlantic. The waves crashed atop her lifeless body as if she were an abandoned piece of driftwood, smacking her with each additional roll of the tide.

A guttural screech erupted from one of them.

There was no mistaking it.

A friend was dead.

*– Excerpt from KILLER BEACH
written by bestselling author Mori Hart*

ONE

Calista

Calista Moore studied the reflection in the mirror staring back at her. Her features remained the same, but everything inside of Calista was different. She was acutely aware that nothing of her life would continue as it was.

Not the brick house, which for the last eighteen years had been the gathering place for family, friends, teenagers. You know the one – everybody knows it. The rambling ranch tucked into the wooded lot with the meticulous lawn lined by deep blue hydrangea. The one where the flowers follow the slate path all the way to the front door, come summer. The garden which Calista had designed and planted with her own two hands. Kirk hadn't helped that day. Somehow, he fails to remember that important detail when visitors wow and ogle the blooming display. And her husband certainly doesn't remember how much convincing he needed at the garden center to purchase them. Instead, what resulted was a downright argument amid the hanging baskets of blood-red begonia and blue lobelia, when she'd stood her ground. Funny how life was like that. Arguing over things that didn't matter. In Calista's opinion, deeper-rooted issues caused senseless arguments to erupt between them at a moment's notice. It had only been the tip of the iceberg.

Her house.

The popular one.

The one in which they'd hosted neighborhood potlucks, too numerous to count.

Calista's *home*.

The refuge she'd meticulously refurbished with monochromatic flair and gleaming hardwood floors on the quiet cul-de-sac in the suburbs of New England was no longer a comforting place to wind down after a long day at work. All the effort and hours she'd labored into creating the perfect home had been futile.

It would be sold.

Calista's beloved job, as a high school English teacher, would likely change too. If it were up to her, she would leave the country altogether and head to Italy where she once dreamed of fleeing in her younger years. If it were only that easy. To go back. A chance at a do-over.

Despite a death-grip hold on the image in front of her, nothing would ever be the same. The stark realization of what was soon to come almost left her breathless.

Calista spun a strand of hair between her fingers. The dark roots of her tinted auburn curls needed color. Perhaps a honey brown? If only she could change the thick rings that surrounded her translucent jade eyes like a rabid raccoon. But given the stress, those would remain.

Could it be as simple as a variation in hair color or a change of her name to just disappear from her life? *Calista*. Meaning *most beautiful*. What a joke. She didn't feel the least bit beautiful as she ran a hand across the bruise left on her right cheek. She had deserved that too. Every inch of black and blue was earned. But her skillfully applied makeup covered where it lay. If she could only crawl into the woodwork and hide, where she could remain – forever.

News would certainly come out into the open; her reputation at Natick High School would be tainted. There would be whispering in the hallways upon her return to the classroom, come fall. Calista's mind had deftly skipped to this foreseen future on numerous occasions to watch it all unfold, rapid fire, before her own eyes. She gripped the sides of the bathroom counter, to steady herself from a sudden rush of vertigo.

There was no way to stop it now. Things were already in motion. The rolling on of her life, like a freight train that she desperately wanted to halt, was already leaping the tracks to fast forward. Nothing would remain.

Every brick.

Of her methodically arranged life.

Would crumble.

Change hadn't been something Calista accepted willingly. But it was as if fate had stepped in and made up its mind on her behalf. So long had she held on tight to *the secret*. To the point that *it* was no longer real – *it* was fiction. Just something she'd scrupulously scripted like a screenplay in a book she'd hoped to pen someday. Time had ticked away, growing faster with each subsequent year, suppressing the secret deeper into her soul. Holding *it* down so tight that she wondered how *it* hadn't made her physically ill or, worse, killed her.

Calista's hair, now caught by the sunlight streaming through the bathroom window, caused her to peer deeper into the mirror. She thought she'd caught a glimmer of grey. But thankfully, it was just a highlight from the mirror shining back at her. It wouldn't be outside the realm of possibility for her hair to turn. After all, her own mother had gone grey prematurely. And her personal calendar had recently flipped to forty, so there was that. She wondered how long her girlish figure would last. At five foot three, from the backend, she could easily pass for a teenager and would often turn to a surprised whistler, while taking a jog down her block.

Her thoughts were interrupted by a hard knock on the bathroom door.

'Mom, you almost done in there? I gotta get to work.' The sound of her son's voice carried through the hollow door between them.

Calista did a doubletake to see if the bruise was completely covered before capping the makeup and tossing it into her cosmetic bag. She then opened the door and greeted her son, Devon, with a smile.

'You ready for your big trip?' Devon folded his arms across his broad chest and leaned his weight on the door casing as he watched his mother collect her things, before following her into the master bedroom.

Calista tossed the cosmetic bag into the suitcase that lay open on the bed, already filled with stacks of t-shirts and tank tops. She added a few swimsuits just in case she cared to cleanse herself in the cold Atlantic. Perhaps an icy baptism would right everything in her world.

'Honestly, Dev, I don't know how I feel about the trip,' she said finally after tucking the swimsuits neatly inside the suitcase. She then sank to the corner of the bed and cradled her head in her hands, wishing to disappear.

'Whaddaya mean? You haven't seen your friends . . . in what has it been? Twenty years, or something like that? Dad told me he worked hard on this surprise for your fortieth, all on his own. Coordinating your friends' schedules in a short amount of time was not easy. Believe me!' Devon's eyes rolled. The eye-roll Calista had come to make peace with, since her boy had grown past a gangly teenager.

'It's complicated,' Calista said quietly.

'What's complicated about it? Moriah Hart handled everything for you, right down to your Airbnb on the Cape. Dad and I thought it would be the motherload of gifts. Hell! It's right on the beach!' he defended.

'Watch your language, young man. You're still not too old to be grounded, you know,' Calista teased, mimicking her teacherly undertone while standing on her tiptoes to bop him on the nose. She knew her correction would fall on deaf ears. And she was right, as he ignored her warning completely with a needless shrug. Calista removed a few t-shirts from the suitcase and re-rolled them before tucking them neatly back inside. There. That was better. Hopefully, that would protect the shirts from unsightly wrinkles. At least that was one thing she could control.

'I don't understand why you're not over the moon about it,' he continued. 'Or why you've been acting so depressed lately. When you have everything in the world going for you.' Devon held his hands firmly on his hips, and his golden eyes searched her face for an explanation. Her son's hair, a darker shade than her own, was set upright off his forehead with gel, and it looked as if his jaw could use a shave. Calista couldn't understand how quickly Devon had grown from a toddler who ran between her legs to a man who now towered over her. She turned completely away from the suitcase and reached for her son's hands.

'I *am* excited, and I appreciate all you've done to help make this happen. A little trepidation is normal, I think. We haven't spent time together in so long. I guess I just want it to go well.' She bit her tongue and held back the elephant in the room. The elephant that was the reason she was making this trip in the first place. And the *real* reason, unbeknownst to her son, that her husband – *his father* – was forcing this trip upon her.

Devon's gaze studied her. And his hands refused to drop hers, but he didn't utter a word. He just waited with his brow creased in deep concern. It was as if he'd finally given up on trying to sway her mood.

'You know I love you, right, Dev? You've always been the apple of my eye. The best son a mother could ask for.'

'Yeah, Mom, I know. Since I'm your *only* child, it's kinda easy to claim that honor. Unless, of course, you count all the students who've been in your classroom over the years – then, I guess there's a little competition.' Devon shared a lopsided grin and gave his mother's hands a squeeze, before releasing them and encasing her in a bear hug. 'It's gonna be fun for you . . . I promise,' he whispered in her ear.

Calista felt the strength in her son's arms, but unfortunately the encouraging words fell flat. At twenty-two years old, he had grown almost a foot above her, and suddenly, she felt quite small. She held back a tear and cleared her throat.

'I'll miss you,' she said, holding him at arm's length.

'It's not like you'll be gone that long.' The infamous eye-roll was repeated. 'But I'll miss you too, Mom,' he said lightly.

Devon didn't know that the brief trip would change everything for him. No, he didn't know that yet.

But it would.

Life, as he knew it, would never be the same. And it was all her fault.

TWO

Remi

Remi Toussaint rolled her overloaded suitcase across the bedroom floor and down the wide-tiled floor, causing a click-clack sound to reverberate from the open-concept hallway. She was just about to drag it across the threshold when her husband dashed behind her with an outstretched hand.

'Hey there, lady! Hold up a sec!' Gabe protested.

Remi didn't stop on command. Instead, she proceeded to push open the door with her toe.

'Can't you just wait a minute?' he asked, gently moving her aside so he could grab the luggage handle in one effortless swing. 'Let me help you with that. I understand you're excited to see the girls, but you need to settle down a bit,' he added with a chuckle. 'We have plenty of time to make it to the airport. Unless, of course, we hit major traffic. But not to worry: we'll get you there.'

'I had it, Gabe. You don't need to fuss.' Remi laced her manicured fingers around her narrow hips and held them there while she defended herself with a raised brow.

'I know you did, honey,' he said with a wide devilish grin. It was the same grin that made her fall in love with him back when Calista had first introduced them after the three had landed in detention. Remi and Calista reported to detention due to excessive chatting in the hallway, causing them to be late for class on numerous occasions. Remi couldn't recall why Gabe had ended up in detention, only that, as a sophomore, she was introduced to another senior and from then on was welcomed into their friendship group. Despite Gabe's mousy receding hairline, he looked as handsome as ever. Back in high school, he was as thin as one of those skimboards she'd seen down at Daytona Beach on spring break. But now, his bulging biceps outmeasured most of the men she knew, and she was proud of how far he'd come.

Gabe pushed past her out the door. 'I know . . . You're a strong woman . . . you can carry your own luggage . . . Yadda yadda . . .' he trailed off as she followed him outside.

The sun was so brilliant Remi needed to tent her eyes the moment she stepped outdoors.

'Phew, it's going to be a hot one today. Are you sure you don't want to fly to Boston with me? Wouldn't you like to see Kirk? I don't think you've talked to him since that last ski trip the four of us went on. That was almost twenty years ago! Wouldn't it be nice to catch up?' she encouraged, pulling him close and taking in the scent of his sweat-soaked muscle shirt after he'd loaded her suitcase into the backseat of their Jeep.

'Don't tease me like that. You know I can't go. Who would work at the gym for us for an entire week?' He wiped a strand of her straight golden hair away from her face and brushed his thumb against her cheek tenderly while their eyes locked.

'I know. I'm sorry,' Remi pouted, leaning into him. 'I appreciate you letting me go and do this on short notice. It's only twenty years overdue,' she laughed easily. 'I honestly don't know how the years flew by so quickly!'

Remi and Gabe had built a thriving yoga studio/gym – Lean on the Matt – a mere mile from their house and rarely took time off. It was a lifestyle more than a job to them, and they often biked there on cooler days. But central Florida in the summer could be brutal. Remi had a sneaking suspicion Gabe would bike there while she was away, despite the growing heat.

'I'm going to miss those baby blues. But know you have my heart with you,' he said, tenderly fingering the heart-shaped diamond pendant around her neck that he'd given her, and which she swore she'd never remove. He then studied her as if he were looking directly into her soul. Gabe had a way of doing that. Making her feel as if she were the only woman who existed on the planet. He confirmed this further when he added, 'Speaking of babies . . . we'll have to plan a trip – just the two of us, because I'm guessing it's not going to be so easy soon.' His eyes then left hers and dropped to her stomach where he lay a soft protective hand on her abdomen.

Remi barely showed a bump. And honestly, it was all still surreal. They had tried for so long; she had completely given up the thought of ever becoming a mother. 'Do you think they'll notice?' She pushed back her shoulders and thrust her stomach deeper into his warm hand.

'Nah, I think you'll still be wearing a bikini on the beach. I sure wish I could be there for that.' He wagged his eyebrows animatedly. 'In fact, maybe I'll see if Rodney can work for us a day or two when you get back, and we'll plan that trip to Clearwater some weekend, like we talked about. How does that sound?'

'Sounds perfect,' she said with a wink, while he held the door for her to hop into the passenger seat before jogging around the front and joining her inside the vehicle. Remi immediately popped the glovebox to reveal their sunglasses and handed Gabe his, before they both slid them on, which was a mistake, because the heat of them almost burned her nose. Another reason to look forward to New England. Hopefully, it would be cooler on the Cape, closer to the ocean. She could almost smell the salt water just thinking of it.

As the Jeep rambled along, Remi asked, 'Do you think I should tell them? Due to the high risk, I'm not sure if I want to. I don't want to jinx it.' She sighed deeply and watched the palm trees roll past. 'Not to mention *how* this happened. It's not really something I want to explain. And you know they're going to ask.'

When Gabe didn't answer, she continued, 'Then the whole trip I'll have to answer questions on how I got pregnant. They all know about your accident and that it's completely outside the realm of possibility for you to father a child. I really don't want to have to explain the lengths we went to, and the unconventional method needed to create this little nugget,' she grunted. 'I'm not sure I'm ready for that conversation, to be honest.'

'So it's unorthodox – who cares? If they're really your friends, they'll understand. They won't judge us. And besides, it's no one's business but ours.' Gabe reached over and laced his fingers through hers. His gaze momentarily abandoned the windshield to encourage her with a look of deep comfort. 'I trust your judgment. If you want to keep it close to your heart, that's totally up to you. I haven't told a soul that you're pregnant, and I won't until you're ready.' He squeezed her hand before releasing it, as his other hand loosely held the steering wheel. 'Again, who cares how we did it? We did it!' he added gleefully. 'We're finally going to be parents!'

'True.' She smiled. 'That's what we need to focus on.'

'Seriously, Rem. Everybody has a secret,' he said evenly. '*Everybody*.'

'Right. No one needs to know the details.'

'That's correct. It's no one's business. So, if you're not comfortable sharing, don't.'

They stopped at an intersection, and Remi interrupted the sudden lull between them with a point of her finger. 'Did you want to stop for a smoothie?'

Tropic of Juice was directly in front of them, and cars filled the drive-thru lane and trailed like a long Florida snake around the parking lot. Remi chanced a nervous glance at the clock on the dashboard, secretly wondering if they even had time for the stop. Gabe must've caught her apprehension at the long line too, as he tapped a comforting hand on her arm. 'I'm good. And I know you don't like to eat much before flying. I packed two protein bars in your bag just in case you get hungry.'

Remi relaxed a little and gave a silent sigh of relief. 'Have I told you how much I love you?' She kissed his palm before he returned his hand to the steering wheel.

'I need no reminding. You show me every single day.' He winked and then changed the subject with a click of his tongue. 'So, who are you most looking forward to seeing after all these years? Calista? Avery? Or Moriah? Inquiring minds want to know.'

'Are you actually asking me to pick a favorite from my old friend group?' she said with a laugh.

'It's been so long; you must be stoked!'

Remi hesitated. 'It's a bit surreal if I'm being honest. I can't believe we'll physically be gathered in one beach house today. I hope it's big enough to handle all our personalities,' she laughed easily.

'So . . . is it Calista? You guys were tight back then. And honestly, if it weren't for you making the varsity cheerleading squad and Calista taking you under her wing, we might've never met,' he reminded her with a raised brow. 'I mean, you were the only sophomore allowed in our group. You kinda owe Calista your life with me.'

'I guess I do, don't I?' She smiled.

'Yeah, you do!'

Remi turned in her seat to face him and eyed him carefully. 'You never had a thing for Calista? I find that weird – she was like the prettiest girl in your class. *Everyone* liked her. At least, you never admitted it to me. If I recall, you asked her out once, didn't you? One of those rare moments when she was in between boyfriends. Before she started dating Kirk?'

'No,' he laughed, 'it wasn't like that. The neighborhood kids all hung out together back then. We were just friends. Besides, her parents were super strict. They didn't allow her to date until she was seventeen, even though she snuck around and did it anyway. They never knew she was dating Kirk until they were practically married.'

'Uh-huh.'

'We were friends of convenience more than anything because her house was a stone's throw from mine. We probably wouldn't have hung out otherwise,' he continued. 'Besides, Kirk made the football team, so her eyes landed on him.'

'Huh. I still don't believe you,' she teased. 'I think you secretly had a crush on her.'

'Believe what you want to believe,' Gabe said easily. 'I just think it's excellent that you're getting this chance reunion.'

'It's bizarre really. The only thing we know about each other now is what we see on social media. I mean, I can't even remember the last time I talked to any one of them on the phone. It's like I'm going on a trip with complete strangers. Hopefully, we'll all fall back into our groove once we reconnect and get past the formality of it all.' Remi chewed on her cheek nervously and added, 'If only I could have a White Claw to take the edge off the first night.'

'That's also up to you, honey. If you need it, go for it.'

'No way. I'm not taking that chance. We worked way too hard to get here.' She laid a protective hand over her abdomen and held it there. 'Not so for Avery, though, I think she has three or four kids now!'

'Right? She's been popping babies out since the ink was barely dry on our high school diploma. Can you imagine Avery growing rows of corn in Iowa? I thought she'd grow up to be a vet or something like that. I don't think we're even friends on Facebook.'

'I don't think Avery is on Facebook much. More on Instagram. She posts a lot of nature pics.'

'Ah, that explains it, then.'

'Out of all of us, she barely posts. I know the least about where life has taken Avery.'

'What a blast from the past this is going to be.' He shook his head in amusement. 'I wish I could be a fly on the wall to see for myself if any of them has changed, and if you'll all revert to your old ways, like the good ol' days. Who are you most interested in reconnecting with?'

'OK, if I must play this game.' Remi leaned in and whispered conspiratorially, 'Since it's just between us.'

'I promise, I'll never tell a soul,' he promised, with a zip of his lips.

'If you're forcing me to pick, I think I'd have to say Moriah. Out of all of us, she has the most glamorous life. She lives on the Vineyard and writes erotica novels. Who of us can top that? We can't even afford to vacation on Martha's Vineyard, never mind live there! I'm dying to talk to her in person to see what it's really like being famous. I hope she's transparent. She could be a little close-lipped back in the day. I wonder if that's changed since her life is so . . . well, you know . . . out there.'

'Wow. That kinda surprises me. I thought for sure you'd pick Calista. You two were joined at the hip in high school. Besties, right? I really had her pegged as your choice. Honestly, I was surprised you two didn't keep in touch all these years. I know we've been busy building the business, and the miles between you doesn't help but . . . we should've made time.'

'Yeah, it's certainly true that Calista and I grew close back then. It seems via her Facebook page that she hasn't changed much. She's still living a very ordinary, organized life, and doting on Devon every chance she gets. Did you know she had someone come into her house and put those organizers in all her closets and label them with a label maker? She posted that once. I wish I planned for things, but alas, here I am, going on a last-minute trip with friends I haven't connected with in decades!'

'Ah, that reminds me. I picked up something for you the other day. Knowing how little you like to fly.' Gabe reached a long arm behind her seat and hauled out a bag and dropped it in her lap.

'What's this?' Remi asked, reaching into the bag to unveil the surprise.

'I wanted you to catch up on reading Moriah's stuff before you see her. You claim you never have enough time. Well, now you do. You can put a dent in it on your flight, or, on the off chance you get stuck on the layover in Chicago, at least you'll have something to read.'

Remi pulled out Moriah's latest novel and squealed with delight. 'Why didn't I think of this?' She held the novel to her heart before eagerly scanning the cover. The name Mori Hart was splashed across it along with a steamy photo of a gorgeous-looking couple tangled in each other's arms. Mori Hart was Moriah's penname, and Remi couldn't help but run her fingers over it in admiration.

'Are you surprised?'

'Am I ever! Although maybe you should have bought me a Kindle. I'm not sure I'm comfortable with people gawking at me while I'm reading smut in the airport,' she admitted easily, pointing out the cover.

'Just think of me when you read it,' he said, nudging her.

Remi brushed him off playfully with her hand. 'That'll only make me miss you more.' Her demeanor then morphed to serious. 'You didn't read it, did you?' She often headed to bed long before her night-owl husband.

'Are you kidding me? Not a chance! However, by the look of that cover, it looks kinda racy. Maybe I should've read it. I might've boned up on some ideas.' Gabe laughed heartily. 'Although I find that rather unlikely,' he continued. 'When I think of the freckle-faced Moriah who *I* remember from back in the day, it's hard to imagine the writer who now is known as Mori Hart,' he intoned with dramatic undertones. 'I guarantee, no one pegged that she'd be writing smut someday! If so, she would've been a lot more popular with dudes back then. If you know what I mean.'

'Oh boy,' Remi grunted. 'This conversation is heading in the wrong direction, fast.' More out of curiosity's sake than actual content, she could hardly wait to read it to see what led her old friend to hit the bestseller list time and time again. She found it utterly amazing. It was true, Remi wasn't much of a reader; it was more of a time issue for her. Running their own business left little time for frivolities. It didn't matter – she wanted to find out what the hype was all about and what had led to her friend's fame. She was now thrilled by the opportunity the plane ride would provide.

'Check out her author photo inside the sleeve,' Gabe directed. 'She doesn't even look like the same person.'

'This is a really nice picture of her.' Remi smiled. 'I can't believe I'm doing this and I'm going to see her tonight!' she gushed. 'This is so crazy!'

'You should've done this ten years ago. Heck, Rem, sometimes I feel like we're still in high school. Where did the time go?'

'And sometimes you act like it too,' she teased with an eye-roll.

Gabe replied with a grunt.

When they arrived at the airport, Remi couldn't determine if it was nerves or the baby causing butterflies to suddenly erupt inside her stomach. It had been quite a while since she'd seen the gang, and she'd been looking forward to it. But now as she was leaving her comfort zone, suddenly she felt gun-shy. Remi hadn't been apart from Gabe since the opening of their business, fifteen years prior. She hardly knew what it was like to be apart from him anymore. And she didn't like the feeling as she kissed him and waved goodbye.

THREE

Avery

'You all better behave while I'm gone. No funny business, you hear?' Avery Williams muttered to the cows. The animals only looked back at her with a blank expression as if she made no sense whatsoever. She brushed the dirt from the knees of her jeans before bidding them adieu and exiting the barn.

'Mom, hurry!' Avery's son, Ike, was anxiously waiting behind the wheel of her Ford pick-up truck, hanging out the driver's side window.

Avery held up a finger. 'Hang on a minute, I've got to go and say one last goodbye to your dad.'

'*Again?* You're gonna be late! There's probably traffic in Cedar Rapids. Don't get mad at me if you miss your flight,' he hollered in singsong fashion before turning up the radio to the point the truck vibrated bass and shook like a mechanical bull.

If only Avery could be so lucky. She wasn't sure how she got talked into this trip in the first place. It seemed like a good idea at the time, but now, with Ike only a month into obtaining his driver's license and needing to be discouraged from hauling kids around in the car, Mandy hoping to win a blue ribbon at the county fair showing her steer, and Jackson . . . well, he was so little and still needed his mama. Jackson's asthma seemed out of control lately, and someone needed to get to the pharmacy to refill his inhaler. Not only that, but Owen was off with his girlfriend looking at engagement rings. To be honest, she didn't want to think about that. Not even a little bit. At least the young couple hadn't picked a date yet. Would grandchildren soon be in her future while she was still raising her own kids?

Time was rushing too fast for Avery. And these precious moments would never come back again, she thought as she watched her daughter, Mandy, pick up a stray cat out in the field and cuddle it close to her neck. She wanted to commit it all to memory. Sooner than later, they'd be memories lost, like a tucked-away photograph catching dust inside a bin beneath the bed.

Avery turned and glanced past the vibrating truck out to the rows of knee-high corn and watched the stalks swaying in the wind. Knee-high on the fourth of July meant the corn was right on schedule. Unlike last year, at least the crop was on target. Hopefully, no tornadoes would blow through while she was gone and destroy it all.

'*Mom!*'

'Fine! I'm going, I'm going!' she muttered before rushing past the truck and hurrying up the farm porch steps, almost catching her foot in the crack in the wood again – the wooden step that needed to be fixed. 'See,' Avery voiced to herself. She didn't have time for this trip.

Besides, what on earth did she have in common with these people anymore anyway? They all had long-standing careers. She was a stay-at-home mom/farmwife/cook/money manager/master gardener/carpool coordinator/PTA president. The list dragged on. Though, she assumed in their eyes, it was not the same thing as a nine-to-five job with a hefty paycheck. They also didn't know her recent predicament. *No one did* – not even her husband and kids. She would keep that information tucked close to her chest until she returned home. And be forced to deal with it then.

The world around her failed to understand how fleeting time was. She was now acutely aware of it, though. The doctor reminded her of that on her last visit. There would be a learning curve. She needed to get her affairs in order. Her life was about to change. Her farming days and all the above-named tasks might be coming to an abrupt end until she could learn a new normal.

'Jack!' Avery yelled, letting the wooden screen door slam behind her and hit her in the backside. 'Jack! You in here?'

Instead, her son Jackson rounded the corner and almost tripped her with the toy car he was wheeling across the crooked wooden floor. 'I told you, not in the house,' she scolded, blinking her eyes and attempting to refocus her blurred vision. 'Where's your father?'

Jackson sped past her and trailed over his shoulder, 'I dunno, eating somethin' . . .'

'You mind your father while I'm gone! You hear, Jackson Michael Williams!'

'Yes, Ma'am,' he said before disappearing into the other room, ignoring her protest to keep the riding toy outdoors. She didn't have time to deal with it, though.

Avery rushed into the kitchen and found her husband leaning over the sink, hungrily wolfing down a sandwich and attempting to allow the stainless-steel basin to catch the dropping crumbs hanging from his mouth. He looked like one of their cows chewing his cud.

'Hey? I thought you took off already?' Jack asked between bites. He turned to her then and wiped the rest of the sandwich evidence from his lips with the back of his hand. 'You're going to miss your flight. Ike's already loaded your suitcase.'

'If only I could be so lucky to miss the flight,' she grunted. 'I really don't have time for this trip.'

'Come on now, we have everything figured out. You don't need to micromanage. We've got this.' Jack downed the rest of the milk from his glass before placing it in the sink and turning to face her again.

Avery stared at him intently. She wanted to memorize every mole on his weather-beaten face. Every hair on his sandy blond head. Every fleck in his hazel eyes.

'Why are you looking at me like that?'

His question broke her daydream. 'It's nothing.' She shook Jack off with a casual wave of her hand and began cleaning up the mess he'd left on the countertop.

He reached out to stop her. 'Don't clean that; I might have another sandwich.'

She blinked a few times and then ignored him and began to fix another sandwich. 'Ham? Turkey? Or did you have both?'

'What are you doing? You need to get going. Ike is waiting!' he reminded her again. 'What's up, Ave? You're acting weird.'

Avery dropped the rag to the counter and faced him. 'When I was asked to go on this trip, I didn't think it through clearly. I didn't realize we'd have a cow ready to give birth, a coop full of new baby chicks, the green beans ready for harvest – which means canning to do. Not to mention Mandy needing my help with 4-H. I want to be there and watch her win that ribbon.' Avery blew out a frustrated breath and shook her head. 'The timing is all off for this trip.'

'There'll be other ribbons.'

'Not for me. I may never see the day,' she cried.

'Oh, don't be so dramatic. You're missing *one* county fair. And we take part every single year. I'm telling you, we've got this. Now go and have a good time. Stop your worrying; it's not going to do you a bit of good. Nor is it going to change anything around here. Besides, we already paid for the plane ticket. And it's not like we have extra money to throw around.' He blew a frustrated breath out the side of his mouth while his eyes noticeably toured the ceiling as if willing her to fly away and disappear like a paper airplane.

Jack was completely missing the obvious, and Avery continued to argue the point. 'Those beans won't can themselves; they need to get in mason jars. And you know once you start picking how it goes. If you don't pick daily, they'll get too stringy. You can't let the kids miss a day of picking. Are you sure you're up to that task?' she warned.

'I'll have my mom come and can them, or Nancy can help. As for the picking, the kids need to earn their keep around here. Believe it or not, the Williams family will survive a week without Mama turning us on our axis.' He shoved her aside and leaned his head into the refrigerator as if searching for something more.

Jack's lack of empathy annoyed her. 'I didn't think I was so easily replaced around here.' She was referring to Nancy, their neighbor who lived down the road. Nancy was constantly one step ahead of them and on top of every task at her own farm, always readily offering a hand. Too readily if Avery had anything to say about it. But *that* argument was for another day.

Jack turned to face her then. 'Look. I'm trying to help. Now go!' he ordered. 'We love you too, but we'll survive a week. Go and see your friends, and we'll see you when you get back. OK?'

'Fine,' Avery huffed. 'There's meatloaf in the fridge for supper, and a strawberry pie for dessert. I used the rest of the strawberries, and I think the patch is just about done anyway. The kids can eat what's left while they're playing outside. Freezer jam is made. Make sure and give your mom a jar of it if she stops by to help with the canning.'

'Thank you. Did you leave a jar in the fridge for breakfast?' He turned to shuffle things around inside the refrigerator in search of the illusive jam.

'Of course, I did.' She grinned then, feeling suddenly proud that she'd handled everything. Her eyes darted to the clock on the microwave which was smeared with something red – most likely spaghetti sauce from the night before. Ike had missed dinner. This place was going to be an absolute mess when she returned. After kissing her husband on the cheek, she turned on her heel and left it all behind.

FOUR

Moriah aka Mori (her pseudonym, and the name she now prefers in everyday life)

After commanding Alexa to turn off the air-conditioning, Mori Hart opened the floor-to-ceiling windows facing the Atlantic to let the Cape Cod breeze blow through. The beach house, which she had borrowed for this anticipated reunion, belonged to her close friend, Jerome Jennings.

Yes – *that* Jerome Jennings. The famous one.

Jerome was currently off in New York at some penthouse flat penning a new screenplay with fellow co-writers. His splendid oceanfront estate was the perfect place to play hostess, filled with more than enough oversized bedrooms and ensuite bathrooms to accommodate each of her guests and more if they chose. The idea of housing a pubescent slumber party like those Mori had hosted back in the day, when this group would stay up half the night due to a sugar high from binging too many M&Ms, no longer held the same appeal as it once had. They'd grown up. People changed. Life had swept her high school friends away like the tide, dumping them off on completely different shores. Now, Mori needed her personal space in which to tuck away like a sea turtle as needed. A place where she could privately chant her morning affirmations after her first cup of espresso. A place to jot down notes in the middle of the night, if need be, for her latest work in progress – which often plagued her more than she'd ever admit to anyone. Not to mention, she needed her own bedroom in case sleep evaded her, as it did most nights, and she found herself pacing the floors like a zombie from *The Walking Dead*.

The estate she'd chosen for the group was a place where she had attended countless parties, and she knew the layout well. When Jerome caught wind that she was gathering her high school friends on short notice to the shores of Cape Cod after they'd recently reconnected on social media, he insisted they use his beachfront 'cottage', and he wouldn't take a dime for it. To Jerome, taking

Mori's money would be considered an insult. He'd been such a good friend to her over the years, and she finally yielded to his suggestion. Even though he was technically one step up in terms of social standing, he never treated her as such. However, calling his home a cottage was putting it mildly. The lawn abutting the vast private beach seemed at minimum a half mile long. And the square footage outnumbered the neighbors by a landslide.

Mori and Jerome had serendipitously crossed paths one day on the ferry. He had been running late and had missed the private charter boat en route to visiting a friend for a weekend stay at the Vineyard, and she was heading home from a book signing on the Cape. He instantly recognized her from the cover of *People* magazine and took a seat on the unoccupied bench next to her. He told her he thought it absurd how the editor of the magazine had the audacity to rip apart her life and divorce (husband #2) in a 200-word-or-less article that had been so edgy and crass. Jerome had confessed, having once worked for the magazine, that he thought the article was in such bad taste, and they had clearly taken a turn, with regard to content, *in the worst possible way* since his departure from the company. She even recalled that he said it was 'trashy' with a flip of his hand which made her smile at the memory. The two became fast friends after that, despite husband #3's grumblings of her kinship with Jerome. She couldn't help it. Jerome was part of the package. The two texted or talked on the phone daily and sometimes even multiple times throughout the day. He'd become her soft spot – and she his.

Looking back, Mori probably should've pushed and opted for the group of gals to travel to her place on the Vineyard, but they all had agreed when planning this great adventure that they should meet on neutral ground and a place they had spent most of their time during their teen years. And so, since she lived in closest proximity to the Cape, it was her job to find a place for which they would split the cost. Her friends didn't yet know that the bill was already covered, and groceries with a chef-on-demand (one who clearly could provide eye candy and research for her next novel) would be delivered ahead of time.

Borrowing Jerome's place worked out better for Mori anyway, as her former friends would all be searching for Adam. And how would she explain that she was on a 'break' from husband #3. It seemed everyone, including *People* magazine, judged her marriages/

divorces and plastered them across the front covers of their tabloids as if their mean-hearted words wouldn't reach her ears or faze her. Nor would they leave a sting. Oh, it stung all right. Worse than stepping directly into a hive without a beekeeper's suit. In fact, the salacious headlines ripped off every Band-Aid she'd carefully stretched over her past. Metaphorically speaking, of course. No one could see the wounds or scratches beneath Band-Aids. These were internal wounds, beneath her skin. The kind of deep insecurities that would rise to the surface for the whole world to see, just as soon as a new tabloid would hit the stands.

Not to mention her author rankings recently sagging on the *New York Times* Bestseller list. Oh yeah, there was that too. She'd need to bathe head to toe in Neosporin if this kept up.

Many a night Mori lay in bed and wished Jerome wasn't gay. Like her, he was a writer and he *understood* her on a level like no other. She couldn't help but wonder because of their deep closeness if she could ever convert him. He was her latest muse. Unbeknownst to him, her fantasies of Jerome were written into her raunchiest scenes. Mori even worked up the courage to ask him one night after too many glasses of Pinot. Which sobered Jerome up immediately and caused him to remind her that she wrote too many erotic novels and being gay didn't work like that. He liked playing for the other team. And it would remain that way.

'What about bi? Would you consider it?' she pushed, heavily under the influence, feeling flirty and fun and leaning into him seductively.

'No,' he replied adamantly, pushing her off him, leaving her flesh to sting as if he'd laid an angry hand on her. He hadn't, of course. He merely put distance between them. But her shame caused her to burn.

This altercation was the only time in their relationship when Mori might've just crossed the line to piss him off completely. She was glad Jerome had forgiven her for that night and never brought it up again, unlike her previous husbands, who liked to constantly remind her of her shortcomings and throw them back in her face whenever the opportunity presented itself.

However, the depressing nature of it all climaxed, especially when Adam had abandoned Mori for Europe. This latest development led her to overeating and binging Netflix for a few months. And now, looking at her bulging waistline, she faced another battle for which she was ill-prepared. She wished she had the time to lose a few pounds before reconnecting with these friends from her past. To her dismay, she'd recently done the opposite and gained another eight thanks to Ben & Jerry's Chunky Monkey. She wondered if she could file a lawsuit against the company for making their ice cream so damn addictive.

Mori's thoughts turned to her friends en route to the Cape. Were they jealous of her money or, at the very least, did they question her unexpected fortune? The windfall had come totally unexpectedly. Seriously. Out of everyone in the group, she was probably secretly voted 'least likely to succeed.' If it wasn't for her celebrity status, would they even have suggested she join them in this mini reunion in the first place? In her opinion, she was most likely remembered as the geek with the freckles on her nose and thick-lensed glasses, her head sunk deep into a book, hiding away in fantasy novels as her parents fought a bitter divorce. (Side bar: *Thank God for contact lenses!*) Reading had been an escape; it was her refuge which continued into adulthood. When she reached her teen years and the boys didn't look at her the way she longed for them to, she began reading romance. And then she started penning stories to create the perfect relationship to live out her deepest desires and fantasies. She always felt writing was a natural progression from reading everything she could get her hands on as a child. Writing was her way of dealing with the stresses of life. Escape life within the pages and ignore the world and drama around her. Never in her wildest dreams did she think she'd hit the *New York Times* Bestseller list and hold the ranking for 102 weeks. And as the saying goes, the rest is history. What she wholeheartedly expected *and never admitted to anyone* was that her published books would sit on a dusty shelf in the back of someone's personal library untouched because they were too embarrassed by the racy covers to display them.

Mori wanted to downplay her wealth in every way possible this week. Maybe it was a good thing they hadn't agreed to take the ferry from Woods Hole to her house after all. But now, looking around the airy room which faced the Atlantic, with sweeping ocean views capped by sand dunes and beach grass, she wondered if she'd succeeded. The shiplap walls painted crisp white which reached the enormous cathedral barn beamed ceiling only added to the glamour of the space. And underfoot, the travertine tile that crossed the threshold leading to the surf met beachy wood floors that probably cost more than one of their yearly salaries. She hoped they wouldn't judge. Jerome was a renowned writer/producer too, and she had agreed not to tell them whose house they'd be occupying while on the Cape. She wished more than ever Jerome was here with her, and they would be the ones spending the next few days together instead. She needed a confidence boost from her bestie as all her insecurities came flooding back.

The group would be here soon, and Mori needed to stop digressing. But she needed him like a parched marathon runner needed water. She moved quickly to the marble kitchen island, picked up her cell phone, and dialed Jerome.

'What is it Mori-love?' he said on the third ring.

'I wasn't expecting you to pick up . . .' Mori bit her lip. 'I know you're busy,' she sighed deeply. 'I just wanted to hear your cheery voicemail and leave you a message.'

'Something wrong with the house?'

'Not even a little,' she admitted. 'Everything is perfect. I owe you the world for this favor. I can't thank you enough.'

'You owe me nothing,' he said airily.

'You're too good to me,' she sighed again.

'What is it, then? I don't mean to cut you off, doll, but I don't have a lot of time. I was just about to go and grab a late lunch with Dante.'

'*Shit.*'

'What's wrong? Talk to me.'

Mori began to pace the oversized kitchen. 'Why did I agree to this? Is it too late to call it off?' She bit at her thumbnail to halt herself from screaming.

'You're getting cold feet again, love. You'll see – it'll be fun for you to reconnect with old friends. Just relax and have a blast! You need this; it'll be good for you.'

'I can't relax. And it's too early for wine.' Mori spied a quick look at the enormous clock on the wall that was more for art than time and had to decipher the exact hour as the numbers weren't present. 'Is that one or two o'clock?' she mumbled.

'It's just about one,' he laughed. 'Hey, if it all goes to hell, just consider it research, honey. You're always looking for new material. Nothing's wasted. Remember that.'

'Nothing's wasted. Research,' she repeated. 'Got it.'

'Yes, you've got it, love. Now I need to run. Kiss! Kiss!' And then, like a hummingbird, he was gone.

If he only knew how *badly* she wanted to feel his lips on hers. She'd take a kiss from him.

Any.

Time.

He offered.

Unfortunately, he wouldn't.

Maybe she should use that thought to bang out a few chapters before her guests' arrival. Instead, she reached into the refrigerator that was hidden behind a large panel inside the wall, plucked out a bottle of age-worthy Chardonnay, and poured herself a tall glass.

FIVE

'*Moriah Hart* as I live and breathe!' Remi squealed as she hopped from the car and tackled Mori in a bear hug. Mori had gone to retrieve the mail for Jerome, the one thing she'd promised to handle in his absence, and found a car parked alongside the driveway. She had hoped for another glass of wine and to refresh her makeup before any of them arrived, but alas it was too late.

Remi held Mori's latest release in her hand and waved the book around dramatically when they finally parted.

'*Girlfriend!* Your words made me blush on the plane. I didn't know you had it in you!' Remi gushed, shoving the cover in front of her as if Mori had never seen her own novel before. 'Where did you come up with this material? Va va va voom! Adam is one lucky man!' she whistled and then grinned, showing the gap between her front teeth that Mori had forgotten about. Witnessing that smile instantly boomeranged her back to their youth.

'You look good, Remi,' Mori said, and she meant it. Remi looked youthful and fit with not a crinkle around her eyes. And her ass? *Fuck!* It was as firm as a soccer ball. Mori secretly wanted to ask if she had an implant put in because Remi's backside looked like it belonged to freaking J-Lo. 'You might have to lead our group in yoga classes on the beach while you're here,' Mori continued. 'I'm sure the rest of us could use a little of your youth dust.' She turned to look at her own ass in disgust. The shorts that she was wearing, *despite the hefty price tag*, looked like two paper grocery bags hanging from her hips. Now, she'd wished she'd chosen something else to wear. 'I just mean to say you fit in those yoga pants nicely. Don't mind me – I'm just jealous, is all,' she added lightly, sucking in her stomach, and wishing she had put on her Spanx as originally planned.

'Oh stop!' Remi gushed with a wave of dismissal. 'Out of all of us, I'm the youngest of the group. I still have a few years before I hit the big four-O,' she reminded Mori. 'I'd be happy to lead a yoga class on the beach if anyone is interested. Sounds fun!' She grinned, toying with a diamond necklace round her neck.

'What a beautiful necklace! Is it heart-shaped? Very pretty.'

'Thanks!' Remi replied. 'Gabe gave it to me for my thirtieth birthday, and I never take it off.'

'I wish I had a man in my life who thought that highly of me.'

'I'm sure Adam can't even compete with Mori Hart!' Remi replied gleefully. 'I mean, you being so famous and all, he probably expects you to pick out your own jewelry.'

Mori suddenly realized that her attempt to fit in was backfiring. Was she always this awkward with the girls in this group? Of course she was. To downplay her wealth, she was already self-sabotaging and talking herself down. Not to mention, she'd drunk too much truth serum and her words needed a rewind button. 'Would you like a glass of wine to unwind after your flight?' she suggested, looping her arm through Remi's and leading her closer to the front door. Maybe if Mori got Remi to loosen up, she wouldn't remember half of the blunders that were bound to erupt from Mori's mouth.

Instead of accepting a drink, though, Remi said, 'You're looking well too, Moriah. I mean Mori. What should we call you this week? I can't believe I'm standing in front of a real live famous person! What a trip!'

'You can call me Mori; most everyone does nowadays.'

They were suddenly distracted by a loud sneeze and movement beyond them. 'Seems your Uber driver could use a hand,' Mori urged with a flick of her finger.

'Oh, I forgot! I was so excited to see you standing out here! Right here in the flesh! I mean, you're the only famous person I know!' Remi squealed again, clapping her hands together excitedly as if she were back to leading the cheer for their high school football team.

After witnessing this, Mori wished she had caffeine running through her veins instead of wine as she felt a headache coming on from all the visible excitement oozing out of her old friend. Mori admired Remi's gusto. She'd always had it. A big smile, a welcoming presence, but she already longed to sneak away and jot down a few notes for her latest work in progress. A plot outside her genre was percolating in her mind, and she wished she could excuse herself to work on it. But she realized that would be totally rude, so she'd force herself to remain.

Remi had effortlessly bounded down the sidewalk to join the

Uber driver, while he proceeded to unload her luggage from deep within the trunk. Mori drew a cleansing breath and hid her fatigue like a ventriloquist, plastering a smile as she watched this all unfold. The high energy, along with Remi's tight-fitting yoga pants, almost made Mori faint with exhaustion as if she'd just tackled a sweaty workout herself. Or maybe it was because she was already feeling the light buzz of Chardonnay. Either way, she needed to get her shit together before the others arrived. Of that she was certain. She clapped her hands to her face to physically wake herself up.

The driver dumped the luggage at the front step and, with a backward wave of his hand, jogged down the cobbled stone path and peeled out of the long driveway hidden from the road.

'Am I the first to arrive?' Remi looked beyond her as if waiting for Avery or Calista to step out the front door and make an appearance. 'I thought for sure Calista would beat me here since she's only driving from Natick.'

'Yep, you're the first one to arrive. Calista isn't coming until tomorrow – something about her son having an appointment she needed to attend.'

Remi's disappointment was obvious as her shoulders sank momentarily, and her smile faded. 'Oh, that's a bummer. I thought we were all arriving today.'

'If you want, you can take your pick of rooms before the others arrive. We'll each have our own bedroom, which is nice. I'd hate to keep anyone awake – I've been working on something, and I might need a bit of privacy to hit the keyboard if the moment strikes in the middle of the night. Snacks are in the refrigerator in case you're hungry from your flight before the chef arrives. Are you? Hungry, that is?'

'I'm good, thanks. I had a protein bar on the way over, but that's sweet of you to ask.'

A protein bar.

That would barely put a dent in the kind of hunger Mori felt as she audibly heard her stomach beg for a Big Mac and supersized fries. There was no McDonalds on Martha's Vineyard, only one located in Woods Hole, which she would frequent when she left the island. Maybe she could escape there?

No wonder Remi's body is firm and fit. She probably doesn't even eat greasy food.

Mori needed to stop this train of thought. What was wrong with her? Why was she acting like a jealous nut? She suddenly felt catapulted back to her younger freckle-faced self with glasses. It was as if Remi had read her insecure thoughts when she broke the silence between them.

'There's something different about you, but I can't put my finger on it.' Remi frowned. 'In a good way, of course.'

'Oh, I don't wear glasses anymore and I've had a few chemical peels, so the spots on my face sorta faded,' Mori admitted easily.

'That's what it is!' Remi leaned in closer to examine Mori's nose. 'Wow! The freckles on your cheeks have completely disappeared too! Beautiful photo on the book jacket. Whoever took it knew what they were doing; the photo brings out your natural beauty. It's amazing.'

Mori shrugged, 'Yep, I guess I've kinda grown up in the last twenty years.'

Remi remained awkwardly quiet for a moment and then cuffed a hand to her ear. 'Goodness! I think I hear the ocean!'

'Yes, we're right on the coast here,' Mori jutted a thumb behind her. 'The water is right out back, beyond the beach roses over there.' She waved her hand to show how far. 'The hydrangeas are a bit overgrown and blocking the view. If I had it my way, I'd probably have them removed,' she pointed out. 'Maybe you'd like to unload your things and take a walk on the beach before the others arrive.'

'Yeah, maybe. By the way, what is this place?' Remi's eyes doubled in size when she finally took in the house in front of them. 'When you said cottage, I thought you meant *cottage* . . . Like a place we might've crashed as kids. Don't take this the wrong way, but this looks like a manor to me. Yes, it has that quintessential New England weathered cedar siding and white trim look to it, but that's about the only part of it that screams *Cape Cod cottage*. And how many windows are there? Too numerous to count!' She giggled nervously. 'How much do we all need to chip in for this place? I hope I can afford it,' she added quietly under her breath. But Mori caught the comment.

'Not a dime. It's all taken care of.'

Remi audibly gasped. 'You're not serious. You can't! We all agreed to split the cost. That wouldn't be fair to you . . .' She trailed off as her eyes returned to the summer home in complete awe.

Just then, a van pulled into the driveway and stopped along the curb. After a moment, a blond woman stepped from the vehicle and looked around anxiously.

'Avery!' Remi squealed and rushed toward her. Mori assumed Avery was the next victim to be tackled in a wide receiver hug.

Mori licked her lips and wished for more wine.

SIX

Calista directed her SUV south to Interstate 95 while she anxiously tried to plan her next move. She knew what she had to do; she just needed to work up the nerve to do it. Her hands clutched the steering wheel, which now dripped with sweat despite the air conditioning running full blast and her legs exploding in goosebumps. A lump in her throat began to form, and tears landed just behind her eyes, ready to erupt at a moment's notice. Traffic was horrendous – cars were weaving in and out at high speeds, causing her even more anxiety.

A sign, indicating a commuter parking lot ahead, brought the first wave of relief. She pulled in, found the first available spot, and jammed the gear into park to catch her bearings.

Calista tipped her head against the steering wheel in frustration but let the engine run while she sucked in a deep breath. She then leaned back into the comfort of the seat and allowed the cool air conditioning to soothe her until her legs numbed from the icy air and she was forced to rub her limbs vigorously to bring the blood flow back again.

She had to do this.

She had to.

Calista gritted her teeth and held back a groan. Kirk wasn't giving her an option. And she hated him for it. She hated that he had this much power over her. And that he was calling the shots.

Before she could talk herself out of it a minute longer, Calista hit the phone number and took a swig of water to clear her throat while listening to the phone ring out from Bluetooth.

'*Hello?*'

'Hey, Gabe, I hope I didn't catch you at a bad time . . .' She paused, taking a breath. 'I need to talk to you.'

'*Calista? Is that you?*'

'Yeah, it's me.'

'*How'd you get my number?*'

'I looked up the name of the gym on Remi's Facebook profile and saw your cell phone listed on the website for personal training.

I was hoping you kept the number, and since it's you on the other end, I guess you did.'

'Oh, yeah. Right. I forgot about that. Boy, I haven't heard your voice in years and it's like I'm ricocheted to high school. How've you been?' Gabe chuckled. 'Aren't you at the Cape? Or at least, on your way?' The sound of his voice escalated then, and his tone came out worried. 'Wait. Is something wrong with Remi?'

'No, nothing like that. I'm not there yet. I told Moriah I wouldn't arrive until tomorrow. I need to talk to you first.'

'*Me?* Why?'

'I'd rather not handle this over the phone. It's rather serious. Can we meet?'

'Meet? You know I live in Florida, right, Calista?' he chuckled nervously. 'That's a little much to ask. Don't you think?'

'I bought you a plane ticket. All you have to do is get on the damn plane.'

'*You did what?* When?'

'It's a red eye. Can you make it? It's a direct flight, and I paid hefty for it. I'll pick you up at Logan first thing in the morning. I'll sleep in the parking lot, if need be.'

There was a long pause on the other end of the line. Calista wondered if he'd hung up on her until she heard a heavy sigh.

'This is important, Gabe. I wouldn't even ask . . . if . . . What I need to tell you is going to blow your world apart. You need to come.'

'Calista, you're scaring me. Does this have something to do with—'

Calista cut him off before he had a chance to say it aloud. 'Yeah . . . hopefully, it scares you enough to come. Please, Gabe . . . we need to meet. I need to see you, before I connect with the girls.' Her voice was urgent now, trying to convince him to do this. She needed to talk to him before she saw anyone else. Especially Remi – despite how Kirk wanted it handled.

Another long pause ensued before Gabe finally begrudgingly agreed. 'Fine. I'll come to you.'

SEVEN

It was hard for Remi to believe she was back in Cape Cod. She spun around the spacious bedroom, taking it all in. She couldn't help but pinch herself at the thought of spending the next five days in the lap of luxury. She hurriedly slipped into a bikini and threw on a gauzy cover-up. She and Avery had agreed to take a morning walk on the beach to get rid of any jetlag left over from the previous day, while Mori graciously insisted on hanging back at the cottage to wait for Calista to arrive. Remi was tired. Avery had been the smart one to excuse herself and head to bed early, while she and Mori stayed up chatting way after midnight. She hoped she didn't crash from all the excitement.

The room was painted an airy blue, and the king-sized bed, drowned in crisp white bedding, faced the Atlantic. Avery mentioned she didn't care which bedroom she was given. As long as it had a bed that wasn't occupied by a husband who snored or a kid that kicked like a bull in the night, she'd be happy. Remi had squealed with delight when she saw the balcony extending from the bedroom and claimed the room immediately. With the door cracked open, the sounds of the sea had lulled her to sleep like a lullaby. She couldn't remember the last time she'd slept so soundly.

Remi stretched into a downward dog and then back up to tree pose before opening the door wider and stepping out to feel the morning breeze. The sound of the surf greeted her with a roar, and she breathed in cadence to meditate. A wave of guilt swept over her that Gabe wasn't along to enjoy this gift of peace. She quickly called him via FaceTime to give him a quick tour, but he didn't pick up the call. When she had informed Gabe that her plane had arrived in Boston, he'd returned a text, so she guessed he was busy at the gym and couldn't stop and talk. She'd try him again later.

She stood on the balcony, leaned her weight on to the railing, and was captivated by the view. The backyard was lush and heavily manicured with beach roses and vivid blue hydrangea which were just hitting full bloom. Typical of the Cape for hydrangea to bloom in July, and somehow Remi had forgotten that. She would have to disagree with Mori; there was no way she would have the shrubs cut down and removed. They provided vivid memories of her time visiting the Cape. A long boardwalk led out from the lawn and met beach sand directly.

It had been years since Remi had returned to Massachusetts, and now, breathing in the heavily salted air, she felt instantly at home. The air was thick here, but not as oppressive as she was currently accustomed to, back in Florida. She watched a seagull fly overhead and closed the door leading to the bedroom when one came near, for fear the bird would fly inside. If that hadn't transpired, she might've never pulled herself away from the view.

Remi removed her toiletry bag from the suitcase and a baseball cap that said *BOSTON* across the bill which she'd purchased at Logan Airport and made her way to the ensuite bath. Just stepping into the stark white marble bathroom made her jaw drop. She had been so tired the previous night that she barely noticed the contents of the room. She ran her hand along the cool, smooth countertop and took in the oversized rain shower that could house its own dance party. She then turned to the white mirror, shaped like a giant ship wheel hanging directly above the sink, and gleefully said to herself as she watched her own grin grow wider, 'Oh, yeah. This will do. This will do just fine.'

Remi splashed cool water on her face and wished for more time to freshen up before they went for a walk, but that seemed silly since they were heading down to the beach. She could shower after.

She heard a knock on the bedroom door and Avery's voice on the other side.

'Hey, you ready to go?'

'Just give me a few more minutes. I'll meet you out there!'

'Sounds good!'

Remi quickly ripped the price tag off with her teeth and then topped her head with the baseball cap, moving her short ponytail to hang out the back end. She then grabbed a beach towel in case they decided to take a dip.

After almost getting lost and finally making her way down a large staircase, she ran into Mori walking toward the kitchen with a wineglass in hand, filled with what looked like orange juice. But Remi wasn't sure. Mori's cheeks were flushed, and she turned at the sound of her name being called out.

'You sure you don't want to leave a note and have Calista meet us out there?'

'No, go on ahead,' Mori insisted with an airy wave of dismissal. 'As soon as she arrives, we'll join you. I promise.'

'If you're sure,' Remi confirmed.

'I'm sure! I was inspired in the middle of the night with a bit of good dialogue for my characters. I need to hit the keyboard and enter it into my work in progress before I lose it,' Mori sang out before continuing in the direction of the kitchen. 'I'm guessing Calista will probably be here soon. She mentioned she was leaving early this morning. Maybe she added a stop or two along the way.'

'OK, then!'

Remi could see through the floor-to-ceiling windows that Avery was waiting for her, seated in an Adirondack chair on an enormous deck that was tucked into the bluff overlooking the sparkling sea. She hurried out the door to greet her.

Avery's head was resting on the back of the chair and her legs stretched out on to a patio table which she'd clearly moved to accommodate them.

'Hey, someone's looking comfortable,' Remi said, finally arriving at her side.

Seemingly embarrassed, Avery moved her feet from the table, set it aside, and sat upright.

'Oh, no! Don't move on my account. We can stay if you want,' Remi suggested. 'We don't have to go for a walk if you'd rather take in the view from here.'

'No, that's OK, I want to stretch my legs. This is the longest I've sat down in weeks!' Avery replied. 'I think my body might be going into shock.' She chuckled then and stood to join Remi. 'By now I would've easily milked cows, fed chickens, weeded the garden, and checked on the corn! Not to mention cooked a hearty breakfast for the family. To be honest, it feels strange to just sit here doing nothing.'

'Sounds like you really need this,' Remi said, shoulder bumping her.

'Yeah, I suppose I do,' Avery grinned. 'I didn't realize how much until I caught a whiff of the sea air.'

'Right? I've really missed New England!'

The two walked amiably along the long boardwalk that led to an empty beach.

'Where is everyone?' Avery asked, breaking their silence.

'Mori mentioned yesterday that this is a private beach. I guess she wasn't kidding,' Remi said, stopping in her tracks and looking in awe at the sweeping view of coastal blue in front of them. Glimmers danced upon the water like sequins on a midnight-colored party dress. In the far distance, Remi caught a glimpse of a sailboat. 'This is absolutely stunning.' She took a deep breath, inhaling the salty sea air to her core.

'I know, right?' Avery agreed with a nod. 'I'm glad Moriah is paying for this because I couldn't even afford the deposit for the garage. It makes me feel a little guilty, though.' She fished her cell phone from her pocket and took a photo of the view in front of them.

'Really? I thought I was the only one feeling that way!' Remi chuckled.

'I wasn't as close to her in high school as you guys were. I dunno. She shouldn't have to foot the bill. It all feels so weird in a way, us being together after all this time, doesn't it? It's like we're familiar but we're not. We know each other . . . but we don't. Life is strange how we all moved away and lost touch, you know? I never expected that to happen.'

'We sure have a lot of catching up to do,' Remi agreed.

'That we do!'

In the moment, Remi didn't realize exactly what that entailed. And that before this trip was over, one of the group would wind up dead.

EIGHT

Calista strolled past the Starbucks at least six times before finally stepping inside and ordering a coffee. She took one sip and dumped the rest into the nearest trash receptacle. She should've trusted her intuition, which had been telling her that she was jittery enough. The added caffeine might put her in cardiac arrest.

There was still precisely twenty-two minutes on the clock before Gabe's flight was due to arrive.

Late.

The red eye had been pushed and his plane was landing a few hours later than planned. As the time ticked closer, Calista's nerves continued to escalate. She took a seat in the nearest plastic chair by the window and tried to concentrate on the world around her. An airline worker in a yellow reflective vest was beginning to load baggage into a plane just outside the window. She tried to focus on the worker's task to no avail. Instead, her mind rebounded to the past.

For years, Calista had replayed the horrific scene over and over in her mind. They'd had a massive fight – their worst fight to date. Tears had flooded her face as she called out for Gabe to *wait*. But he refused. In front of his childhood home, Gabe jumped on his ten-speed to escape from their argument, while Calista had chased him down the block. She remembered how her chest had heaved from the effort to catch up to his bicycle. The rolling of the garage door when he'd sped past two houses, before reaching hers. Calista's father backing the SUV out of the driveway. The sound of twisted metal. Gabe writhing in pain. And blood. *So much blood.*

Calista squeezed her eyes shut, trying to squelch the memory. She rose from the chair to stop this nonsense. She no longer wanted to relive the event that had sealed their fate. Knowing she would soon see Gabe, everything was dredged back up again as if it just happened yesterday.

She needed to walk.

And breathe.

Away from the window, Calista attempted another distraction by stepping inside a gift shop where she found herself smack dab in front of the paperback novel display. After searching for it, she noted Moriah's was not on the shelf. She asked the clerk about it and was told Mori Hart's book was sold out, which caused Calista to smile with pride. She aimlessly plucked a mystery novel from the pile and tried to focus on what was written on the back, but after rereading the first line three times, she gave up. She opted for a pack of mint gum before abandoning the shop completely and popping a stick into her mouth. The cooling sensation helped replace the sour taste of bile that had resulted from that one sip of coffee.

Without warning, out of the corner of her eye, Calista caught a familiar burgundy polo shirt above perfectly pleated khaki slacks coming toward her, causing her to do a doubletake. Stopping mid-stride, she faced the figure directly, slipped her hands on her waist, and waited. The anger rose in her chest as she watched each fucking step of Kirk Moore's approach.

Her husband stopped roughly a foot from her face. 'What are you doing?' he demanded. 'You should be at the Cape by now! Not wearing a hole in the floor at Logan Airport, pacing around like some kind of caged animal.'

So, Kirk noticed. How long had he been watching her? And from where?

'Are you seriously following me?'

'I needed to make sure you'll follow through with this,' he said evenly. 'And it seems to me, you're looking for a detour instead of actually doing what you're supposed to do.'

'You've got to be kidding.' Calista met his stare. 'You can't control this. Or me. Those days are over. *Kirk.*'

Kirk's jaw twitched in response to her standing up for herself. She hated it when he looked at her like that. His eyes cold and heartless, as if they'd never had anything go right in their life together. Like their bodies had never touched or been intertwined beneath the sheets. Kirk was almost unrecognizable to her now.

'Oh, I can't? Watch me. I fucking own you. And you know it. You can't reorganize this one to meet your perfectionistic expectations,' he seethed in a threatening tone. A tone Calista had never heard spoken to her in their entire married life and which shook her to the core. She refused to allow him to see that he'd gotten to her.

'Did it ever occur to you that I was trying to be perfect for *you*? Trying to live up to your impossible expectations. Just to get a scrap of love from you. All these years, I was like a mouse begging for cheese. I see that so clearly now.' She huffed and added an eye-roll to drive the point home. 'Honestly, I'm just wondering what took me so long.'

'Don't give me that line of bullshit. Now that I know who you really are and what you're actually capable of.' He flung up a hand of defense and shook his head wildly. 'Just don't.'

'Go home, Kirk.'

'I can't. I have a business meeting. And I won't lose my job over you.' He looked at his Apple watch then and grimaced as though he desperately wanted to skip the meeting but couldn't. She knew he had a big account this week, and all the drama was a wrinkle in his plans. His work *always* came before her. This was no surprise. For the first time, though, she was glad of it. Maybe it would cause him to disappear. *If only.*

'You'd better get moving then,' she said coolly. 'I'd hate for you to be late.'

He took a step closer and thrust a finger dangerously close to the tip of her nose. 'This time, I'm controlling the narrative. You need to hurry up and get to the Cape and talk to Remi. Stop wasting time. I'm warning you.'

Calista took a step backward, trying to reclaim her personal space. She wanted to run.

Run from him.

Run from the airport.

Run from meeting Gabe.

Run from *all* of it.

Instead, Calista squared her shoulders and replied through clenched teeth, so the entire airport wouldn't overhear. 'Then go! You're the one wasting precious time! There is no reason for you to be here!'

'There's no reason for you to be here either!' he volleyed. 'So, why are you?'

Calista noted the passing of time, and with each volley, she knew she was losing leverage. She didn't want Kirk to know Gabe was coming in less than fifteen minutes. 'You need to go.'

'I'm not leaving until you explain why you're here. You looking for the next flight out of Boston, or what?' He studied her then. His beady eyes peered at her with expectancy to show he was right. As if he could read her naked soul. 'If you don't explain everything the way we had planned, Devon will learn it from me. Is that what you want?' He pressed hard, like a twisting knife into her heart. He knew her soft spot. He knew her son meant everything to her. He knew it. And he used it against her. This caused her to hate him all the more.

'I'm picking up Remi, you idiot!' she spat. The lie coming out so easily now. She'd had many years of practice behind her belt. Lying was something she excelled at.

Kirk looked taken aback.

'Yeah,' she threatened, taking a step closer into his personal space. 'You need to leave before you blow this whole thing up. I've got this handled. I said I would, and I will. Now promise me, you'll trust me with this at least. Just once, give me the benefit of the doubt. I'll deal with it.'

'You never told me you were picking Remi up?' He sounded a little weaker now, as if she'd finally won the argument.

'You never asked. And besides' – she wagged a finger angrily between them – 'this is what divorce looks like, Kirk. You don't get to know everything in my world anymore. You got that?' She met his stare down evenly.

Kirk faintly cowered at her response, a slight sign of weakness that surprised her. She never stood up for herself. Never. She was half expecting him to slap her across the face again, not to shrink back. When she knew she had the upper hand, she pushed. 'Go!'

'Call me when it's done.' Those were the last words she heard utter from his mouth before he turned away from her. Her eyes lasered in on him as she watched him walk away and step out the door leading to the parking lot.

NINE

By the time Avery and Remi had returned from their walk along the beach, Avery was beyond starving. She was accustomed to a hearty breakfast, especially on the weekends. Farm-fresh eggs, bacon, fruit, toast with peanut butter or homemade jam. Or both. Her stomach was begging for sustenance, and she was secretly glad Mori had mentioned a chef would be arriving soon to cook for them. As awkward as that sounded to her own ears, she'd take it. The only person standing behind a stovetop back at the farm was her. Couldn't they each chip in to help cook? Or go out to eat? But right now, she didn't care if someone waited on her; she was desperate for food and put her own reasoning aside.

As soon as the two stepped inside the cottage, Mori beckoned them toward the kitchen, where apparently the chef had already arrived, as the smell of bacon and fresh baked muffins wafted through the air, causing Avery's stomach to respond with another anticipatory roll.

'Ladies, Brody is here to make omelets. Any. Kind. You. Want.' Mori's eyes traveled up and down the handsome *'boy'*, whom Avery assumed was not much older than her son Owen. The way Mori ogled the chef as if he were something to devour made her feel embarrassed for the lot of them. He was *clearly* half their age. Avery couldn't help but wonder what Mori's husband, Adam, would think of her hiring a 'boy toy' for the week.

Remi didn't seem to notice as she said, 'How lovely! Can you make an egg-white veggie one with avocado oil? I don't do butter, unless it's grass-fed.'

Brody smiled wide, showing perfectly white virgin teeth. His grin was so white, in fact, that Avery could envision him in a toothpaste commercial.

'You bet!' he said, clapping his hands together as if excited to get started. His blond hair was buzzed short and gelled spiky on the top. His perfectly sculpted jaw supplied zero facial hair, and Avery wondered if he was even old enough to grow any. But his azure eyes were captivating and alert, and he seemed completely in his element. As if he'd just stepped off the set of one of the latest *Top Chef* competitions.

'That's right, ladies! He can make *anything*. Your wish is his desire – right, Brody?' Mori asked seductively, plucking a piece of cooked bacon off a nearby plate and popping it into her mouth as if she were starving for him. Avery almost had to hold back her gag reflex. From what she remembered of Moriah and her shyness around boys in high school, her behavior was quite the opposite of what she was witnessing now. A noticeable turnaround, in her opinion. She wondered if she was working out one of her latest books in real time.

'We also have mimosas if you're interested,' Mori continued as she waved a hand airily toward a bottle of expensive-looking champagne and a jug of orange juice. It looked as if she'd already helped herself.

'I'll just have the OJ,' Remi said, pouring herself some into a champagne flute.

Avery couldn't help but look around the kitchen in search of a red SOLO cup. The last time she drank out of a champagne flute was at her own wedding. And even that was only filled with house wine. She decided to pass on the orange juice; the glasses had a decorative etch to them which made them look expensive. Her luck, she'd trip and break one and need to replace a pricy piece of crystal; Jack would never forgive her.

'Cheers!' Mori said, lifting her glass to clink with Remi before taking a drawn-out sip.

Avery turned her attention back to the chef. 'Where'd you learn to cook?' she asked. Her curiosity piqued as she leaned into the vast kitchen island where Brody had every fresh herb and chopped vegetable known to man assembled in front of him. She reached for a leaf of cilantro, rubbed it between her fingers until it oiled then took a whiff, centering herself as if she were back on the farm tending her own herb garden and preparing to can a batch of fresh salsa.

'I'm a student at Johnson and Wales,' he said proudly. 'Graduating this year. I do these types of gigs to make a little extra ching in the summer. My uncle has a place down Cape where I couch-dive while I'm working here.'

Down Cape. Avery hadn't heard that term in years. It meant his uncle's place was farther down the tip of Cape Cod, toward Provincetown, she surmised.

Mori swiped her phone from the countertop and sang into an app, 'Use the term "couch-dive" in context of sleepover when sexy male character is talking,' she chirped aloud. Loud enough for Brody to overhear and grin wide. And then his face momentarily flushed cherry-red.

Avery wanted to crawl inside the floor. She hadn't read any of Mori's work, though she'd heard of it after a quick search on the internet, back at the farm. When she found out how famous Moriah had become, she felt proud to have gone to school with her, and envious of how far her childhood friend had come. But when she realized the kind of stuff Moriah wrote, the proudness fell off like an unwanted coat on a hot summer day. It sounded to Avery like her friend was making money by writing porn. Remi and Mori had giggled about her success long into the night, and Avery opted to head to bed early after the long day of travel, so she could avoid the subject completely. She honestly didn't know how she would respond regarding the subject, if cornered. Just thinking about it made her want to run to confession before her priest.

'You mind if I make a cup of coffee?' Avery asked hesitantly, looking around for a coffee machine and finally locking eyes on an expensive-looking Keurig/espresso gadget. She had no idea how to use that contraption. At home, she often made a large pot of coffee from which the entire family could grab refills after the morning chores were completed.

'Whatever is here, consider it yours this week. This is your home away from home. Help yourself to anything and everything,' Mori said kindly, waving an exaggerated hand around the enormous kitchen. 'And if there is anything else I can do to make your stay more comfortable, just say the word. I'm like a genie in a bottle,' she sang out Christina Aguilera-style.

Avery's veins suddenly coursed with shame. Mori was being so nice, and here she was being a jerk and judging her livelihood harshly. Maybe she was the one with an attitude problem. 'Thanks, I really do appreciate that, and all you've done to make us comfortable here. And finding us this place to stay so we could all meet up again after all these years. Seriously. It's absolutely stunning and more than I could've ever imagined!'

'Aww,' Mori came and wrapped an arm around her shoulder and brought her in. 'Of course – that's what friends do for each other,' she smiled sweetly.

Then Avery felt even more like a jerk. It wasn't her business how someone else made their money or led their life. She was there to reconnect, not disconnect from everyone with her harsh judgments. Avery decided then and there to drop her holier-than-thou attitude and support her old friend. She blinked at the sudden wave that hit her eyes and blurred her vision. And then shook her head to clear it.

'Hey, Ave, you OK?' Mori must've noticed, as she leaned in to examine her closely.

Avery rubbed her eyes with both fists. 'I'm fine.' She held back a yawn. 'I think I just need my caffeine to wake up. You mind showing me how to use this thing?' she added with a laugh, pointing to the fancy coffee machine.

Mori's expression turned to one of confusion. 'Huh?'

'I have an old-fashioned coffee maker at home. You know, the kind that fills in an actual glass pot? I don't know where to begin here,' Avery explained as she explored the sleek machine in front of her through blur-filled eyes.

'Ah, you really *don't* leave the farm much, do you?' Mori teased and then proceeded to show her various flavors of these K-Cup thingies. Avery marveled at how quickly the coffee filled the mug and immediately took a sip of the black brew the moment the machine stopped.

'No creamer?' Mori asked. 'There's a couple of flavors in the refrigerator if you want some.'

'Thanks, I'd love some.' Avery took another sip before topping it with hazelnut creamer. The next sip she took was slow and mindful, letting the hug of caffeine soothe her. 'Wow. This hits the spot. This machine might be my new best friend,' she grinned, wrapping her fingers around the mug more tightly.

'Yeah, you might need to invest in one of those,' Mori said with a nod before moving to refill her mimosa. 'Once you have one, you'll never go back. I can promise you that,' she declared.

'She's right about that!' Remi added with a grin.

'Did you want an omelet?' Brody asked Avery as he handed Remi a loaded steaming plate.

'Sure, I'll take your specialty. I'll eat whatever; I'm not fussy. But I'm certainly hangry!' she said with a chuckle.

'Now we're talking!' Brody exclaimed, reaching to gather ingredients and popping a squirt of olive oil and then a hint of butter into the pan. He then added the liquid scrambled eggs to let them set.

Avery waited while the chef crafted her omelet while the others stepped outside, so they could enjoy their breakfast on the deck facing the ocean.

'What made you pursue cooking as a career?' Avery asked as he loaded the semi-cooked egg mixture with various vegetables, bacon, and cheese, before folding it over in the fry pan. Jack barely stepped inside her kitchen back in Iowa. Her mother often scoffed that she lived a 1950s lifestyle, where the husband was the head of the farm, while Avery handled all of the housework. It made her wonder if Nancy was delivering meals to him and the kids this week. In her world, it was so foreign to see a man standing behind the stove. 'You look as though you'd be pretty good at something like construction, too.' Avery felt her face burn then. She hadn't meant it, but the boy did have a solid build, and she couldn't help but think he'd make a great farmhand. She cleared her throat and didn't prod further.

'I was raised by my grandmother, and she taught me when I was very young to fend for myself. I always had dinner ready for us when she came home from work,' he said as he plated her omelet and topped it with fresh basil and fanned slices of avocado off to the side. The avocado was so incredibly chartreuse, not like the half-black ones she often came home with after a visit to her local Hy-Vee.

His candid revelation caused a whole new appreciation for the young man standing in front of her. 'Sounds like you have a wonderful grandmother.'

'Had,' he corrected. 'She died last year.'

Avery seemed to be putting her foot in her mouth at every turn. 'Oh, Brody, I'm so sorry . . .' she stuttered. 'I didn't know.'

'No worries. How would you know?' He handed her the full plate after finishing his design. 'This one was her favorite; she requested it all the time. I hope you enjoy it.'

'I already do,' she said with an appreciative nod, reaching for a blueberry muffin to add to her plate. 'Thank you for this. It looks fabulous,' she added over her shoulder, before leaving him and rushing to join the others.

The sun was causing the Atlantic to glisten like a disco ball, and the tranquil sandy beach off in the distance made Avery feel miles away from Iowa – in a good way. 'What a view,' she said, setting down her coffee, then her plate, and taking a seat under the umbrella-covered table. 'Man! I could get used to this.'

'It's incredible,' Remi agreed with a nod between bites and then she, too, took a moment to regard the sea before sipping her orange juice.

'I feel a bit spoiled to be honest,' Mori said. 'Sometimes I don't even notice the view here or at home on the Vineyard. I'm so caught up in my own head.' She broke off a piece of muffin and then popped it in her mouth. 'Always under deadline or agenda,' she added with a grunt between chews. 'I need to learn how to stop and smell the roses now and then.'

'The deadlines are hard on you, huh?' Avery asked before taking a bite of her delicious omelet. She'd need to get the recipe before returning home. The fresh basil on top was not something she'd ever thought to do.

'Sometimes. Right now, I'm plotting a book, different from what my agent and publisher expect of me. I want to write a suspense novel, exploring deception and the impact it has on relationships. Maybe it should be True Crime,' Mori admitted and then held a finger to her lips. 'But don't tell anyone I've been working on something new. It's our little secret.'

The author's eyes had filled with so much excitement and fresh enthusiasm that it caused Avery to prod further. 'Why don't you pursue it?'

'Yeah? What's stopping you?' Remi asked between bites. 'I'd totally read that!'

Mori laughed effortlessly. 'It doesn't exactly work that way.'

Avery took a sip of coffee and then asked, 'What do you mean?'

'I mean my agent, publishers, they want me to stay in my lane. This is where the cash flow is. You have to understand, they've made a *ton* of money off my work,' Mori said openly. 'They want me to keep going with it. I can't tell you how exhausted I am from writing sex scenes. But I keep writing them!' she said with an eye-roll. 'Especially when it pays the bills.'

'Well, that doesn't seem fair,' Remi interjected. 'I mean, if you want to write something else, why don't you? I'm siding with Avery on this one.' She shot Avery an agreeable nod which caused Avery to smile back at her.

Remi continued, 'I for one say don't stunt your creativity! I wish

I had the creative gene. I can barely draw a stick figure,' she chuckled.

'Yeah, and I was always taught to go with your gut. If it's leading that way, then you ought to go for it,' Avery encouraged. 'What if you were really on to something? What if it becomes better than anything you've ever written?'

'It's just hard to fit in time for what I want to write when I have deadlines and expectations constantly looming,' Mori explained. 'It's really a time-crunch issue.'

'Hey, you should write a book about four friends who get together on the Cape after not seeing each other for a long time,' Avery teased. 'That book could practically write itself! We can give you some good material, I'm sure. Right, Rem?' She shot Remi a wink.

'Indeed, we can,' Remi replied, suddenly looking down at her stomach. Avery couldn't fathom why; the girl was fit as a button.

'It is what it is,' Mori shrugged. 'I need to stay in my lane.' She wiped her hands of muffin crumbs as if wiping the conversation off the table completely.

'Now that's just sad,' Remi said, turning toward Mori and landing a comforting hand on her arm. 'Don't give up, girl.'

'Well, no. It's not all bad. Now that you two are here and changing my perspective on things, you're reminding me to slow down and take life in,' Mori said pensively, gazing beyond them out toward the water. After a long pause, she added, 'Which reminds me, Calista promised she'd arrive before breakfast. I told her Chef Brody would be here, and she should just grab a snack for her travels. I wonder what happened?'

The three looked at the empty spot at the table, and concern grew among them.

'Maybe one of us should give her a call,' Remi suggested.

'Since I needed to share the address of where we were staying, I have all your numbers plugged into my phone.' Mori scrolled through a bunch of numbers before ringing their friend.

But Calista didn't answer.

TEN

Calista wrung her hands while she waited for Gabe to show up at the baggage claim. When the overhead screen finally confirmed that his flight had arrived, and the bags began to flow on the conveyor belt, she felt like running to the bathroom and throwing up. She yanked her cell phone from her pocket and ignored all the missed calls and messages. She only wanted to search Remi's Instagram page and find a recent photo of Gabe, so she could instantly recognize him. He had changed so much in the last twenty years, and she had forcibly erased him from her mind. She didn't think she would know him if he literally knocked her over.

'Calista?'

She heard a familiar voice behind her and spun on her heel toward him. She might not initially recognize his face, but the baritone sound – she could peg that voice anywhere.

'Gabe!' Calista threw her arms around his neck and held him tight; her body began to tremble beneath the solidness of him. His rock-strong arms were unlike anything she'd ever felt from Kirk. She hadn't expected the butterflies to erupt inside her stomach at the sight of him, or all her old feelings to rush back like a tsunami. Suddenly, she was seventeen again, disobeying her parents and sneaking off to be with him. Breathing him in, she couldn't believe he still wore Curve. Did they still even make that cologne? Or was she imagining things? The scent of him almost catapulted her to the forest behind his childhood home, where he'd built a treehouse for them to escape to. It was there he promised that one day he'd build her a bigger house in another city, far from Massachusetts. His treehouse became their secret space, hidden beneath the tall pines, and only the two of them knew of its existence. The place where they'd hide, explore each other's virgin bodies upon the carpet remnants, until they couldn't take it anymore and their desire climaxed. A place where they'd become each other's 'first' beneath the stars. A place where her overprotective parents couldn't stop them. Calista's mother had found a morning-after pill still in the unopened package which she'd hidden beneath her bed and had assumed the worst. Calista was forbidden to date. Not Gabe. Not Kirk. Not anyone.

'Oh my God, you're shaking,' he said, pulling her death grip off his body and bringing her back to the present moment. Calista was desperately clinging to him like saran wrap – the Costco kind, the stuff that *really* sticks like glue.

'I'm sorry. I'm a little nervous,' she admitted, giving him a onceover. His face was tan and beautiful. The person standing in front of her was no longer the boy she remembered; instead, Gabe's jawline had matured into manhood, and he clearly had grown into his muscles. Instantly, Calista was reminded of an NCP USA Championship bodybuilding competitor whom Devon had once pointed out to her on a YouTube video. Gabe's physique was comparable, and she thought her son would be equally impressed. She had to blink her eyes to take her high school sweetheart in again.

'I can't believe how nervous I am,' she repeated.

'I see that. I've got you – just take a breath.'

Calista breathed deeply as commanded and was surprised at his nonplussed demeanor. He was much different from the skinny shy teen she remembered from her old neighborhood. And he was so relaxed, despite this forced reunion.

'Where are your bags?' She looked beyond him to the conveyor belt where the rest of the weary travelers were eagerly watching for their luggage, like hawks ready to pounce.

'I'm not here on vacation, Calista,' he reminded her, holding up a backpack carry-on. 'I'm only here because you bought me a flight. And I'm getting on the next one heading back south. So . . . you mind telling me what this is all about?'

'Right.' Calista breathed deeply. She was beginning to hyperventilate, and she needed to remind herself to keep breathing before she literally caused herself to pass out smack dab in the middle of Logan Airport. She could already envision an ambulance ride and her secrets spilling out on the nightly news instead of the way she intended.

'Does this have to do with our parents? Last I heard, they were still arguing over some damn thing. I've tried to get mine to accept your father's apology. It was a long time ago, and look, I'm fine!' He held out jazz hands dramatically as if to prove it.

'Umm.' Calista looked at the crowd that was swarming the area around the baggage claim and pressed her lips tightly together before retreating a step backward.

Gabe must've got the message as he asked, 'Where do you want to talk? Can we find a private place here at the airport? I'd rather not leave if we don't have to. And I really want to know why you dragged me out here right before your reunion with the girls. Unless one of our parents is going to be brought up on charges for taking this long-standing ridiculous argument any further, I really don't understand the need for a face-to-face . . .' he trailed off, searching her eyes.

'Yeah, umm, sure.'

Calista led the way to the escalator, and they rode to the next level. 'There's an area past the food court where I think we can talk privately. I noticed it earlier when I walked by; a mechanic was working on a plane, like one's out of commission,' she said over her shoulder.

Gabe stood behind her, and she could feel the weight of his stare on the back of her head. Her heart thumped erratically due to what she was soon about to share. She disagreed with Kirk over this. Gabe had the right to know *first* before she told Remi the truth.

The two walked in silence until they reached the area by the window overlooking the tarmac, which was vacant. Even the rows of chairs around them were empty. Calista took a seat, and Gabe took the one directly next to her. He turned to her, causing their knees to knock together.

'OK, what's this about? And don't mince words. I have a flight back to Florida to catch.' As a reminder, he pointed to the overhead screen listing the flight schedule above their heads. 'Don't beat around the bush, Cal. Hit me with it. Will you, please?' His tone came out as if he was pleading with her now. As though he'd been pondering what this was about ever since she'd begged him to come.

Calista was stunned by his forwardness but appreciated the fact that he probably felt she'd led him on a wild goose chase. So she went for it. 'You fathered a son.' She looked down at her hands, and they were visibly shaking. Her voice was unwavering, however, and she lifted her gaze to see if he understood.

His dark eyes narrowed in on her, and he looked stricken. 'What the hell are you talking about. I don't have any biological children. Have you lost your mind, Calista?'

'Yes, you do. You have a son, Gabe,' she whispered. 'Living here in Massachusetts.'

'*What?* That's impossible.' Gabe shook his head in denial. 'Who? Who told you this garbage? Is this some sort of joke?' He leapt off the seat then and spun on his heels as if he were ready to bolt.

'Gabe, *wait!*'

Unlike the day of the accident, this time Gabe froze on command and didn't run from her. Instead, he collapsed defeatedly into the chair. He slumped forward, so that his back faced her, and then leaned his arms on to his knees as if willing his arms to physically hold him upright.

Calista reached for him to turn around and forced him to meet her gaze by gently moving his chin to face her. 'It's not impossible. And you know it.'

'Um, yeah, it actually is. Remember the accident? Calista . . .' He breathed out her name as if he'd done it a million times in his head. 'I can't have kids. I lost that opportunity a long time ago. You of all people should know that!'

'I was pregnant the week before your accident,' she said quietly.

'Wait.' He held up a hand and red crawled from his neck to his face. 'What did you say?' His eyes narrowed in on her.

'You really want me to repeat it?'

'*Devon?*'

Calista nodded.

'*Your* Devon?'

She nodded again.

'Your Devon . . . is *my* Devon,' he confirmed aloud.

'Yes.'

Calista could tell Gabe was desperately trying to even his breath before he said, 'You mean to tell me you knew this all these years and kept it from me? And you decide to drop this in my lap now when your son is like eighteen or nineteen years old? Fuck! I don't even know how old he is!'

'He's twenty-two,' she murmured quietly.

'Oh, so you decide to tell me now that you have this reunion planned. Is that it? Is getting together with the girls somehow forcing you to look at the past? A reminder that Devon is my son! No wonder you've avoided seeing Remi and me all these years. You were hiding the truth from me!'

'No . . . that's not it . . .'

Gabe ran his hand nervously through his hair and then scrubbed his face with his hands as if hoping to wash away everything he'd just heard. 'How could you do this to me?' His eyes were wild now. They darted around the room, nervously looking for a place to land.

'I know this is a lot to take in.'

'I don't believe you . . .' he stuttered. 'I'm going to need proof. What is this? Some kind of truth-or-dare game? Did the girls down at the Cape prompt you to do this? It's some kind of reunion fun game? Let's get Gabe to squirm. Huh? Because, Calista, this is far from funny.'

'Is Ancestry.com all the proof you need? Or do you want more than that?' she asked softly.

His eyes widened further still. 'You matched my DNA? How the hell could you do that?'

'I didn't have to. The father's DNA didn't match Kirk's, and you're the only other person on the planet I slept with. There's only been two. You and Kirk . . . so do the math.'

'*Oh. My. God.* I can't believe this.'

'I know and I'm sorry. I promise you; I didn't know. All these years . . . and how much you and Kirk sort of look alike, I never even questioned it. Why would I? But then Kirk was looking for a long-lost cousin . . . he started using Ancestry.com . . . and we kind of tripped over the results.' She didn't mention that Kirk and Gabe looked nothing alike, now that they'd grown up. Gabe's body was flawless. Kirk looked as if he'd held an office job and sat at a desk most of his adult life – which he had. Exercise had never been high on Kirk's radar.

Nonetheless, Calista wondered if Gabe could detect the lie stamped all over her face. She knew all along that Devon wasn't Kirk's son; she'd just never voiced it aloud. She was the only one who knew about those slip-ups with Gabe. And, of course, Gabe knew it too. But they'd never spoken about their time in the treehouse. *Not to anyone.* It was their secret. Even after he and Remi moved to Florida and settled their lives there, she had never shared that secret with another soul. Gabe was the one who'd made the decision for them. Their parents were such rivals at that point; they both knew a relationship would never work. Especially when they were forbidden to see each other. Heck, if she'd told Gabe back then, he probably would've ended up with Remi anyway, and then where would she be? All alone? A single mother? Barely making ends meet? The only reason she pushed Gabe and Remi together in the first place was as an excuse to still hang around him despite her parents' warnings. She used Remi as a pawn to keep him close. Calista was desperate for him back then. And looking at him now, sitting in front of her, the feelings were still there, causing her heart to break into a million fresh little pieces.

Gabe kneaded his forehead with his hands, leaving a mark, and then his fingers traveled to his temples where he slowly massaged. His face turned an unnerving shade of white. 'Does Devon know I'm his father?'

'No, not yet.'

'When? How is that going to happen?'

'I don't know that yet, but we must tell Remi. Kirk won't keep this a secret and he's going to tell my son, but I asked him to wait. I suggested to Kirk that we talk to *you* first, but he refused to agree to that. It's like he wants to control how all of this comes out. He told me to tell Remi first and he gave me this week to do it. That's my deadline; otherwise, he's going to tell Devon everything.'

'Why is he in such a rush? I mean, clearly your son hasn't questioned? Has he?'

'No, Devon has no idea. The mere thought would be ludicrous to him! Kirk assumed it would be a good idea to plan this reunion and tell Remi face to face. I guess he felt that you didn't *deserve* to know first, since it was Remi who'd been betrayed – not you. Personally, I think he's just pissed that you and I slept together, and no one knew it. Anyhow, we're getting a divorce. Not over just this . . . other things as well.' Her eyes dropped to the floor to the worn carpet below. She wondered if this was what her new life would look like. Worn carpets and outdated appliances. She once had it all – the best of everything. And soon it would all be gone. What would happen to her now?

'He's divorcing you? You're telling me Kirk never found out about us? I always wondered why he didn't reach out to keep in touch with me all these years. I just assumed you told him we shared a past, and he didn't take the betrayal well.'

'No, I never told a soul.' She made the sign of the cross as if it meant something. At the moment, it meant absolutely nothing. She would not easily be absolved of this. No. This was life-changing. A mess. A hot mess.

'You swear?'

'Of course. That was always our dirty little secret.' As soon as the words were out of Calista's mouth, she wanted to hit the rewind button. She said *dirty* but there wasn't anything dirty about it in her mind. If she closed her eyes, she could still feel his tender touch and taste his kiss. It's a funny thing, the passing of time. It doesn't change feelings. She still recalled the way he looked at her back then, as if she were the only girl on the planet. He had seen her soul, like no other human being had. Kirk didn't hold a candle to Gabe in bed, but she needed someone to help raise her baby. And the someone she needed was in love with Remi. But she never wanted to be someone's second best. She wanted to be someone's first. And if Gabe couldn't stand up to her parents, how could she? She wanted him to fight for her. And he didn't even lift a fist.

'Does Remi know we shared a past? Did you ever confess it to her? Ever?'

He didn't answer. Instead, her comment seemed to remind him of his wife.

Gabe adamantly shook his head, 'No! This isn't fair. It's like some cosmic joke! Why is this happening now. Tell me, why *now* of all times?' He slammed a closed fist on his thigh. Calista wondered if that would leave a bruise. Which reminded her of her own. She was so numb to everything that she'd forgotten about it.

Calista pointed to her cheek. 'When I told Kirk that I wanted to keep this a secret until I had a chance to talk to you, he hit me. He's never done anything like that to me before. I guess I deserved it.'

Gabe peered closely at her face as if he were trying to remove her makeup with his eyes to view the bruise firsthand. 'It's never OK to hit a woman,' he said firmly. 'Never. You understand that, right?' He held her gaze until she agreed with a slight nod. 'I'll fuckin' kill the bastard if he lays a hand on you again,' he added through gritted teeth. 'That's not how things get handled!'

Calista didn't share that the bruise inside her heart was far more painful than any physical pain that had been inflicted. She could sense Gabe's resentment escalating, his energy palpable now, and that was not her intent. 'It's OK,' she soothed, laying a hand on top of his. 'We'll figure it out. We'll all get through this.' She hoped by saying the words aloud, she would come to believe them too.

'I'm telling you, if he touches you again,' he warned. And Calista took the warning seriously.

'I believe you,' she said, meeting his gaze. The hurt she witnessed in his eyes almost destroyed her. 'I'm so sorry, Gabe. For all of this. I never meant . . .'

'We'll figure it out.' He mimicked her words back to her, so it seemed as if what she'd shared had finally registered in his mind. And he was perhaps entering the accepting phase.

'We have to tell Remi before Kirk does,' Calista cautioned. 'She needs to hear it from one of us. Or both of us. Honestly, I'm not really sure which one of us should tell her. Do you have a suggestion? She's your wife; I will do whatever you say. It's your call.'

'Yeah, and she used to be your best friend,' he scoffed. 'What happened to that. Huh?'

His outburst stung. Calista didn't need a shameful reminder again of what she had done to Remi. Or why she had backed off their friendship all these years. Nor did she need a reminder from Kirk; the bruise helped with that. Yet didn't Gabe take any responsibility for their little secret? Their betrayal? Suddenly, it all felt dirty, and she was now the one growing frustrated.

'This is just poetic. It really is the worst possible timing for my wife,' he continued, standing now and beginning to pace circles in front of her. It was as if the chair was too little to contain him and he needed to get rid of the excess fight-or-flight energy.

'Why? Is something wrong with Remi?'

'She's pregnant.'

Calista sucked a breath. 'How? You just said . . . Oh! In vitro? You guys finally attempted that route?'

'Something like that.'

'What do you mean, *something like that*? If it wasn't in vitro, then how?'

'She slept with a guy at the gym.'

'Wait. Now I'm confused! Remi *cheated* on you?' Calista rose from her seat and grabbed one of his hands sympathetically. Maybe this wouldn't be as damaging as Calista initially thought. Maybe this would lessen the blow somehow. Maybe she and Gabe and Devon would end up one happy little family, after all. Maybe she could pick up the pieces of her life and glue them back together. Sure, the idea had cracks. But—

'No, it wasn't like that. She didn't cheat on me. I watched,' he said, interrupting her hopes and dreams and shattering them all over again. He dropped Calista's hand and then raked his hands through his hair nervously. He then weaved his fingers behind his neck and held them there as he studied her. He looked at her helplessly as if he wanted her to toss him a life raft. But she couldn't because she too was drowning.

'*Well?* Say something!'

Calista let out a nervous cough and chuckled before taking a seat once again. 'Excuse me, I'm trying to recalibrate my brain here. I thought I just heard you say you *watched*. What the hell is that supposed to mean? I'm really not following here!'

'Remi and I paid him to sleep with her. It only took like five or six times.'

Calista had no words; she just stared at him in shock.

'Don't look at me like that! It's a ton cheaper than in vitro and we know what we're getting. The guy's in good shape, he takes care of himself, he follows strict nutrition – he's a perfect match,' he defended, ticking off his fingers like a grocery list and not another man sleeping with his wife *while he watched*!

As if this checked-off list made it all rational.

Calista didn't know what to say. This was not what she was expecting – even a little. It was amazing how quickly the tables turned. If Mori got wind of this, she'd have another bestseller on her hands. Only this wasn't fiction; it was their own hellish reality.

'Say something,' Gabe urged. 'Tell me how we're going to fix all this.'

Calista deflated in the chair and put her head in her hands. The pressure along her temples made her want to reach for a bottle of ibuprofen. 'I don't know what to say at this point.'

'Do I just get on the plane and head back to Florida?'

'Just like you to run. Go ahead, Gabe. Run home to your perfect life while I stay back and pick up the pieces as always,' Calista murmured under her breath.

'That's not fair.'

'Is it not the truth?' She locked eyes with him again. 'Are you not the runner? Why the hell are you living in Florida? You left *me* for Remi? Remember?' As soon as the words were out of her mouth, she regretted them. He might be the runner, but she was the liar. She'd held the secret of Devon's paternity so tight it almost suffocated her. She reached out for his hand then and took it in hers. 'I'm sorry. I didn't mean that; I'm just stressing out, is all.'

Gabe shook her off. 'It's fine.'

'It's not *fine*,' she said gently. 'Nothing will ever be fine again!'

'Then what do we do now? Tell me,' he begged eagerly. 'I don't even know where we go with this.'

'I have no idea,' Calista replied wearily. 'I just know that we have to get to Remi before Kirk does, because he'll ruin everything.'

ELEVEN

Evening had come, and Mori had planned for Brody to return and prepare stuffed quahogs. The quahogs or clams – native and freshly dug from the shores of Cape Cod – are commonly served oceanside and often cooked directly on the beach. However, Mori opted for linguica-stuffed quahogs, and a side of New England clam chowder to remind her friends of their high school days when they would all pile in the car (whichever car had enough gas in the tank) and, unbeknownst to their parents, make the hour-and-a-half trip to the Cape. They'd spend the night camping out on the beach somewhere in Falmouth and eating clam chowder takeout from some hole-in-the-wall eatery. Therefore, Mori opted for the chef to bring the food down to the sand where a beach campfire was already ablaze, despite the fact the sun hadn't dipped fully below the horizon yet. Chairs were surrounding the campfire, thanks to Brody's earlier efforts, and all the ladies had to do was show up.

Mori looked up to see Remi and Avery walking towards her on the boardwalk leading to the beach.

'Surprise!' she said when they finally joined her at the campfire.

'What is this? I just passed Brody in the kitchen, and he didn't utter a peep!' Remi asked excitedly, laying her sweatshirt on a chair. 'I thought you said you wanted to walk the beach before dinner; I wasn't expecting this! How fun!'

'Yeah, this is awesome!' Avery joined in. 'Just like old times!'

'I'm glad you both approve.' Mori smiled appreciatively before scrolling through her texts to see if she'd missed an update from Calista. 'We're only missing one person.' She was trying not to be distracted by the obvious, but she couldn't help it. 'It's really bothering me that we haven't heard from her. Where the hell is she?'

'Seriously?' A look of shock washed across Remi's face. 'She never called or texted you back? I just assumed—'

'No, I honestly don't know what to make of it. It's not like we have poor cell service out here. There's no reason for it.' Mori checked the full bars again on her phone and tried not to sound anxious, but she couldn't help it. A pang in the pit of her stomach made her feel that something was very wrong. 'Has she reached out to you, Avery?'

Avery shook her head, and the three exchanged a look of concern.

'That's weird . . . and now that you mention it, Gabe hasn't called me back either,' Remi frowned. 'I've been checking my phone too. I would've seen it if she reached out. That's really strange,' she added, clicking her tongue.

'My phone is back in my room. Should I go and take a look and see if maybe she texted me?' Avery asked.

'No, it's OK. I think she would've responded to me first, since I'm the one who reached out to her this morning. Unless you've been in touch with her recently? Are you close with her nowadays?' Mori asked.

'Not really,' Avery admitted. 'Out of all of us, I'm probably the most out of the loop. I don't go on social media much.'

'Let me try her again. I'm sure it's fine.' Mori called Calista's phone, and this time when she heard Calista's voicemail, she left a message: 'Hey, girlfriend! We're all here at the beach house, excited to see you! We understand if maybe something came up. Just shoot me a text that you're on your way, OK? We're starting to worry. OK, bye for now.'

Brody came into view juggling an armful of stuff, and Avery said, 'I'm gonna go and help the poor kid out.' She sprinted over to assist, leaving Mori and Remi alone to tend the fire.

'Gosh, I hope she's OK,' Remi said worriedly. 'It's weird for her to be so late and not call. Or text, at the very least.'

'I'm sure we're overreacting,' Mori said. 'Probably something came up to do with her son. Maybe the appointment went on longer than expected and he needed a follow-up or something.'

'Yeah, I suppose,' Remi answered as she rubbed her abdomen. Mori wondered if she was hungry.

'You ready for some New England clam chowder, Missy?' she teased.

'You bet I am! I can't get that kind of treat in Florida!' Remi grinned. 'It's just not the same as the soup from here. It never is.'

Brody set down a large cooler and Avery placed an oversized picnic basket beside it.

'Plates, bowls, napkins, cutlery – all are in there.' Brody pointed to the basket. 'And the cooler has all the wine it can handle.' He winked at Mori.

She returned the wink and cooed, 'Good boy. You'll get a tip for that.'

This caused the chef to laugh heartily. 'I'll be right back with the clam chowder,' he announced.

'Let me help you,' Avery called after him, but his feet were already kicking up sand in his wake as he jogged back to the house. 'I got it!' he said over his shoulder. 'Just relax!'

Avery began to follow despite his words, and Mori stopped her with an outstretched hand. 'Oh no you don't. I paid him extra for this, and I paid him *well*,' Mori confessed. 'You just sit back like he suggested, and relax, Avery. This treat is for you to enjoy. I'm sure you have enough cooking to handle in your own kitchen back in Iowa.'

'I'm not sure I know *how* to relax,' Avery admitted, looking around her feet as if she needed some way of being of service.

Mori handed Avery a wineglass. 'Here. Hold this while I pour.'

Brody had already popped the cork and pushed it back inside just enough to stop the alcohol from dripping, per Mori's earlier request of not having to use a bottle opener on the beach. *Good lad.*

After pouring the glass of wine, Mori instructed Avery to sit and handed the glass to her. 'Drink,' she ordered.

Avery laughed and, in good spirits, took a sip of the wine. 'Oh, this is quite good!'

'Perfect.' Mori nodded approval, then handed Remi a glass to hold. After she had filled it, Remi refused it and instead handed it back to her.

Mori pushed back.

'Nah, I can't tonight.' Remi shook her head and pushed the wineglass aside again. 'You have it.'

'Oh yes, you can,' Mori insisted. 'I remember you could outdrink us in high school!' She shot a knowing glance to Avery who responded with a chuckle.

'No, really. I can't.'

'Look, doll.' Suddenly, Mori was talking like Jerome, whose vocabulary was surely rubbing off on her. He was never far from her mind. Just using his words made her miss him like crazy. She shook her head to recalibrate her brain once again. 'Let's just relax and catch up in each other's lives, enjoy a glass of wine while we wait for Brody to return with our chowder. Can we do that? *Please?*'

Her tone almost came out as begging. And she knew, based on past experiences within this group, she didn't need to beg.

'I'm pregnant,' Remi blurted out.

Mori was stunned and didn't utter a word. She looked toward Avery who stopped frozen midway from setting the wineglass down in the sand beside her. The two exchanged a look of shock. Neither seemed able to find the words to speak.

'Yes, you heard correctly. I'm pregnant. Aren't you guys happy for me?'

Mori and Avery rushed to join Remi in a group hug. 'Of course we are! Congratulations!' Avery shouted, and Mori echoed the sentiment.

'I'm just shocked!' Mori said, holding her heart when they finally parted. 'Why on earth didn't you say anything when you first arrived?'

'It's early,' Remi confessed. 'I didn't want to jinx anything.'

'And Gabe's bike accident? The doctors were wrong back then?' Avery asked hesitantly. 'I guess it was the shock of the great news that caught us off guard. We didn't think . . . it was possible. We'd heard . . .'

Remi cut her off. 'No, the doctor was right.'

'Gosh, that was a horrible accident,' Avery said pensively. 'I remember standing at my locker the next day and hearing about it at summer school. Calista's dad had backed his SUV into Gabe's bicycle. I don't think Gabe and Calista were allowed to hang out after that, or even utter each other's names at the dinner table for weeks. They definitely caught the brunt of that.'

The three were quiet momentarily as each relived the horrible memory in their own minds.

'I don't want to talk about the accident anymore. It is what it is, and Gabe is sterile from it,' Remi said despondently. 'That accident turned into a life sentence for him. For *us*, really. But we've managed.'

'Is that why you and Calista didn't keep in touch over the years after you married Gabe?' Mori asked. 'Out of all of us, I always thought you two were the closest. Wasn't she the one who convinced the coach to put you on the varsity cheerleading team? And became your mentor?'

'No, I don't think that was why we lost touch. It's true, their parents still haven't mended fences. I remember Calista visiting

Gabe in the hospital when I was sitting at his bedside, and she mentioned their argument was over me. I have no recollection of why they'd be fighting over me in the first place. I never really heard the full story. It was pretty traumatic for Gabe. Something he doesn't like to talk about.'

'Well . . . the good news is you're pregnant now!' Avery reminded them, lifting her glass. 'Congratulations, Remi. Cheers to you guys. I'm so happy for you!'

Remi's earlier enthusiasm seemed to deflate, and she was far less excited. Mori pressed, 'What? There's something else we're missing here?' She hoped it was just reliving the accident that caused Remi's mood to shift, but she felt there was something more. Her writing senses were prickling all over. Normally, she would grab a notebook and jot notes when this happened. Instead, she'd have to remember it for later.

'Yes, there's something more.' Remi sounded defeated and yet hopeful at the same time.

'What?' Avery asked.

The look on Remi's face was not what Mori had anticipated, and she couldn't exactly read her expression. She waited with bated breath before Remi suggested, 'Pour yourself a glass or two, Mori, and hopefully neither of you will remember what I'm about to tell you. Let's just say, we got creative.'

'Sounds juicy,' Mori said as she topped up her glass of wine. 'Something I could use in one of my books?' She moved her seat closer and made herself comfortable, readying herself for what Remi was about to reveal.

Meanwhile, Avery covered her ears. 'Oh *Gawd*, Remi. If you're going to talk about Gabe and your sex life, I might have to move my chair further down the beach. What I remember of Gabe is watching him play on my brother's little league team. I don't need to hear this. This is gross.'

Remi rubbed her abdomen tenderly. 'Gabe didn't technically make this baby,' she announced shyly.

Avery lifted the wineglass to her lips and took a huge gulp, causing beach sand to sit on her thigh where she now rested the bottom of the glass. She lifted the glass and brushed it away.

'Go on,' Mori said with a roll of her hand. 'We're waiting . . .'

Remi bit her lip and, with a shy smile, said quietly, 'I slept with the trainer at our gym a few times.'

Mori flashed a look to Avery whose eyes at this sudden revelation expanded to the size of sand dollars.

'And Gabe knows?' Avery spurted. 'He has to know that baby isn't his!' she said, pointing an accusing finger to Remi's stomach.

'Oh, yeah, he knows,' Remi said, nonplussed. 'He watched, sometimes.'

'Now *this* I can use!' Mori exclaimed before taking another sip of wine. She could hardly wait for more details. She really hoped Remi would be forthcoming.

'Don't tell a soul!' Remi exclaimed and put a finger to her lips. 'No one has to know.'

'Of course not. Our lips are sealed, right, Avery?'

Avery looked as if she wanted to crawl beneath the chair, and she kept blinking her eyes rapidly as if she couldn't clear her vision.

'Avery? You OK?' Mori asked.

'Yep. Just taking this all in,' Avery said with a deep breath, before draining the entire glass of wine in one go and then holding out her wineglass for a refill. Mori readily obliged.

'Now we're talking! Get the party started!' Mori said, elated, as Avery sat back in the chair with a topped-up glass.

'So, how was it? The sex, I mean?' Mori asked. 'We want details.'

'Speak for yourself,' Avery said, taking another huge gulp.

'Just keep drinking and hopefully you won't remember this conversation,' Remi teased.

Avery didn't argue this time. Instead, she drawled, 'Don't mind if I do.'

Mori leaned forward in her chair expectantly before Remi squashed the conversation with three little words.

'Oh, hey Brody.'

Avery sighed with relief. 'I've never been so happy to see New England clam chowder in my whole life.'

Sadly, Mori didn't feel the same.

TWELVE

The three licked their bowls of chowder clean as the sun dipped in the horizon and the heat of the day was replaced by a cool breeze.

The sky morphed into a glorious shade of violet. Deep burgundy clouds streaked across it, mirroring atop the water. As the waves methodically lapped to shore, and the tide crawled in, the fire continued to crackle, keeping Mori's bare feet warm on the cool sand.

After wiping his lips with a cloth napkin, Brody collected the dirty dishes on a tray. 'Hey, thanks for letting me crash your party . . . I was starving. I don't normally eat with guests, but you ladies were all so gracious to allow it.'

'Hey, you made it. And by the way, it was the best darn chowder this side of Boston! I'm so full!' Avery said. 'You're gonna have your pick of jobs after graduation. I guarantee it.'

Brody beamed.

'Maybe I'll hire you as my personal chef. What do you think about living on the Vineyard after graduation?' Mori asked.

'Oh, I couldn't afford it. It's *really* expensive living over there,' Brody countered. His gaze traveled toward the water where the stretch of land called Martha's Vineyard lay just beyond the bay. There was an unexpected longing in his eyes that Mori couldn't read.

'I can convert my writing cottage, located behind my house, to your living quarters. And turn my library back to an office,' Mori suggested. 'I agree. It's hard to find inexpensive housing over there. But think about it.'

'I will.' He smiled then and jutted a thumb toward the house. 'I need to head back and work on dessert.'

'Ooh! What are we having? I have no problem splurging on dessert. Diet begone!' Remi shared a look of knowing with Avery and Mori. Now that the group knew she was pregnant, Mori assumed Remi was letting her guard down and not watching every single calorie that she put into her mouth.

'Cannolis – just like you'd find on the North End. I've been practicing,' Brody said proudly, slipping his hands to his hips.

'I think I'm in heaven. Pinch me,' Avery said enthusiastically. The wine was turning her nose a shade of pink and her demeanor was a ton more relaxed.

Mori was happy her wine was kicking in.

'I haven't had a cannoli in years! Thanks for thinking to make a Boston favorite. My memories are flooding back,' Remi agreed with a nod. 'I can't wait to try your work of art.'

'Bring it on, Babe,' Mori chimed in.

'I'm on it!' Brody laughed and turned toward the beach house. Mori watched as he jogged easily across the sand. Man, he was a thing of beauty! She needed to get to her laptop quickly before she lost the words forming inside her mind as she followed the chef with her eyes all the way back to the boardwalk.

'What a nice guy. It's been really fun getting to know him and hearing that strong accent again. It's catchy. I feel like all my New England feels are rushing back to me now,' Remi said, breaking the silence. 'I've been gone far too long.'

'I agree!' Avery said. 'It's fun to be back home again.'

Mori turned to Remi then. 'OK, before Brody crashed our party, you had something to add. Sidebar – I love his company and didn't at all mind that he joined us for dinner. I was just looking forward to more details.' She wagged her eyebrows teasingly. 'Come on, now; don't you dare hold back.'

Avery held out her wineglass. 'I have a feeling I'm going to need more for this conversation.' Which caused Mori to easily oblige and top off the glass once again. Luckily, Brody had more than one bottle ready in his arsenal.

Remi took in a calculated yoga breath before she spoke. 'Are you sure you want to hear this? Maybe Brody's interruption was a good thing. It stopped me from oversharing.'

'Um, no! We love oversharing!' Mori encouraged. 'You're not getting out of it that easy!'

'OK. But just like the old days, this conversation doesn't leave this campfire. Truth or dare?' She held out a fist, and the three exchanged a fist bump before releasing it like an explosion.

'We want the truth. Don't we, Ave?' Mori turned to Avery who had sunk back in her chair while she herself sat upright in utter anticipation.

'Yeah, truth,' Avery finally agreed with a lift of her chin.

They both looked at Remi who confessed, 'Truth? OK. Here

goes. I loved. Every. Single. Minute. Of making this baby.' Remi looked down at her stomach and folded her hands across her abdomen protectively. The sparkle in her eyes reflected across the campfire. And the look of delight was undeniable.

'Oh boy,' Avery uttered.

Mori leaned forward in her chair. '*Explain.*'

'I'm thinking there's more truth coming than I can handle,' Avery said with a hiccup. 'I might lose my chowder.'

Mori play-slapped Avery with the back of her hand. 'Oh, don't be such a prude. You've got a houseful of kids. Don't act like you're a virgin! We know what it took between those rows of Iowa corn to grow your family!'

Avery responded with an eye-roll.

'Sorry for the interruption, doll.' Mori grinned at Remi. 'Please. Continue.'

'Let's just say . . . Gabe wasn't *always* present.' Remi curled her lip as if she wanted to stop a moving train. But she'd already said too much.

'Oh my God! You're in love with him?' Avery asked tentatively. 'This trainer guy – babymaker. You're in love with him?' she repeated. Her eyes were blinking mechanically.

Though it didn't need repeating, they all understood what Remi was attempting to say. At least Mori thought so.

'No. I wouldn't take it that far, exactly.'

'What would you say, then?' Mori prompted.

Remi's expression twisted. 'I would say . . . I can't stop,' she admitted quietly with a smirk.

'You can't stop what exactly?' Avery asked.

'The sex.' Remi bit at her thumbnail. 'I can't stop having sex with him.'

'You can't stop having sex with the babymaker. Is that what you're saying?'

'And Gabe doesn't know?' Mori confirmed.

'Yeah, Gabe doesn't know,' Remi nodded.

'This sounds like a problem,' Avery said.

Remi visibly winced. 'Is it?'

'Why can't you stop?' Mori had to know. This was too good not to. She *wrote* this stuff, for Pete's sake, but she didn't live it. This was a firsthand account, being expressed in front of her very eyes. It was as if one of her characters had leapt from the page and come to life. Her ears begged for more. She wanted synonyms, antonyms, verbs! She wanted it all!

'The way he touches me is electric.' Remi reached to her collar bone, leaving a rub mark, and then toyed with her necklace. 'He kisses me, right there and just the whisper of his lips on my skin almost makes me scream. It's like being kissed by a feather. And my lower back . . . he licks it like a popsicle until I'm covered in goosebumps.' She bit her lip before continuing. 'Let's just say he knows how to use his body. Or drive mine mad! We've even tried a little bondage with some equipment at the gym. I didn't think I'd be into it. But it's incredibly erotic and addicting.'

Avery slapped her forehead. '*Oh Gawd.*'

'How do you mean *bondage*? What else does he do to you? Or you to him? I want it all, girl. Don't stop,' Mori said gleefully. 'Don't you dare stop!'

Avery giggled like a schoolgirl then. 'Yeah, don't stop. I think Mori's about to have an orgasm right here on the beach!'

Remi seemed to suddenly back out of her trance and stated evenly, 'You're not using this in one of your books. *Swear to me!*'

'Why not?' Avery chimed in. 'Maybe you can collect some of her royalties out of this.'

Mori couldn't make promises; this was all too good. 'What if I change your name?' she asked, tentatively chewing her lip.

'No!' Remi shouted.

'I'm just kidding . . . I won't write it.' Though her toes were digging deep into the sand to hold herself back from feeling every little sensuous detail.

'How old is he?' Avery wanted to know.

'Honestly? I'm not sure.'

'I don't believe you,' Avery said. 'He's younger than Gabe, isn't he?'

'Maybe,' Remi shrugged. 'We never really talked about it.'

Avery raised a brow. 'I'm guessing he's not much older than Chef Brody. Am I right?'

'Probably,' Remi admitted with a sly smile. 'I mean, this guy's body is impeccable. He's in *great* shape. I mean, it's not my fault. Gabe was the one who picked him and approached him about it.'

'Oh, good for you! I'm impressed!' Mori giggled now. She couldn't help it. The wine, the salty breeze, the conversation – it was all just going to her head. She wished Jerome were here to see her like this. All flushed and happy. 'What's his name anyway?'

'I'm not telling you that. We signed a confidentiality agreement.'

'Oh, juicy!' Mori said, steepling her fingers. 'A confidentiality agreement – this just keeps getting better! It's like a written permission slip for secret sex! For the sake of this conversation, though, what shall we call him?'

'Call him Taz,' Remi suggested. 'I call him that sometimes.'

'As in the Tasmanian Devil?' Mori confirmed.

'The very one,' Remi nodded with a devilish grin.

'I love it!' Mori squealed, rocking back into her seat.

'Are you going to end it?' Avery asked. 'With this Taz guy.'

'I've tried,' Remi said. 'I'm hoping it'll be easier now that I'm pregnant. Maybe I won't feel sexy, and it will help me stop.' She frowned. 'Do you think? Once I get bigger, I'll be able to stop? Right?'

'I dunno, I've never been pregnant,' Mori said and then they looked to Avery for counsel. 'Iowa girl is your babymaker, over there! She might be able to help with this.'

'Don't look at me!' Avery said. 'I'm not explaining my sex life to you two. I'll take the dare instead!' she declared. 'I'll run naked across this beach if I have to! Or chug another bottle of wine till I puke! Or eat a raw quahog! But I'm not sharing Jack stories with you guys. No way!' She physically drew a line in the sand using her toe. 'We're done here,' she added firmly.

Mori addressed Avery's dare. 'Oh, don't worry, we'll have time for that. I'd like to see you run naked across the beach. But in the daylight, of course. When the world can see you bare it all! Thanks for the suggestion!' she grinned.

'You guys aren't helping,' Remi whined like a petulant child. '*How* am I gonna stop? He's like an addiction. A fix I *need*. He's like a drug . . . an addictive drug!'

'You just stop. Cold turkey,' Avery suggested. 'Buy a dildo if you have to.'

'Ah.' Mori turned to her. 'A dildo? Unlike the Keurig machine, our prudish Iowa farmer here knows what that contraption is! Isn't that a surprise! They have adult toy shops like that out in the sticks, do they?'

Avery slapped her forehead with the heel of her palm.

'I'm hoping the time away will help me end it. If he'd only stop sending me hot Snapchats,' Remi continued. 'He's so freaking hot! I would show you guys, but he'd kill me!'

'Taz snapchats you? Does Gabe know?' Mori begged to know.

'Well . . . he hasn't sent me any Snaps since I've arrived in Massachusetts.'

Something in her voice sounded disappointed, and Mori didn't push. But she knew she was right when Remi continued, 'Maybe I'm outta sight outta mind.' She shrugged.

'You should delete him and pretend we never had this conversation. Give me your phone, I'll do it.' Avery gestured for Remi to hand it over.

Remi refused by patting her pocket as if she was keeping her phone tucked safely inside. 'No, it's fine.'

Mori could see Remi shutting down and it was confirmed when she said, 'OK. I'm done talking then. You two need to keep this in the vault. I swear, if you tell Gabe that I'm still sleeping with Taz, I'll never forgive you.'

'When would we ever talk to Gabe? We haven't seen each other in over twenty years!' Avery pronounced with a chuckle.

'Don't worry, your secret is safe with us,' Mori confirmed. Her thoughts turned to their minus-one. 'I'm really starting to worry about Calista.' She reached for her own phone only to confirm no missed calls or messages. The volume had been turned all the way up, just in case. But it didn't matter. There was nothing.

'Maybe we should reach out to Kirk and ask if something happened. Hopefully, we're all just overreacting, and her phone died or something,' Remi said, finally pulling her phone from the safety of her shorts pocket under Avery's watchful eye.

'Yeah, I think we should. Calista said she was going to be here already. I was trying to give her the benefit of the doubt, but honestly, I'm getting worried. This is hard because we really haven't been in each other's lives in a long time. But I never saw Calista as being rude like this and not responding.' Mori frowned. 'Something's not right. Something's definitely going on.'

'I agree. There must be a reason why she's not responding. It's not like her,' Avery agreed. 'Something must've happened.'

Remi typed out a message and within seconds she had received an alert. She smiled to the group. 'I messaged Kirk via Facebook messenger because I don't have his phone number. Looks like he responded!' Mori and Avery abandoned their chairs to join her. They looked over her shoulder and waited.

Kirk's message read: **Calista left the house early yesterday morning.**

THIRTEEN

'Wait. That can't be right,' Remi said, pointing to the screen. 'How can Kirk say that Calista left *yesterday* morning? That's impossible! Where the hell is she?' Her pulse quickened with each additional comment.

'Message him back!' Mori said. Her words were coming out slurred now.

'Yeahhh, do . . . Moriah says.' Avery's words were coming out wavy too. 'Tell . . . him she'ssss not here.'

The timing for learning this information from Kirk was a little off as Remi was the only sober one left in the group. And his message left her reeling.

'Go ahead, ask 'em!' Mori pointed to Remi's phone.

Remi shot out a quick message hoping he'd instantly respond: She's not here. And then waited. The little white checkmark circled in blue next to Kirk's name on Facebook stared back at her absently. 'I think he's offline,' she said finally. 'He's not reading it.'

'Now whaaat we do?' Avery leaned forward in her chair, and Remi wondered if she soon might be sick. The thought of it only made her own stomach churn. The last thing she wanted to deal with right now was holding Avery's hair back, above a toilet, for the rest of the evening.

Remi decided since the two next to her were inebriated, she was the only one with a level head to make a plan. 'I guess, all we can do is wait.'

Avery hiccupped. 'Wait for what?'

'Wait for Kirk to respond.' She looked from Avery to Mori for help, but they were too drunk to let the enormity of this sink in. She was the only one feeling the weight of it.

Where was Calista?

'That's a good idea. We'll wait,' Mori said before weaving away from them and walking toward the water, leaving a zigzag pattern in the sand in her wake.

'Where are you going?' Remi hollered after her.

'For a midnight swim!' Mori giggled.

'It's barely nine o'clock,' Avery clucked, looking to the sky as if she could tell the actual time from the position of the moon and stars. Remi didn't doubt that Avery, after spending years on a farm, most likely had that talent.

'I'm going, no matter what time!' Mori continued. 'I have to pee.'

'Oh no you don't!' Remi rose from her seat to follow, and Avery stumbled toward her.

'Yes, I doooo,' Mori sang out. 'I have to peeeee!'

'I'm comin' too,' Avery slurred. 'Wait for me!'

By the time Remi had caught up with Mori, she had already stripped off her clothes piece by piece and left them littered behind her. Thankfully, Mori had kept her underwear and bra on. If Brody happened to rejoin them on the beach, he was in for a slap of 'over-forty' shock and awe.

'You're not serious!' Remi yelled, wading behind Mori who, a minute ago, while standing in knee-high water, had fallen backwards on her ass as the tide rolled in, causing her to erupt in a fit of laughter.

'Woah!' Mori shrieked as an unexpected wave came up and hit her on the side of her head.

She deserved that, Remi thought with a shake of her head. Mori stood up, stunned, as if the cold water had finally knocked her back to reality.

'I'm soaked!' Mori looked utterly startled, which made Remi break out in laughter. Before she could warn of another pending wave, Avery ran past her, buck-naked, yelling over her shoulder.

'I'm doing my dare! But not in the daylight!'

Remi didn't know what to do except watch her friends like a teacher on recess waiting for one of them to fall off the monkey bars. Avery ran waist-high and then dove in expertly. She swam over to Mori. Within moments, the two were skipping through waves below the light of the rising moon, laughing and having a good time. Remi just stood there, holding her abdomen protectively. 'Don't go out too deep!' she hollered after them.

Where was Calista?

Now, more than ever, she wished she had kept in touch with Calista over the years and understood her better. In her mind, this behavior was out of character for her friend, but then again, she hadn't seen her in over twenty years. She thought back to high school when they'd been almost inseparable. Nearly every weekend was spent at each other's houses, choosing whichever had the better dinner option. Even when she was dating Gabe, Calista would tag along as a threesome. But when Gabe and Remi moved to Florida, it was as if they were wiped completely from Calista's life. Like they never existed. Remi always thought it *strange*.

She watched as Mori and Avery played and splashed in the water like ten-year-olds. Maybe she should go slip on her bikini and join the fun instead of focusing on the one friend who didn't show up for them or even bother to send a text. So like Calista, to put her own needs before everyone else's. She recalled her friend could show a selfish streak back in the day. She hoped for her sake that's all it was, and they could all laugh about it when she arrived.

Remi turned momentarily and noticed Brody was returning to the campfire with a box in his arms, most likely their dessert. She needed to head him off at the pass.

Remi cuffed her mouth and hollered, 'Hey, you two!' after turning her attention back to the sea. 'Sit tight beneath the water where you can't be seen and look out for each other. I'll be right back!' She jogged as fast as she could before Brody could catch on to what was happening. As soon as he was in earshot, she yelled out a warning: 'Naked women in the water! You may want to turn around!'

Even in the dark, Remi noticed Brody's face redden.

'Yikes!' he said, averting his eyes and turning his attention to the embers left over in the campfire which was just about snuffed out. 'I'd better get this going again so they can warm up after their dip in the ocean. It's OK when you stay below the water, but once the sun goes down, it gets pretty darn cold out here.'

He set the box of cannolis down on a chair and immediately added more wood to the fire and poked it with a long stick to reignite. Large flames flicked out from the top, bringing the campfire back to life and setting Brody's face aglow in the rekindled light.

Meanwhile, Remi noticed a single red rose sticking out of the box he'd delivered.

'You're too sweet!' Remi said, lifting the long-stemmed rose and taking a sniff. 'Some girl out there is going to be so lucky to snap you up.'

'I can't take the credit,' Brody admitted easily, dropping the stick he was using into the fire and watching it burn.

'Huh?'

'Flowers were delivered to you back at the house.' He plucked a card from his back pocket and held it in her direction.

The card read: *Remi, think of me, Taz.*

Now it was Remi's turn for her face to redden. 'Oh, thanks.' She had sent Taz a Snap of the house as soon as she had arrived, with the address attached to let him know she'd made it to the Cape, and noticed he'd read the message, but to her disappointment he hadn't responded to it. Now he'd sent her flowers. Gabe hadn't responded to her arrival on the Cape yet either, which she found odd. Maybe she wasn't the only one with a secret affair. The thought made her burn with fury. After all, in a few months they'd be parents. How much would their world change when two became three?

'You OK?' Brody asked, shaking her from her reverie.

'Yeah, sure. You?'

'Uh-huh,' Brody said, keeping eye contact with Remi as if he didn't want to catch sight of what was happening beyond them, out in the Atlantic.

Remi wondered if Brody, now studying her so carefully, could see the shame readily apparent on her face. She quickly changed the subject. 'Can you do me one last favor before you head out for the night?'

'Sure, what do you need?'

'Can you bring back some beach towels?' Remi jutted a thumb behind her. 'I don't think it's safe for me to leave those two alone and go all the way back to the house,' she added with an exaggerated eye-roll. 'I'm afraid one of them might drown without parental supervision.'

'You got it. No problem.' Brody immediately turned on his heel and jogged away from her. Remi couldn't help but wonder if the poor kid was looking for a quick escape from the nonsense happening on the beach. If only she could be so lucky. She stifled a yawn. If it was safe to leave them, she would go and crawl into bed, exhausted from all the adrenaline leading up to this trip. The last few days were finally catching up with her.

Remi turned to watch Mori and Avery frolic in the water for a few moments longer and noted they were safe before quickly checking her phone. No message on Facebook from Kirk, but there was a new Snap from Taz. It revealed a picture of him seductively looking into the camera as if he were standing right in front of her. Remi sucked in a breath to squash the longing pulling from deep within. She moved her thumb and then he was gone, and she instantly felt regret for not saving the photo. He was already slipping away from her, and she desperately wanted to hang on.

FOURTEEN

The next morning, Avery stumbled into the kitchen with her head in her hands, desperate for a strong dose of caffeine. She was thankful that the only thing required was to put in a K-Cup and hit the start button. Jack had better come through and fulfill her Christmas request this year, as she was already envisioning a Keurig machine in her foreseeable future. She didn't care how much it would set them back.

The last time Avery drank this much alcohol was back in Iowa, three years prior when they'd decided to host a party in the barn for New Year's Eve. Stacks of hay lined the walls, while her son Owen's band had played, and they danced until two a.m. It had been so much fun until it hadn't. She'd spent the entire next day cleaning up after the party, feeling ill, and had made a promise to herself that she'd never make that mistake again. Yet here she was, blinking behind blurred vision, desperate for coffee while her fingers massaged her temples.

'Morning, Ave.' Mori stepped into the kitchen and immediately poured herself a glass of orange juice and topped it off with a splash of champagne.

'Oh, gross! How could you drink that after last night?' Avery whispered. Just the sound of her own voice made her head hurt. This might be a two-K-Cup morning.

'Try a little. It'll help with the hangover,' Mori suggested, taking a sip.

Avery held back a gag with the back of her hand. 'Not even a chance.'

'Brody will be here soon; maybe a slice of toast will help settle your stomach.'

Just the thought of breakfast almost sent Avery running for the bathroom.

A cheerful Remi sauntered into the room with a rolled yoga mat tucked under her arm. 'Mornin', ladies,' she sang out. 'Care to join me for a yoga set on the beach?'

'I'll try it. If you wait until after breakfast,' Mori said. 'Brody's on his way.'

'I think I'll sit this one out,' Avery replied, lacing her hands around the mug and inhaling all the goodness seeping out of it. Ah, the scent of coffee was almost as intoxicating as the alcohol the night before.

Mori's phone dinged on the counter, catching her attention. She smiled wide the minute she read the message, causing Avery to ask, 'Adam? Or better yet please tell me it's Calista.'

Mori breathed deeply and sighed, 'No. Not Adam.' She chuckled downheartedly. 'And sorry, not Calista either.' She frowned.

'Wait. I just caught that. Everything OK between you and Adam?' Remi asked, resting her hip alongside the counter. 'I'm sorry I haven't asked about you two sooner.'

The abrupt change in demeanor wasn't lost on Avery either. She wasn't sure if the mood shift was due to Adam or Calista, so she moved closer to join in on the conversation – despite her throbbing head.

Mori chewed her lip. 'Adam's in Europe. He and I are on a bit of a break.'

'Oh nooo. I had no idea!' Remi said, dropping the yoga mat to the floor and reaching out to Mori for a hug. 'Are you OK?'

'Yeah, I'll be fine,' Mori said with watery eyes once they'd parted.

'I'm sorry to hear it, Mori.' Avery moved closer to pat her encouragingly on the arm. 'So, the good news that made you smile – was that your agent, then?' she prompted, hoping to lighten Mori's mood. 'Are you going to be able to write that book you always wanted?'

'No, that was a text from Jerome.'

'*Jerome?* That's a new name we haven't heard yet. Is he your latest muse?' Remi asked, her smile growing wide. 'Tell all!'

'He's not my Taz, if that's what you're asking,' Mori replied. 'Although not because I haven't tried,' she uttered under her breath so low they could barely catch it.

'Come again?' Remi asked.

Mori waved a hand of dismissal. 'It's nothing.'

'You can't leave us hanging,' Remi encouraged. 'I believe someone owes us a truth or dare after last night.'

Avery thought she might need ibuprofen for this conversation, so she changed it by turning her attention back to Remi.

'Hey, did Kirk ever get back to you?'

Remi's expression fell. 'No, he didn't.'

'Did he read the message?' Avery pushed.

Remi shook her head. 'No. I keep checking but nada.' The sound of disappointment was evident, and Avery felt it too. 'Apparently, he doesn't keep up with Facebook much.'

'We need to do something. We're on day three here,' Avery said, kneading her forehead and blinking her eyes as she attempted to get them to focus.

'I agree,' Mori said, setting down her empty champagne flute.

Just then, a new wave crossed Avery's vision, causing her to lean on the counter for support. The mug slipped from her hand and crashed to the floor, splashing what remained of her coffee everywhere.

'Avery! Are you OK?' Mori came to the rescue by immediately reaching for the paper towels and mopping up both the floor and Avery, deep concern riddled upon her brow. 'I thought you were going to pass out or something.'

'Yeah, I thought that too. Did you burn yourself?' Remi asked, jumping in to aid with the clean-up by carefully picking up the remnants of the porcelain mug and tossing the broken pieces into the trash.

'I think the only thing that's burning is my pride,' Avery admitted. 'I'm a bit embarrassed.'

'Oh, not to worry, we'll clean it up!' Mori replied empathetically. 'I'm just glad you're not hurt.'

'No, it's not that . . .' Avery sighed.

'What is it, then?' Remi asked.

'I suppose it's time to spill the beans.'

'I thought you just did,' Mori joked with a wink. She always had been good at breaking the tension.

Avery smiled ruefully, grateful. 'The truth, not coffee. Because it's getting harder and harder to hide this. Right before this trip, I was diagnosed with advanced-stage macular degeneration. I'm going blind, guys,' Avery muttered. 'I don't have much time left before I'll see hardly anything – if I can even see at all.'

Mori cupped her hand over her mouth, as if holding back her words. The inability to figure out the Keurig machine, the times when Avery was excessively blinking or wiping her eyes, appearing dizzy. Mori clearly was putting it all together.

'I'm so sorry, Avery,' she whispered finally. 'The idea of never being able to watch a sunrise again, or see your children's faces as they get older and watch Jack age alongside you . . .'

Hearing Mori voice these things aloud only compounded more bad news that Avery wasn't prepared to share or comprehend. It wasn't as though she hadn't thought about them the minute the doctor shared the horrible truth. But hearing them voiced hurt, and it must've shown on her face because Remi's brow narrowed in deep concern.

'"Sorry" seems a tremendously inadequate word. I don't know what to say except . . . we had no idea,' Remi uttered finally. 'Why are you hiding it?'

'Honestly, I can't even think about my diagnosis right now. Maybe I'm hiding it because I'm in denial. Today, I can see. Tomorrow, who knows? But right now, all I *want* to think of is . . . anything other than this!' Avery threw her hands up in frustration.

Mori placed a supportive hand on Avery's arm. 'OK, like what? What do you want to think about?'

'Maybe we should focus on Calista. We need to get to the bottom of why she never arrived. This is getting out of hand.'

'Would it help if we try to video-chat Kirk?' Remi suggested. 'Maybe the ring tone will force him to answer us.'

'You can do that?' Avery asked.

'Yeah,' Remi and Mori blurted in unison, and then the two shared a knowing grin.

'Yes, do it! Try it, then,' Avery encouraged, leading Mori by the elbow back to the counter where her cell phone was connected to the phone charger.

They watched as Mori hit a few buttons. Before long, a male voice sung out, and Remi and Avery joined the call over Mori's shoulder.

'Kirk!' Mori shrieked. 'Hey! It's the girls calling from the Cape! We've been trying to get ahold of you!'

Remi bumped Mori aside and pushed her face into the video-chat. 'Sorry, Kirk, but we needed to reach out. Calista hasn't made it to the Cape yet. Did she return home? Is something wrong?'

The color drained from his face, and he looked visibly shaken. 'You're kidding,' he said.

'Wait. She's not home?' Avery confirmed.

'And you haven't heard from her?' Mori asked.

He slowly shook his head.

Heavy silence fell over the room. Receiving firsthand confirmation from Kirk that their suspicions were correct, and Calista was somewhere between Natick and the Cape, caused Avery to falter like a cod out of water.

'Kirk,' Mori said evenly, 'you need to call nine-one-one and file a missing persons report – right this second.'

'OK,' was all Kirk said before he hung up.

FIFTEEN

The three stood motionless, unable to speak. Finally, Mori broke the silence and said, 'I need to call Brody.' Her cell phone shook wildly in her hand, and her sweat-soaked palm caused her to fumble with it like she was corralling a wet fish. She dried her hand on her shorts before continuing with her task.

'Why are you calling him?' Remi asked.

'To tell him not to come today. If it's all right with you guys, I think we should skip breakfast and head out right away. Don't you?'

'Of course,' Avery agreed. 'What are you thinking?'

'We can pick something up along the way. A smoothie or an egg McMuffin or something. I don't care; it's up to you two. I for one have lost my appetite.'

'No, I'm not talking about food. I mean, where are we *going*? What's the plan?' Avery asked.

'Natick! We really don't have any other choice. I can't just sit around here waiting! Can you?' Mori exclaimed. She looked at her iPhone to unlock the screen using the face recognition again. She seriously needed to adjust her settings because the dang phone kept locking her out too quickly. Then she scrolled for Brody's name and sent him a quick text message informing him not to come and that she would still pay him.

'Do you really think we should go there?' Remi asked, throwing her hands to her head and holding them there, as if the roof might cave in. 'This is awful. I don't know what we should do.'

Mori dropped her phone to the counter and began pacing the floor while her eyes darted around the kitchen like an out-of-control pinball game. She stopped to face them and set her hands firmly on her hips. They looked to her expectantly. 'Don't you think we should go? We need to find her! The last thing Calista mentioned was that she was on her way, after finishing up an appointment with Devon.'

'Yeah, of course you're right; we can't just sit around here and wait. We need to do something. Maybe we'll find her car on the side of the road, if she broke down. Perhaps she started walking and her phone died,' Avery said, biting at her thumbnail nervously. 'Do either of you know what kind of car she drives?'

'Avery, it's been a few *days*! Wouldn't someone report a car on the side of the highway? Especially if it had been sitting there abandoned?' Remi countered. 'I mean, yeah, a car might sit on a country road back in your state of Iowa for days, but you're forgetting, we're talking about a busy Massachusetts interstate here. Someone would've reported it, no?'

Avery just threw her hands up. 'I don't know; I'm grasping here! I'm only trying to help. What do you suggest?'

Mori took a calculated breath. 'It's OK, Ave. Right now, we all need to stay calm. Take one of your yoga breaths, Rem. You too, Ave.'

'She's right; we're not going to be any good to anyone if we start freaking out,' Avery agreed with a nod. But her expression remained riddled with worry.

Mori took her own advice and breathed deeply. 'Right. We need to make a plan.'

'Maybe we should call all the hospitals close to the highway, you think?' Remi suggested.

'There's an hour and a half's worth of hospitals between here and Natick. But I suppose we can make a list in the car. We'll take mine,' Mori said and then realized that was a stupid thing to say as she was the only one with a vehicle because the two standing in front of her had flown into Boston. 'Go pack an overnight bag, in case we don't make it back tonight,' she directed. 'And I'll load a cooler with some water bottles and snacks. We'll meet back down here in ten minutes or so. Does that give you both enough time?'

Avery and Remi confirmed with a curt nod before leaving Mori alone in the kitchen, which was just as well. She needed to digest what had just transpired in the last few minutes. How had their lives taken such a drastic turn? This was supposed to be a fun reunion and yet it was turning out to be a distressing experience. She reached for her lifeline and texted Jerome: Something horrible has happened and one of our friends seems to be missing. No worries. I'll put the security camera on before I leave the cottage. Might be gone overnight.

Within seconds, her lifeline's photo was lighting up her screen.

'Jerome!' Mori wailed.

'What's going on, doll?' The concern in his voice was palpable, and she loved him even more for it. She would consider FaceTiming him if the eye liner wasn't pooling around her tear-filled eyes. But alas, even without a mirror, she was certain she looked like absolute shit.

'Our friend, Calista, who was supposed to make the drive down from Natick never arrived! Her husband said she left *days ago*. And now we're on morning number three!' Mori squeezed the bridge of her nose to stop the tears from coming, but it didn't work; instead, they flowed freely. The realization that Calista was actually missing was hitting her hard and fast, and her stomach flipped like she'd just taken a ride on a rollercoaster.

'It's OK,' he soothed. 'Everything is going to be OK. Try to catch your breath.'

'How can you say that it's going to be OK? None of us have heard from her! This is not OK, Jerome; she could be in some hospital dying somewhere from a traumatic brain injury!' Mori said dramatically. 'Or maybe she's lost her memory!'

'Is this woman married?'

'Yes,' she hiccupped. 'Why?'

'If she is in a hospital somewhere, and her identification was inside the car, her husband would've been contacted by now. I'm sure of it.'

'Oh. Right. Good point. I hadn't thought of that. I'm just panicking.' Mori reached for a nearby paper towel holder, ripped off a piece, dabbed her eyes, and then blew her nose into the harsh paper.

'So, you see, love, I'm sure she's OK. Maybe she didn't tell her husband she had to make a stop before joining you all on the Cape.'

'Calista did; she said she needed to take her son Devon to an appointment.'

'See? I'm sure she's fine. Maybe things took longer than anticipated.'

'She would've texted or called, though,' Mori cried. 'I'm sure of it. She would've told her husband!'

'Maybe? Then again, maybe not. Try not to jump to conclusions, love,' he soothed. 'You don't really know her and what's going on in her life anymore. Do you?'

'Jerome?'

'Yes?'

'I miss you.'
'I'm right here.'
'I know.'
'It's all going to be OK; you'll see.'
'Jerome?'
'Yes?'
'I love you.'
'I love you too, doll. Keep me posted, OK?'
He waited for her to say, 'I will,' before he added, 'Kiss, kiss!' and was gone.

Talking to her bestie was all that Mori needed to get back on track with a solid plan. Jerome was like ointment on sunburned skin, and she was now prepared to get moving. She snagged an insulated cooler bag that she knew Jerome kept in a nearby closet for their beach picnics and began loading it with random snacks and a few bottles of water from the refrigerator. Before long, the three worried faces met back in the kitchen, and Remi and Avery followed Mori somberly toward her vehicle.

'Do you even know where to go? I've never been to Calista's house in Natick,' Remi asked, as she assisted Mori with getting the cooler and overnight bags into the trunk of her cherry-red Mercedes SUV.

'Yeah, do you?' Avery asked.

The four of them had grown up in Hopkinton, so Natick, although only a twenty-five-minute drive north, was like a world away from where they were raised. It was a place the four had rarely spent any time, save occasionally shopping at the Natick Mall.

'Yeah, before I moved to the Vineyard, I went to a barbecue at Calista's. It was a long time ago, but I still have her address in my contacts.'

'I guess we're ready, then,' Remi said, looking for a button to close the trunk and coming up empty.

'I got it here.' Mori hit the automatic button on her fob to shut the trunk before Avery called shotgun.

The ride to Natick was eerily quiet as each was preoccupied with her own thoughts. An hour and a half of almost complete silence hadn't happened since Remi and Avery had landed in Boston. The shock of it all had left them utterly speechless. By the time they arrived in front of Calista's house, newscasters were peppered across the front lawn. And it looked like complete chaos. Mori couldn't believe what she was witnessing.

'Shit's getting real,' Avery said, breaking the silence.

This was the first obscenity Mori had ever heard uttered from Avery's mouth.

'This is unbelievable,' Remi muttered, unclicking her seatbelt and sliding her body between the front seats to accompany them.

'Actually, this is good, though. Right?' Mori said grimly. 'White suburban wife and local teacher, missing. I guess, in a way, having the press out here and everyone looking for her might help.'

'Help what?' Remi asked.

'Finding her. Dead or alive,' Avery replied ominously.

SIXTEEN

Remi's legs noticeably shook as the SUV pulled along the sidewalk to park. She hadn't seen Kirk in decades, and here he was in the flesh – front and center, on his perfectly manicured lawn, with a microphone shoved in his face, being filmed by a local news crew. The vision outside the window was indeed surreal. Kirk had aged quite a bit since Remi had last seen him, which was to be expected. Heck, they all had aged. But his solemn expression and pale face amid the bright sunshine made him appear even older than an early-fortyish man wearing a business suit.

Mori interrupted her thoughts when she asked, 'Is that her son, Devon, over there? I recognized him from Calista's last Instagram post. I'm guessing he wasn't with her when she disappeared.'

Devon, his face as ashen as his father's, towered over Kirk. A girl with bleached blond hair stood beside him, their hands tightly woven together. Possibly a girlfriend, or at least someone close enough to the young man to hold his hand through this horrible ordeal. Remi was thankful Calista's son had support at a time like this. She wished Gabe were here. Or Taz. Then shook her head to rid it of the thought. It was awful of her to think of Taz at a time like this. But an escape into his sturdy arms would feel *really* good about now.

After unclicking her seatbelt, Avery turned to Mori. 'You think Calista lied to you about having an appointment with Devon? Maybe there was a different reason she was running late. Is that possible?'

'She must've,' Mori pointed out. 'Clearly, her son is here, despite what she texted me.'

'Yeah, thankfully. It would be awful for Kirk if both of them were missing,' Avery said woefully. 'His whole world would be in a shambles. This is hard enough to deal with.'

Remi shifted closer to join the conversation. 'We need to find out if Devon left with Calista the other morning and what time she brought him back home before leaving for the Cape,' Remi proposed. 'So we can establish a timeline before jumping to any more conclusions,' she added, slipping back into the rear seat and then searching for her purse to check her phone.

'Yeah, Mori, maybe you shouldn't share that little tidbit with Kirk. I mean, that Calista texted you and mentioned she had an appointment with Devon. Perhaps just share that information privately with the police so we can do a little digging,' Avery offered. 'We might find out more if we compile our own side investigation. Do either of you know how things were going between Kirk and Calista? Have they been getting along lately?'

Mori shook her head. 'Sounds to me like you've been watching too many true-crime shows back on the farm. But in answer to your question, I have no idea how they've been getting along. You, Rem?' Mori turned her attention to Remi through the rearview and waited for an answer.

Remi quietly said, 'No idea.' Now more than ever, she desperately wished they had kept in touch. She would know then how to act and what to say at a moment like this. This was just an inconceivable way to reconnect with Kirk. What was she to say? *Hey, nice to see you again. Sorry your wife is missing.*

'Shall we?' Mori prompted, breaking her reverie.

'I'm not sure I'm ready for this,' Avery said under her breath.

'Me either.' Remi turned her attention to the two squad cars with *Natick Police* splashed in large white letters across the side. Three uniformed police officers were conducting a door-to-door, talking with neighbors from the cul-de-sac. Her stomach took a queasy flip. What if something really bad had happened?

What if they never saw Calista again?

No.

Remi wouldn't let her mind wander. *No!* It just wasn't possible. There was a reasonable explanation for all of this. They just needed a little more time to get to the bottom of it.

'You're sure I shouldn't mention anything to Kirk about the appointment? Last call before we exit this car,' Mori asked.

'Yeah, I think Avery's right about that,' Remi confirmed. 'We always covered for each other back in the day. No sense getting in the middle of her relationship woes if she was hiding something. When we find her, she might get pissed. Don't tell Kirk anything,' she added firmly.

'When or *if*?' Avery added somberly.

'OK, don't talk like that. Let's go. But we stick together – you got that?' Mori mumbled.

But her words came out hollow to Remi's ears. As if Mori felt she was already getting sucked into something seedy that she didn't want to be a part of. And she really wasn't sure what to do or how to act.

Apparently, Remi wasn't alone. None of them knew how to behave or what to expect. This was outside anything they'd ever experienced.

'Fine, let's do this,' Avery said, opening the door, making the final call, and pushing them into action. 'The newscaster just left them. Let's hurry. It'll give us an opportunity to talk to Kirk before he gets cornered into more questions from the police or neighbors.'

Remi wasn't ready but had no other choice than to join the others in this small window of opportunity.

The heat of the day was a bit of a shock to the system after being trapped inside the air-conditioned vehicle for nearly two hours. Remi's numb legs wobbled when she followed the others toward Kirk. She felt as if she were floating in someone else's body. Her head caught up in a wild spiral of rapid succession thoughts of how she should greet the poor man whose wife was now missing. Kirk's expression barely shifted when they reached his side. If anything, the reality of them being there only reminded him of whom he had lost.

'What are you all doing here?' Kirk asked after releasing Mori from an embrace and mechanically sharing hugs with the rest of them.

Remi was taken aback. They hadn't seen Kirk in so long and this was his greeting? Given the circumstances, she needed to give him leeway, though. 'We're here to help,' she said quietly. 'Provide support.' She didn't add, 'Good to see you, Kirk.' If anything, the message came across loud and clear that he wasn't in the least bit happy to see the three of them. Tears suddenly formed in her eyes.

'I'm the one that should be crying,' Kirk said, staring blankly at her.

'Give her a break, will you? Remi's pregnant!' Mori uttered, coming to her aid.

'Yeah, please let us know what we can do. Hand out flyers?

Whatever you need,' Avery said, trying to downplay the escalating tension. She then wove her thumbs through the belt loops of her cut-off shorts and looked mildly uncomfortable.

'What you need to do is to get back to the Cape! What if Calista shows up there and you are gone!' Kirk said nervously. 'Why didn't at least one of you stay back? How could you be so careless!'

'Oh, shit. I didn't think of that,' Mori grimaced. 'Honestly, it was a knee-jerk reaction. We got in the car and started driving . . . We wanted to help . . .' she trailed off, as if hoping for a lifeline.

'Yeah, well, you should've called first. Get back in that car and don't stop until you hit the Cape. Do you hear me?' Kirk commanded.

'Seriously?' Avery hissed.

Remi thought Avery's tone was a little harsh given the circumstances. She reached out to hold Avery back as it looked like her friend wanted to wind up and hit Kirk straight in the mouth, farmgirl-style. She understood everyone handled stress and grief differently, so Remi decided in that moment to remain as calm as possible for the rest of them.

'Yes! Seriously!' Kirk spat with equal venom at Avery. 'That's how you can help. Get the hell outta here! And stay put once you get there until you hear from my wife.'

Devon must've heard the conversation escalating as he moved quickly to his father's side. 'Dad,' he said, attempting to calm his father by resting a hand on his shoulder and then giving him a little shake. 'Dad!' he repeated louder this time, as if willing him out of the angry trance. 'What's wrong with you?'

'This is what's wrong. There's no one on the Cape to greet your mother when she arrives. *If* she arrives!' Kirk flung a hand toward the group of three who cowered at his reaction. 'Maybe your mother wouldn't be missing if this whole trip was never planned,' he added through gritted teeth. 'What a mistake!'

'Please don't say that,' Remi murmured. 'It sounds like you're blaming her . . . and this is hard enough on all of us.'

'Hard on you?' Kirk cackled venomously. 'You don't know the half of it.'

'I'm sorry . . .' Remi choked out. 'I didn't mean . . .'

'How could you lose her? Where the hell did she go? Didn't Calista pick you up at the airport?' Kirk studied Remi closely as if she were answering a question on a test and she needed to pick the right answer.

'No! I took an Uber, and so did Avery!' Remi defended, gesturing a hand to her friend standing next to her. 'We haven't seen her, right, Ave?'

Avery nodded.

'I promise you, I haven't seen her since arriving from Florida,' Remi continued. 'We're not hiding her from you, Kirk. Goodness, we're here to help!'

'I knew she lied to me; the question is *why*,' Kirk seethed under his breath, but not so quietly that Remi didn't catch it.

'What did you say?' Remi had hoped for an answer to this, but Devon interrupted.

Stepping between them, he said, 'Oh, hey.'

Kirk leaned forward, and Devon placed a defensive hand between him and Remi to encourage his father to take a step backward and mentally cool off.

'Hi, I'm Devon. I apologize for my father's behavior.' Calista's son extended a hand in greeting, and Remi took his sweaty palm in hers. 'You must be friends with my mother. All I can say is, we're just a little worried about her. So please don't mind us. I guess we're not handling any of this well.'

Devon's girlfriend reached his side and interrupted, saying, 'Hey, Dev, I just need to head inside for a minute. Do you want me to bring you back a soda or anything?'

Remi couldn't help but wonder what Calista thought of Devon's girlfriend. The girl seemed deeply empathetic and kind, not to mention strikingly gorgeous. Now Remi might never be able to ask Calista how she felt about her son reaching dating age. Or anything else, for that matter. A fresh lump formed in her throat.

'Thanks. If you don't mind, grab one for my dad too, please,' Devon said, interrupting Remi's trance before the girl squeezed his hand and moved away.

'Hi, I'm Mori. Nice to meet you, Devon.' Mori continued the introductions. 'I'm sorry it's taken these circumstances to finally meet you. I met you as a baby, but I'm sure you don't recall.'

'Yeah, I'm sorry, I don't.' A brief smile crossed Devon's lips, but the smile never reached his eyes as he continued to cordially shake each of their hands.

Remi couldn't help but think the young man quite composed despite what he was going through. He was the opposite of his father, who was now running his hands nervously through his hair and looking absolutely fit to be tied. Calista would be proud of her son. Not so much of her husband, she surmised.

A police officer approached and removed Kirk from the equation to question him further. Meanwhile, Devon beckoned the three of them out of earshot a few steps from the rest of the group that had settled and continued to multiply on the lawn.

'Again, I'm sorry about my dad. He's a bit stressed out. I swear, he didn't mean anything by it.'

'Understandably,' Mori said. 'We probably should've thought it through and called before making the trip. We just wanted to help.' She looked to Avery and Remi then, and they agreed with a nod.

'Totally,' Devon replied.

'Hey, we're gonna take off. But if you need anything, or have any updates, please don't hesitate to call.' Remi removed her cell phone from her purse. 'Can you put your contact information in, and I'll share it with the others just as soon as we get back in the car.'

'Yeah, no problem. Good idea.' Devon took her phone to input his name and number.

Remi continued, 'We're going to do everything we can to find your mother. May I ask you something?'

'Sure, what is it?' he replied, not taking his eyes off the iPhone keyboard.

'How was your mom the morning she left? Did you talk to her before . . .' Remi let the question dangle in the air.

'Yeah.' Devon's expression pinched. 'She was good. A little nervous. After not seeing you guys for so many years, she wanted the reunion to go well.' He chuckled. 'I take that back, I shouldn't say she was *nervous*. Perhaps a little apprehensive. More like excited.'

'And that was the morning she left for the Cape? Was that the last time you saw her?'

'Yeah, she was in her bedroom packing, and I had to go to work. I said goodbye before I left the house. That was the last time . . .' His voice cracked and his eyes began to fill.

Remi reached out and touched him gently on the arm. 'It's OK, Devon. It's all going to be OK. We'll find her, I promise,' she encouraged, and he gave a brief weary smile.

'Yeah, I'm sure there is a perfectly acceptable explanation,' he sighed. 'At least I hope so.'

'And your parents? They get along OK?' Avery asked.

'Oh, yeah. They're tight.' Devon nodded, wiping his eyes with the back of his hand. 'My dad was excited to put this trip to the Cape together for her fortieth. And he was glad you all came on board with the idea to help celebrate the milestone birthday. This is just . . . well . . . not at all how we pictured things would go, you know?'

'We understand,' Remi said, touching him gently on the arm again.

Devon handed back Remi's phone. 'And my mom didn't text any of you? To say she was running late?' he asked, studying them. 'That's the weird part. It's like she just vanished without a trace.'

The three shared a glance before all mumbling an assenting 'Sorry, no.'

The police officer who had been talking to Kirk moved in their direction and stepped into their circle, interrupting the conversation. 'I'm Officer Novack,' he said with a tip of his cap. After flashing his badge, he added. 'May I have a minute with you three before you leave?'

'I'd better go. Nice meeting you all.' Devon shared a quick wave goodbye before turning on his heel and moving across the lawn toward his girlfriend.

The young officer looked as if he was barely out of the academy. Remi couldn't help but think a trip to her gym might man up his scrawny biceps a tad before he headed out on patrol. She bit her lip to stop herself from saying so.

'I understand Calista Moore was en route to visit with you ladies?' he asked, studying them. 'And she never arrived?'

Remi looked to Mori to be the spokesperson of the group, and she took the cue willingly.

'That is correct,' Mori said. 'She was due to arrive at the Cape on Saturday.'

'And I've heard on cop shows that the first forty-eight hours are crucial when leading a missing persons investigation. Isn't that right?' Avery interjected.

'Unfortunately, that is correct,' Novack said, regarding Avery with a nod. 'Have any of you heard from her in the last forty-eight hours?'

Mori handed her phone to the officer to share the last text. 'That's the only text I received from her, saying that she had an appointment the morning she was due to leave. But we just spoke to her son, and something isn't adding up. According to Devon, he didn't have an appointment. He was heading to work the last time Calista saw him. I'm not sure if that means anything. We can't determine why she lied to me, but we collectively decided not to share that information with her husband. In case she was having an affair or something we weren't privy to. We thought it might be best not to add fuel to the fire. You know?'

The officer's brow rose, and his tone turned to questioning. 'Calista was having an affair?'

'No! Wait. Hold up. That's not what she said,' Remi interrupted. 'We are just keeping the text close to our chest, as we think you should too. Just in case. You never know what goes on behind closed doors.' As it was, Remi, for one, was very aware of what went on behind closed doors. And it was often things that would cause a neighbor's jaw to drop.

Did anybody ever really know anyone? Transparently? Or was everyone in the world just putting on a façade? Were people all living their lives as they portrayed on social media or was it all just a bold-faced lie?

The officer regarded Remi with a smirk as though he didn't like being told how to do his job. 'May I have the address of where you are staying for the next few days? We will be sending out the local police department to canvass the area just in case she made it that far.'

Mori shared the address with the officer, and he plugged the information into his phone.

He then handed each of them a business card. 'Call me if you hear from her. And her husband is right: the best place for you three right now is back on Cape Cod.'

This was the last thing Officer Novack said before escorting them back to Mori's car.

SEVENTEEN

'Now, that was bizarre,' Avery said, slipping into the backseat so that Remi could ride shotgun on the return trip to Cape Cod. 'I'm not sure what I was expecting, but that wasn't at all how I thought today would go. You guys?' she asked while buckling her seatbelt.

'No kidding,' Mori uttered with a grunt while starting the engine. 'That didn't go the way I anticipated either.'

'What did you two expect?' Remi asked.

'I dunno. But I didn't think we'd be kicked to the curb almost immediately.' Avery snorted. 'Rather shocking. Kirk certainly has a stick up his ass. We were treated like complete strangers!'

'Realistically, we are,' Remi said. 'I mean, we haven't spent time together in decades. It seems to me that we're a small piece of a much larger puzzle. I guess we never should've left the Cape and let the police come to us. We're a little out of jurisdiction here.'

'Speaking of that,' Avery interjected, 'we probably should head straight home, like Kirk demanded, just on the off chance Calista shows up. Anyone need a snack? Mori, do you want to pull over and I can put the cooler in the backseat with me before we get on the highway?'

'I don't think I can eat. Despite being hungry, I'd rather have a drink. Pour me a stiff one please. And make it a double!' Mori exclaimed. 'I should pick up a bottle of wine and have one of you drive the rest of the way home, while I down it from the backseat,' she added with a chuckle.

'I don't think I can eat either,' Remi said quietly. 'Even though I should.'

'You need to take care of that baby,' Avery cautioned.

'I know, and I will. I just don't have an appetite right now. I think if I ate something, we'd have to pull over so I could vomit.'

'We'll wait then,' Avery encouraged, ruffling the back of Remi's head. 'No offense, but I don't think I want to smell that for the next hour and a half.'

'So why did Calista lie? Anyone have a guess?' Mori asked, meeting Avery's eyes in the rearview mirror. 'It's very odd.'

'Very odd indeed,' Avery agreed.

When Mori merged on to the busy highway and headed south, traffic was thick. Avery hoped they would make it back in a timely manner. The idea of being stuck on the Sagamore Bridge for hours on end didn't sit well with her, and she knew it was a common occurrence during summertime. Avery was already growing weary from the stress of it all. The fatigue was harder than a physical day at the farm. She sighed audibly, evidently loud enough for the front passengers to overhear.

'You OK back there?' Remi asked.

'Yeah, I'm just trying to make sense of all of this,' Avery admitted, kneading her forehead to clear her blurry vision, even though all the massaging in the world would do little to improve it. 'I'm not sure if it means anything, but I caught something interesting when we were talking to Devon.'

Remi shifted and turned toward the backseat to physically look at her. 'What's that?'

'Devon mentioned that Kirk planned the reunion on the Cape. But I thought the initial idea started with you, Remi – right? Kirk didn't have anything to do with the planning, did he?'

'Ah, she's right,' Mori chimed in. Her eyes momentarily met Avery's in the rearview mirror again.

'You think it was just a misunderstanding on Devon's part?' Remi asked. 'Perhaps he's a little confused about the details. Calista was the one who reached out to me about the idea to reconnect on the Cape, and I ran with it.'

'Yeah, I agree with Ave; that was weird,' Mori said. 'What would've given Devon the idea that Kirk planned our trip?'

'An oversight?' Avery gnawed on her lip. 'It didn't seem like it to me, which is why I brought it up. Something about Devon's demeanor was unnerving to me too. I mean, why was he so calm and collected? Meanwhile, his father was completely losing his shit. It's almost like he knew something was going on with his mom. Or he wasn't sharing everything. Or maybe he knows where she is.'

'Really? I didn't take it that way at all. I found Calista's son to be very mature. Maybe he just handles himself in situations more like his mother. From what I can remember, Kirk was always more of the drama queen,' Remi replied.

'It was also strange that Kirk asked if Calista picked us up at the airport. Did you catch that?' Remi continued. 'When I tried to probe further, Devon interrupted, so I missed getting a firm answer about it.'

'I did – I caught that too,' Avery nodded. 'It sure seems Calista is hiding a lot about her perfectly manicured life. Something's just not adding up to me. I think Devon knows more than he's letting on.'

'Speaking of manicured, did you see that house!' Remi exclaimed. 'Every bush was so well trimmed; not a branch was out of place. It looked like something out of a magazine.'

'Not one dandelion in the lawn!' Mori added. 'I noticed that too.'

Although she thought it highly unlikely, Avery couldn't help but search out the window, looking for an abandoned car that was potentially Calista's. All glimpses of hope were dashed, though, as each additional mile rolled past and nothing was discovered. 'Yeah, unfortunately, something is strangely amiss in her perfectly arranged life. *Where* is she?' she groaned.

'Don't know where she is, but one thing I do know: this is all very heartbreaking,' Remi replied.

'It sure is,' Mori added. 'It's not at all the way any of us envisioned this reunion would go.'

'No kidding!' Avery said.

By the time they made it to the Sagamore Bridge, Avery breathed an inward sigh of relief. Traffic was moving, and they wouldn't be stuck for as long as she'd anticipated. The sun was still brilliant as they crossed the Cape Cod Canal, sparkles erupting on the water below. It was such a beautiful sight that Avery needed to stop and take a moment to soak it all in. Before long, she'd be back in land-locked rows of corn and this Northeast visit would be but a memory.

'Anyone getting their appetite back? I can text Brody and see if he's available to whip us up some dinner?' Mori suggested. 'I'm sure he wouldn't mind.'

'Actually, that sounds terrific now that we're back on the Cape,' Avery said. Her stomach was beginning to rumble. Surprisingly, because of all the stress of the day, she barely thought anymore of her hangover and decided at that moment another glass of wine might even be warranted.

'Hand me your phone, Mori, and I'll do it for you,' Remi said. 'You just concentrate on getting us home.'

By the time they pulled up to the cottage in Falmouth, a collective sigh of relief rushed over them. The only car parked out front, though, belonged to Brody. And all hopes that Calista might magically appear vanished with the stark realization that she hadn't arrived in their absence, as Kirk had hoped.

The scent of tomato sauce greeted them the moment they stepped inside the house, sending Avery's empty stomach into overdrive. She breathed it in willingly. 'Are we having spaghetti?'

Brody was standing over the stove, stirring the sauce, and turned to them with a grin. 'Evenin', ladies!'

'Brody, you're a miracle worker. It smells amazing! I can't wait to try some,' Avery said, meeting him by the stove and taking a lick off the spoonful he held up.

'Yeah, it smells like the North End to me!' Remi added, joining him on the other side of the oversized pot in search of her own sample.

'I concur! Have I told you lately how much I love you?' Mori asked in her swooning voice, which caused the boy to throw his head back in mock laughter. She reached for the pile of grapes resting on the counter, plucked a few, and popped them one by one into her mouth seductively while keeping her eyes on the chef.

Avery couldn't help but wonder, if she and Remi weren't around, how far would Mori take this little charade? Would she *actually* sleep with this kid? Or was this all just flirty play?

'Salted water is boiling and ready for fresh pasta. The noodles only take three minutes, so just say the word and I'll drop it in the pot,' Brody said, interrupting Avery's thoughts.

'Word!' Remi exclaimed, clapping as if starting a high school cheer, causing them to all break out in laughter. It was good to have a moment of release. A glimmer that made Avery feel for just a second that life was normal again.

'You got it! There's a bottle of wine in an ice bucket waiting for you ladies out on the deck. Go ahead and relax, and I'll bring dinner out as soon as it's ready,' Brody replied.

Mori gave them an encouraging nod toward the door. 'You girls go on ahead. I'm going to explain our day to our chef here, and I'll be out to join you in a minute.'

'Don't have to tell me twice!' Avery looped Remi by the arm and led them outside. She really didn't want to see or hear any more of Mori's inappropriate behavior with the boy anyway.

The sun was just starting its descent in the sky, and a pinkish hue glowed above the sea, causing the water to appear lavender. They both plopped heavily into their seats, and Avery was just pouring a glass of wine when Mori rushed outside and beckoned them to return indoors.

'Hurry! I just turned on the news to catch the weather forecast, and they're talking about Calista! I have the TV on pause. Come quick!'

Avery and Remi rushed inside, and the three stood in front of the television in wait. Mori immediately hit the play button and turned up the volume extra loud.

A recent photo of Calista splashed across the screen.

Local police are searching for a popular Natick High School English teacher, Calista Moore. Calista was reportedly en route to Cape Cod on holiday when her husband, Kirk Moore, reported her missing to the Natick Police Department. Sources say she never arrived on the Cape. Local authorities are asking for the public's assistance in this case. Calista was last seen at Logan Airport with this man. He has a noticeable sleeve tattoo of the American Flag on his left arm. If you know this man, or have any information on either person's whereabouts, please contact the Middlesex County Police Department. Earlier reports suggest that Kirk Moore has no understanding of why his wife would've been seen at the airport. Her car, a 2019 silver Nissan Rogue with Massachusetts license number BG4 512, has yet to be found. If you have any information in this case . . .

The camera then zoomed into a blurry couple exiting the airport.

Remi gasped.

Avery turned to see her friend's complexion turn eerily white while mouthing the words '*Oh my God. Gabe.*'

EIGHTEEN

Although her mind was in a haze, Remi felt herself being physically escorted to the sofa, and then Avery encouraged her to place her head between her knees as soon as she took a seat on the luxurious fabric.

'It might be the shock or the lack of food that's making you feel like you're going to faint,' Avery urged, rubbing a tender hand on her back as if Remi were one of her children.

Remi was appreciative, though. She needed all the encouragement she could get. It was as if she was catapulted into someone else's life – a life of unknown territory. Everything was a shambles, causing her mind to work on overdrive. So much so that she couldn't catch her bearings. Nothing was clear. Suddenly, it was as if her world was covered in a mist of heavy Boston fog.

'I'll get a glass of water. Brody!' Mori shouted before hastily abandoning the living room.

Remi lifted her head from her knees and felt the blood swooshing back to her brain. She then held her head steady in her hands. Beads of sweat poured out of her despite the air conditioning. If only her world could stop spinning like a tilt-a-whirl.

Mori returned with a wet washcloth and a bottle of water. 'Drink,' she ordered. And then she rolled a cool washcloth and hung it along the back of Remi's neck, sending a fresh shiver down her spine.

'Have you spoken to Gabe since your arrival?' Avery asked gently, taking a seat next to her and reaching for her hand.

Remi could tell Avery was attempting to treat her with all the sensitivity in the world, but it was clear she was also searching for answers. Answers that Remi clearly wasn't privy to. 'No, I haven't,' she managed to choke out.

'Why not?' Mori asked.

Remi knew Mori wasn't being accusatory either, just curious, but the implication still stung yet again. 'I assumed he was busy with the gym. I thought he was holding the fort while I was gone, and that's why he wasn't responding to my calls. He replied to my text when I arrived at Logan, though, so I didn't think anything more of it.' She blew out a breath of frustration. 'Until now.' Her eyes rose to the television which thankfully was now turned off. She wasn't aware who had switched it off. But at least *someone* was trying to protect her feelings.

Avery soothed, 'Don't worry. We'll figure this all out. You're going to be OK. I'm sure there is a perfectly good explanation for all of this. I promise.'

'How can you say that? You can't promise that.' Remi hastily looked around the room in search of something – anything – to get her mind away from this new reality.

Noting her predicament, Mori asked, 'What do you need, hon? Tell us, and we'll do whatever we can.'

'I need my purse. I need my phone.' Her tone reached near hysterics. 'I need to call my husband. Right. Flipping. Now!' she hissed through gritted teeth, slamming her fist atop her knee.

'OK. I think you left it in the kitchen. I'll be right back,' Mori said before disappearing again.

Remi shook her head, trying, but failing, to quiet the agitation growing within her entire body. She combed her fingers through her hair, attempting to make sense of the situation. 'What the fuck is going on?'

'You have no idea why Gabe would've made the trip to Boston? Maybe he wanted to surprise you?' Avery encouraged. 'Could that be it? Perhaps he's concerned about you traveling alone – you know, with the baby on board and all? It's his first kid. He might be nervous. You both waited so long. Maybe his manly overprotective nature took over . . . and he met up with Calista to surprise you . . .' she trailed off.

'No. I *asked* him to come. I practically begged him! And he was quite firm on the *no*. He said he wasn't comfortable leaving the gym. And I believed him.' Remi looked at Avery eye to eye then, hoping for a hint of understanding but coming away with more fear based on the mirrored look in her friend's eyes.

'Here it is!' Mori hurried into the room and flung the purse at Remi, which she caught with one hand. She immediately plucked her phone from it and dialed Gabe.

Of course, he didn't answer.

Of course, he didn't.

'Are you going to text him?' Mori asked. Worry riddled her face, and she began pacing in front of her friends.

'And say what? What the hell are you doing with Calista? Who, by the way, is supposed to be here, at this very moment, at the Cape, with us!' Her voice rose with each additional comment, nearing hysterics again. 'A missing woman who the whole country is going to be looking for by day's end! Where the fuck are you two? You think he'll respond to that?' she added sarcastically. 'Maybe I should add a few pissed-off emojis to drive the point home.'

Avery blew out a slow breath. 'You know your husband better than anyone. You handle this exactly how you think you should – to get him to respond.' She shared a look with Mori that made Remi feel even smaller.

'How about you call an employee at your gym and see what they have to say? Someone must be covering for him,' Mori hinted. 'Perhaps they know what his plans are.'

Remi dialed Rodney's cell and he, too, didn't answer. 'Now what?' She frowned at her phone and willed it to respond with anything from Gabe, but she was continually met with a blank screen.

'Taz?' Mori asked with a smirk. 'Would that be wrong? To reach out to him? He might know something?'

Remi hemmed and hawed before finally acquiescing. She dialed Taz and he picked up on the second ring. 'Hey, Babe, how's your trip out east?' he asked. The sound of his voice was like liquid honey on a sore throat. Remi could instantly imagine his tender touch upon her skin, causing her to erupt in fresh goosebumps. Desperately, she wanted him to hold her. She needed to feel his strength now more than ever. Instead, she cleared her throat.

'Hey,' she sadly choked out.

'What's wrong, Babe?'

Remi cut to the chase when she noticed Mori and Avery hovering over her, looking for answers. 'Do you happen to know where Gabe is?'

'Huh?'

'Have you seen Gabe at the gym?'

'No, only Rodney. Why?'

'Did Rodney mention anything to you?'

'Yeah, he asked if I could help at the gym if he got in a pinch. He said Gabe wasn't going to be available for a few days. I just assumed he was coming to see you. Oh no. He didn't see the flowers I sent, did he? I hope I didn't cause a problem—'

Remi stopped him cold. 'No, don't worry about that. It's fine. And thank you.'

'Babe, hey. I really miss—'

'Look, I gotta go. I'll talk to you soon, OK?'

'Yeah. I get it. Rem, look—'

'I have to *go!*' she said firmly.

'Got it,' he clipped.

Remi could tell from the sound of his voice that Taz felt dejected. But she couldn't deal with that now; she had bigger fish to fry. She banged her forehead with her phone, wishing it to ring.

'Now what?' Mori asked.

'I need some air. Let's go outside. I need to breathe!' Remi's demands were now coming out like pants of desperation. She fanned air toward her face with her hands, but it wasn't helping the anxiety and the sudden rush of heat she was feeling growing inside. She would be on the verge of a full-blown panic attack if she didn't get herself together.

'Sure. Of course,' Mori said companionably, looping her by the arm.

Avery held the door while she and Mori pushed through ahead of her. They all gathered around the patio table where Brody already had their supper waiting below covered plates.

'I don't think I have much of an appetite,' Remi sighed.

'Do you think you could hold down a piece of bread? You need to eat something,' Avery suggested.

Remi shot her a look, aghast. 'Seriously? How can I eat at a time like this?'

'Remi,' said Avery, her eyes filled with concern. 'You haven't eaten all day, and the baby needs something.'

'OK. Fine.' Remi complied but she only took nibbles of the toasted bread. Even though the crusty garlic bread was another testament to Brody's amazing skills, her stomach began to churn.

Meanwhile, Mori and Avery each downed an entire glass of wine in mere minutes. If she could only join them for one glass to ease the jitters growing inside of her. Instead, she put her hand protectively on her abdomen. On Gabe's baby. No. On Taz's baby. *Oh God, what had she done?* Now more than ever, she wished she wasn't pregnant. Remi wanted a complete rewind of her life, to handle everything with different decisions. But she was also acutely aware it was a little late for that. She held that thought deep within her. It was not something she'd ever admit to the two sitting next to her.

'You holding up OK?' Mori asked, as if reading her like an open book.

'Yeah,' Remi said, trying but failing to swallow the dry bread that was now lodged in her chest. She pounded it down with a closed fist. Suddenly, a ringtone interrupted them. Remi sprang for her phone on the table and noticed it wasn't Gabe calling – it was Devon. She eyed the phone as if it were a live grenade. 'What do I do?' she cried.

Both Avery and Mori had leapt to their feet, to see who was calling. The three shared a discouraged look before Mori ordered Remi, 'Answer it!'

'But he's gonna ask! I'm sure Kirk told him . . . that Calista's with Gabe,' she stuttered. 'They must've seen the news, too. Or the police asked them who Calista was with. Oh, I can't . . . I can't do this.' She put her head in her hands and let the phone go to voicemail while the other two looked on in defeat.

Devon never left a message.

NINETEEN

Mori rolled over and fluffed the pillow for the umpteenth time. On a good night, she didn't sleep well, and this was not a good night. It had taken hours for her and Avery to calm Remi enough to part ways and get some rest. Normally, a shot or two of tequila would've done the trick. But due to her friend's pregnancy, that wasn't an option. Her brain was working overtime trying to make sense of everything that had transpired in the last twenty-four hours. But the more Mori thought about it, *nothing* made sense.

If Gabe and Calista hadn't seen each other in decades, why now? And where were they going? If they were somewhere safe, why wouldn't they at least notify the police of their whereabouts? The TV and local radio were relentlessly blasting missing persons reports all over the state of Massachusetts. Hell, the story had reached them clear on the Cape! By now, someone would've approached Calista or Gabe, explaining that their faces were plastered everywhere. How could two grown adults virtually disappear off the face of the earth? What was the deal? What rock were they hiding under? And why were they seen exiting Logan Airport of all places? They clearly didn't take an outbound flight; the police would've informed the press if that had happened, and they would've announced that during the broadcast.

The Ring doorbell alerted. Mori squinted to check the clock beside the bed which read 2:17 a.m. A buzzing doorbell in the wee hours of the morning never brought good news. Her stomach did a flip-flop as her toes reached the floor. She threw on her bathrobe before making her way quickly down the stairs to see who had arrived. A handful of uniformed officers showed up on the camera, and Mori briefly hesitated, wondering if she should wake the others before opening the door. She turned and looked toward the staircase. Evidently, she wasn't the only one whom sleep evaded. Avery and Remi were making their way down the steps as she opened the door to greet the officers. She instantly recognized one of them from Kirk's front lawn. Before she could remember his name, he flung out his badge and reminded her.

'Hi, we met yesterday. I'm Officer Novack. And this is my partner, Officer Hamilton.'

A third man stepped out of the shadows and held up his badge. 'I'm Detective John Reed. Can we come in?'

Mori knew it was a rhetorical question. Seriously, what choice did she have but to invite them in? It reminded her of penning one of her books. She would interrupt this with text to halt the reader from learning the bad news too soon. She would drag it out a paragraph or two further, until the reader was screaming for her to continue the words on the page. But alas, this wasn't a page from her manuscript: it was truth standing before her. 'Yes, please step inside.' She opened the door wider. 'Do you have any news on Calista?' she asked hesitantly, afraid of their answer.

'No, ma'am. I'm sorry, I don't,' Novack said.

A brief sigh of relief escaped Mori. The police would keep her wondering; just like her books, they wouldn't climax yet.

After crossing the threshold, the detective said firmly, 'We need to speak with Remi Toussaint.'

He was the only one of them not in an official police uniform; instead, he wore a short-sleeved dress shirt and slacks. It looked as if the job had taken its toll on Detective Reed. His curly hair was peppered grey, though if Mori could gauge by his physique, she would guess, at most, he was mid-thirties. The lines around his eyes and forehead were deep, as if the detective frowned excessively. Knowing the kind of work he handled day in and day out, she could understand why. Her own face had been sculpted in a frown ever since the prior morning when they'd left Kirk's front lawn. If things didn't change soon, she'd be adding permanent creases to her own complexion and would need a round of Botox.

'I'm here,' Remi said quietly, stepping forward.

'Please. Make yourselves comfortable in the living room. I'll be right in with some beverages,' Mori said before she encouraged Avery by the arm in the direction of the kitchen and watched as Remi led the officers away from them.

As soon as they were out of earshot, Mori whispered, 'This is getting worse by the minute. What do you think they're going to confront Remi about?'

'What do you think?' Avery said sarcastically. 'Gabe, of course! Like we said last night, it's probably why Devon called her – to find out what she knows. We need to hurry so we can be there for her. Remi might need a little handholding throughout this whole ordeal.'

'True,' Mori agreed with a nod before they rushed into the kitchen and loaded their arms full of water bottles to hand out.

Remi looked so small sitting on the sofa with her hands folded neatly in her lap. Her head rose when Mori and Avery entered the room, but her face remained expressionless.

Mori's memory boomeranged to when the four of them were called to the principal's office for getting caught skipping school. But this was so much worse than a slap on the wrist they'd received for misbehaving in high school. 'Here we are. Let us know if we can help you with anything else,' Mori said before unloading the contents of her arms onto the nearby side table. No one stepped forward to take a bottle of water.

Detective Reed didn't waste any time. 'It's our understanding that Devon Moore contacted you last night?' He studied Remi carefully, and she suddenly looked as if there were red ants crawling beneath her seat as she began to excessively fidget.

'Yes, he called while we were eating dinner but didn't leave a message. I didn't call him back.'

'Why?' the detective pressed.

'I don't know. I guess I was trying to process.'

'Process.' He nodded slowly as if he too was trying to make sense of her answer. 'So, you saw the news report and didn't call the police to inform them? Why?'

'Inform them of what exactly?'

'That your husband is in Boston.' His brow noticeably rose. 'With Calista.'

'I'm assuming Kirk shared that after watching the news report,' Mori interrupted, causing all eyes to land in her direction and wait expectantly. 'That Remi's husband is the man escorting Calista out of Logan Airport. That's how you learned who she was with – correct?'

This time Officer Novack answered, 'Yes. Kirk informed us of the identity of the man in question when we found them on CCTV.'

All eyes returned to Remi when the detective continued, 'When was the last time you had contact with your husband?'

'He drove me to the airport in Florida. I haven't talked with him since.'

The detective's eyes widened in surprise. 'You haven't spoken to him since you left Florida? Wasn't that four days ago?'

Remi looked as if her face had been slapped. 'We trust each other, Detective. He knew I was vacationing with friends whom I hadn't seen in ages. I texted him when I arrived in Boston, and he responded to that text. That's all I needed.' She folded her arms protectively across her chest and closed her lips in a grim line.

'Has it been four days already?' Avery mumbled under her breath to Mori. 'Calista's been missing that long? The time sure seems to have gotten away from us.'

Mori yawned and shared an agreeable nod. 'Yeah, it's been a little nuts around here, hasn't it?'

The detective's eyes volleyed between them as he eavesdropped on their side conversation before returning to Remi. 'To confirm. You haven't had *any* contact with your husband since leaving Florida. I'm assuming that's where your husband lives with you. Is that correct?'

'Yes, on both counts,' Remi said quietly. 'Do I need a lawyer?'

'Whatever for?' the detective asked quickly. A little too quickly in Mori's opinion.

'I dunno. My husband is missing, our *friend* is missing. And you seem a little . . . judgy? Asking me all these questions.'

'Do I?' the detective asked.

'Yeah.'

'That's not my intention, Mrs Toussaint,' he replied flatly. 'I'm only trying to locate your husband and your friend. Who are missing. Together. You understand?'

'Right,' Remi said, her eyes meeting the detective's squarely. 'I get it.'

'Do you know if your husband and Calista Moore were engaged in an extramarital affair?'

Remi laughed mockingly then. 'Seriously? All the way from Florida? They haven't seen each other in decades, *Detective*,' she scoffed.

In Mori's opinion, her tone was a little harsh, when saying 'Detective,' and it made her wonder if it was lack of sleep, lack of food, or pregnancy hormones that led her friend to sound a little out of character, different from the Remi she recalled from her youth who was all joyful and bubbles. This was a one-eighty from her arrival on the Cape.

Detective Reed shrugged. 'Wouldn't be the first time. I'm sure you're very well aware that social media has changed the way relationships operate in the last decade. Isn't that how you all planned this reunion in the first place?' His eyes traveled between them. 'People keep in touch in a myriad of ways – FaceTime, email, texting, Snapchat, you name it.'

Mori noticed that Remi's cheeks immediately flushed at the mention of Snapchat, and she began to squirm again in her seat. She wondered if the detective noticed it too.

'Is this what you drove all the way to the Cape to discuss, Detective Reed? You could've called. It's almost three in the morning,' Remi stated matter-of-factly.

'Time is of the essence when dealing with a missing persons case. The first forty-eight hours are critical, and we're way past that,' he replied, meeting her gaze.

'I've heard that. About the first forty-eight hours – actually, when we were in Natick, it was brought up,' Avery interrupted. And then shrank back as if she shouldn't have spoken.

'Are you not concerned about your husband's whereabouts, Mrs Toussaint?'

'Of course I am!' Remi exclaimed. 'What kind of a question is that? Instead of looking for him, you're here challenging me! When you should be out there running around Massachusetts with a search team! Go do your job!'

The detective's phone buzzed, and he held a finger to the air before stepping aside and taking a call. 'Please excuse me for a moment.'

Mori and Avery took the cue of the interruption to move and sit like bookends beside their friend. 'Are you OK?' Mori asked, patting Remi gently on the leg.

Avery reached for a bottle of water and handed it to her. Remi accepted it willingly and immediately popped the cap and took a sip.

'Yeah, I'm OK,' Remi replied, wiping her lips.

The detective walked deeper into the room. A grim expression riddled his face.

'You have news?' Officer Novack asked.

'Yeah. They found the car.'

TWENTY

Remi leapt from her seat. 'Did you just say someone located Calista's car?'

'Yes. It's been confirmed,' Detective Reed said calmly, holding up a hand as if attempting to soothe her without sharing additional information.

His calm demeanor didn't help. Not when Remi's anxiety was escalating, and she was on the cusp of hysterics. She continued to dart questions at the detective without waiting for a response. 'Where is it? Did they find Gabe? Did they find Calista? Where are they? Did someone find them too? Are they together?'

'No, neither of them was with the car. The Nissan was found in a parking lot at Horseshoe Mill. It's a nature reserve located in Buzzards Bay,' he explained.

'I'm familiar with it. Walking trails, that sort of thing,' Mori said, moving to Remi's side. 'What's her car doing there of all places?'

'Wait. What?' Remi's heart leapt in her chest. 'You mean to tell me they were literally just on the other side of the canal? Heading to the Cape? And stopped at a nature reserve! That doesn't even make sense!' She began to pace in circles, trying to take in the news while her mind spun wildly.

'Maybe they had car trouble and pulled in there?' Avery suggested, moving to stand at Remi's side to rub her back in comforting circles. Remi believed her friend to be an excellent mother, as Avery's maternal instinct kicked in once again to comfort her.

'Then why didn't they call?' Mori asked, looking pointedly at Avery. 'If they had car trouble, they'd know we're a stone's throw away. That doesn't make sense.'

'I don't know.' Avery shrugged. 'I'm just suggesting . . . there must be a plausible explanation.'

Detective Reed shared a look with his fellow officers and then gestured with his head toward the door.

'You're going there now?' Mori asked. 'While it's still dark? How will you search?'

'Yes. We're heading there now. Time is of the essence.' He turned to Remi one last time before walking toward the door. 'Thank you for your time. We'll be in touch, Mrs Toussaint.'

'Wait!' Remi grabbed the officer by the arm. 'You'll call me, right? If you find anything? Anything at all? Please don't leave me hanging like this!' she begged. 'I'm starting to lose my mind.'

'Absolutely. And please do the same if you happen to hear from your husband.' Reed turned his attention back to the officers then. 'Gentlemen, let's get a move on.'

The tone of the detective's last comment and his placated expression led Remi to believe Reed doubted Gabe would get in touch with her. And she wondered more than ever why he hadn't. Maybe her husband knew more about her relationship with Taz than she'd thought. Perhaps Gabe thought she was in love with Taz and was going to raise the baby with his or her biological father instead. Was she? She shook her head to get rid of the thought. She needed to find Gabe. Where the fuck was he?

After the officers had left and Mori closed the door, the three friends stood frozen, shock overtaking them.

'What now?' Avery asked, breaking their silence. 'This is crazy.'

Mori moved closer to Remi and put her arm around her shoulder and looked her over to make sure she was all right. 'You holding up OK, kid? You look like you've seen a ghost.'

'I don't even know how to answer that,' Remi admitted, as her shoulders slouched in defeat. 'I feel like I'm in a movie that I'd like to hit the rewind button on. Can we get a do-over? What the hell!'

'We should probably go over there, shouldn't we? I've been to Horseshoe before; I know how to get there. Let's get dressed and follow them, hon. Good idea or no?' Mori asked hesitantly.

Remi wasn't convinced. 'Will they let us? Or will the place be surrounded by police tape? Maybe we should just go back to bed and deal with it when the sun comes up. Aren't you all exhausted? It's been a very long day. I can't ask that of you . . .'

'What do you mean *let us*? Your husband is missing, Remi!' Avery said a little too harshly. It was as if she was trying to wake Remi from the current trance she had found herself in.

'I don't think any one of us is going to be able to sleep under these circumstances. I think we need to be there to see firsthand what they discover,' Mori added. 'Don't you think, Rem?' she said a little bit more gently, looking daggers at Avery and giving her a nudge to pipe down.

'Yeah, OK . . . let's go,' Remi answered, marching toward the stairs. 'I'm just going to throw on a pair of yoga pants and put on a bra,' she added over her shoulder. 'Meet you back here in a few.'

When Remi opened the door to the bedroom, it didn't have the same appeal as it had just a few days prior. Now, it reminded her of everything that was wrong with her life. A bed that she alone had slept in. At a place where this hellish nightmare began. She wondered if she'd ever share a bed with her husband again. Had he been having an affair with Calista? She'd point-blank asked Gabe on the way to the airport if he'd ever had a crush on her, and he'd vehemently denied it. *Hadn't he?*

Remi tried to replay the conversation in her mind to determine if she'd missed something. She hadn't. Gabe was faithful. And he wanted to have a baby with her. So why didn't Calista or Gabe text anyone? And what were they doing together? Remi wanted to throw open the doors and scream bloody murder from the balcony. The unanswered questions were spreading like a cancer within her.

She dug through her suitcase and changed from her nightshirt and shorts into yoga pants and a pink tank top. After lacing her hair into a ponytail, she decided this time to forego the baseball cap. She tossed a zip-up sweatshirt over her shoulders for the air-conditioned ride, before abandoning the bedroom.

Within minutes, Avery and Mori met Remi in the kitchen. They too were fully dressed and ready to go. Mori even hauled a cooler back to the vehicle, but Remi doubted any of them would eat anything out of it. Perhaps Mori had filled it with alcohol in case they couldn't handle what soon might come.

The ride across the bridge to Buzzards Bay was so quiet, only the hum of the tires hitting the road filled the space between them. It seemed no one wanted to utter a word regarding the chaos that was plaguing each of them. Not surprising at that hour, traffic was light on the bridge, and they made good time.

When they arrived, Remi was amazed by the level of police presence, as several Buzzards Bay police vehicles had been added to the group along with the officers who had interrogated her back at the beach house. The fact that Gabe was involved with any of this was still hard to compute in Remi's mind. Since he hadn't flown to Boston with her, she wanted to pretend Gabe was still back in Florida, running their business. None of what was happening before her very eyes felt real, especially that he too was now missing.

None of it fit.

Mori searched for Remi in the rearview mirror. 'You OK back there?'

Before she lost her nerve, Remi reached for the door handle. 'Yeah. Let's go and see if they discovered anything.' She walked directly toward the first available officer and introduced herself and was told that the local PD were organizing a grid search at first daylight. Apparently, the thick brush where they had initially wanted to investigate had made it difficult in the dark. Without warning, Remi felt the bile rise in her throat to the point she could vomit, so she excused herself and darted for the woods.

She leaned an elbow against a tree to catch her bearings and wiped the beads of sweat off her forehead. When she looked down, she caught something lying in the long grass a few feet away. She moved it over with her foot.

A cell phone.

Remi looked over both shoulders to see if she was being watched before picking the phone up and shoving it into her back pocket.

It was then, out of the corner of her eye, that Remi noticed Detective Reed exiting the woods toward the parking lot. She hurried to corner him.

'Did you find them?'

'No, we haven't located anyone yet,' he said grimly.

'Any updates at all? Did you find anything of value out here?'

The detective held up a clear evidence bag in his hand. 'Does this look familiar?' He revealed a gym lanyard with *LEAN ON THE MATT* printed across it for her to examine. A hint of red blood was smeared on it.

Remi's stomach flipped, and she could feel the bile rise in her throat once again. 'I recognize that. I believe that belongs to my husband.' She pointed to the lanyard. 'Where'd you find it?'

'On the ground, a few feet from the vehicle.'

'Oh.'

'It looks like it was torn off his body or an altercation might've occurred,' he said grimly. 'Look at the rip,' he pointed out.

Remi shook her head. 'No . . . that can't be. He's so strong . . .

I don't . . . know . . . how that could happen . . .' she stuttered. 'You don't know him. He's built like a brick house.'

A sinking feeling of dread took over all rational reasons why something belonging to her husband was found on the ground. She could feel the detective's eyes on her, determining her reaction to this sudden piece of evidence.

Detective Reed stepped forward and eyed her closer. 'We will get to the bottom of this. Don't you worry about that.'

'None of this makes sense. I don't understand it,' Remi admitted with a defeated shrug. 'I don't know why Gabe wouldn't tell me he was here. I wish I could tell you more, Detective. I don't understand why he hasn't gotten in touch with me. We're best friends. This is so unlike him.'

Reed gave a brief look of compassion then, as if he finally felt for her having to go through all of this, but he remained mute.

'Now what?' she asked.

'I'll put this into evidence. At some point, we'll have to determine why your husband was here.'

Remi rubbed the back of her neck. 'Gabe wouldn't hurt anyone. I promise you that,' she said confidently.

The detective looked as if he hadn't slept in quite some time as he ran a hand across his weary expression before he shared a look of caution. He seemed not to believe a word out of her mouth. He confirmed this by saying, 'I've seen a lot of things in my line of work that would come as a surprise to you. Things that family members never saw coming or expected from their loved ones.'

'Anything?' Avery was out of breath and Mori right on her heels when they reached Remi's side.

'Detective Reed found Gabe's gym lanyard – and there's blood on it.' Remi was saying the words, but it still didn't seem real.

None of this did.

TWENTY-ONE

By the time they arrived back at the house, the three were emotionally spent. Detective Reed had encouraged them to get a few hours of shut-eye before rejoining the search team mid-morning. They only acquiesced when the detective agreed to strict instructions to phone Remi with any developments. Avery still couldn't believe that Gabe and Calista were missing. *Together.* What were they doing together in the first place?

Since Iowa was only an hour behind due to the time zone difference and Jack was normally up before dawn to handle farm chores, Avery texted her husband on the return ride to explain she might have to extend her trip. No surprise, his response had been very accommodating; he would do whatever it took on his part to help her out. Including changing her airline tickets. He even took it as far as encouraging her to stay in Massachusetts as long as she needed. Indefinitely.

Avery couldn't help but wonder how many times her neighbor, Nancy, had paid a visit in her absence. But then she brushed it aside. Seeing Remi's reaction at the nature reserve had depleted her emotional energy, and she couldn't deal with anything else on her plate right now. She couldn't imagine what Remi was going through if she was feeling this distraught herself over the police locating Calista's vehicle – yet not finding a trace of either one of the two missing people.

Avery departed from the kitchen where the center island had physically been holding her upright and sluggishly moved to the living-room window and peered out at the incredible view beyond. She stopped to take it all in through blur-filled eyes. The sky was playing tricks with the early-morning dew. A pinkish hue and wisps of purple clouds waited along the horizon for the sun to make its appearance, while seagulls flew in tandem overhead. She positioned her phone to take a photo and seal the sight into her brain for eternity.

'Wow, that's beautiful,' Mori said, coming up alongside her.

'Remi, come check this out!' she beckoned. 'The sky is incredible this morning.'

When she joined them, Remi was holding a banana in her hand, which was good to see. Avery knew that the baby inside of Remi needed sustenance. She also understood how hard it would be under the circumstances to provide it, as her own stomach churned from all the stress.

'Oh, that is so pretty. Witnessing that view outside this window reminds me that everything will work out in time,' Remi sighed. 'I'm just not sure I'm ready to go to bed now, though; I'm too riled up,' she added, breaking the smallest piece of banana and popping it into her mouth.

It looked to Avery as if her friend was willing the fruit to go down.

'I think my adrenaline is running in overdrive,' Remi continued.

'That's totally understandable,' Avery said, taking her hand and giving it a comforting squeeze before releasing it. 'I'm not sure I can sleep yet, either. We're here for you as long as you need, right, Mori?'

Mori nodded assent as she was fighting back a yawn.

'Oh, gosh, I feel so guilty,' Remi murmured, kneading her forehead until it left a mark. She seemed to be taking all the responsibility for what had transpired in the last few days heavily on her shoulders.

Avery couldn't blame her. She imagined that Remi carried a lot of guilt where Taz was concerned. She knew that if she had stepped out on Jack and had been hiding that type of secret, it would plague her. But wasn't she holding out from Jack on her own personal big secret? Wasn't that basically the same thing? Was keeping a dark secret the same as lying about the truth? Regardless, the timing of all of this did little good. It wouldn't bring back Gabe or Calista. 'Don't do that to yourself,' Avery finally encouraged.

'Wait. Guilty? For *what?*' Mori asked. Evidently, their friend's writer-mind was on the prowl again, and she wouldn't let it go.

Remi bit her lip. 'I have a confession, you guys. And you're not going to like it.'

Avery interrupted with a shake of her head. 'If this is about that guy Taz, I don't think I can handle it right now. This is not the time—'

Remi raised her hand to stop her. 'No. Of course not. But leave it to me to make another bad decision. I think I really blew it this time.' She had uttered the words so quietly that Avery had to strain her ears to hear her.

'What did you blow? Now, you've really got me wondering!' Mori said, landing her hands firmly on her hips. 'And you know when I'm curious, I won't let go until you tell me. So spill it.'

'It's regarding something I found at the nature reserve.'

'Yeah?' Avery leaned in closer and studied her and thought she caught a little more than a hint of guilt. 'Goodness! You're not talking about the lanyard, are you? You found something else?'

'Seriously! What is it?' Mori added excitedly. 'Did you find something else that might be relevant?'

Remi sighed, 'I think so.'

'Then *what* is this big secret that you're ashamed of! You're making me crazy!' Mori yelled. 'Spill it!'

Avery wondered if Mori was past exhaustion and patience too. They all seemed to be hanging on by a thread, on their very last nerve.

'I think I found out why Calista isn't returning our messages. I found her phone. Initially, I thought it was Gabe's phone and that's why he hadn't gotten in touch with me. But it's not – it's Calista's,' Remi said quietly.

'Wait. What?' Mori asked, shaking her head wildly. 'What are you talking about?'

'You found a cell phone and you took it? From a crime scene!' Avery pressed. 'Is that what you're admitting to us?' Her heart began to pound in her chest.

Remi shrugged sheepishly and then visibly winced. 'Yeah, I know . . . probably not a smart move. Huh?'

'How do you know it's Calista's?' Mori asked pointedly. 'If you haven't seen her in years? Please, explain!'

'Who else could the phone belong to?' Remi defended. 'I found it on the ground not far from her car and it was clean, like it hadn't been there for long! And it's not Gabe's. It doesn't take a rocket scientist to put two and two together! Does it?'

'I can't believe this,' Avery murmured. The realization of Remi tampering with evidence made her extremely nervous. It could get her friend in a heap of trouble, so she stated that aloud, without a hint of judgment and as matter-of-factly as she could muster. 'You know, you can do time in jail for this.'

'I know!' Remi put her head in her hands then. 'I fucked up, OK?'

'Wait, so is there face recognition on it?' Mori asked.

'Uh-huh.'

'Shit,' Mori uttered.

'How were you planning to guess her code?' Avery asked. 'I mean, besides the face recognition, she has a number passcode too. We just need to guess correctly. Am I right? I don't know, I have an outdated Android, so . . .'

'Um, yeah. That's like trying to pick the right lottery numbers, Avery.' Mori was deflated. 'Not going to happen.'

'Perhaps you should give the phone back to Detective Reed, and apologize and say you made a mistake,' Avery suggested. 'Tell him you thought it was Gabe's, but it was dark outside. And after closer review, you realized it probably belongs to Calista instead. That could work.' She nodded slowly, chewing her lip.

'I can't.'

'Why?' Mori asked.

'Let me go get it. And I'll show you why.'

When Remi left them, Avery mouthed, 'This is so not good. Not good at all.'

'I agree,' Mori whispered. 'She's probably going to be arrested for tampering with evidence, like you said. Or, at the very least, slapped with a hefty fine and probation on top of everything else she's dealing with.'

When she returned, Remi shared the phone with them. 'Gabe's Otter case is black – this one is red. The detective is never going to believe I didn't recognize the color of the Otter case, no matter how dark it was outside!'

'And Reed or any of the other officers didn't see you pick it up in the woods?' Mori asked.

'No! Trust me, I looked around before I stuffed it in my back pocket! I'm not that stupid!'

'You really have learned to lie, haven't you? Your time hanging with Taz has not been wasted,' Avery spilled and then wished she could hit the rewind button. The look on Remi's face turned her to a puddle of shame. She immediately begged for mercy. 'I'm so sorry, Rem, I didn't mean that. I'm overtired – it just came out.'

Remi's gaze cast downward in defeat.

'*Again*, I'm sorry.' Now Avery was the one ashamed.

'It's fine. And I deserved it,' Remi said flatly.

'No, you don't deserve any of this,' Avery defended, reaching for her. 'I'm so sorry, Remi; please accept my heartfelt apology. I shouldn't have said that. I really didn't mean to hurt you. It was not my intention.'

'No worries; we're good.' Remi cracked a weak smile. 'Maybe we should go and get some rest and deal with this later. I think we've all officially reached our wits' end.'

'I don't think I can. I'm pretty wired too. Are you guys up for a walk on the beach first?' Avery asked. 'Maybe some fresh air would do us a world of good. It might help us sleep if we physically work this out.'

'That actually sounds like a good idea,' Mori agreed with a yawn. 'Let's go for a therapeutic stroll and then take a nap before we head back to help with the grid search. I'm up for it if you are?'

'What about Calista's phone?' Avery asked. 'What are you going to do, Remi? Try to guess her passcode?'

'No. I'll just wait and see what today brings. Hopefully, the police will locate them, *alive*, and this will all be in the rearview. In the meantime, you're right. Let's get some fresh air and walk. I need a break from all of this.'

The sun was just beginning to peak, causing the sea to dance animatedly with magical sparkles. It was going to be a hot day as the air was already feeling sticky. A soft breeze tickled Avery's skin, though, as they headed further down the boardwalk. For just a moment, she allowed the scent of the salty sea air refresh her spirit. When they reached the end of the boardwalk, Avery said, 'I don't get this opportunity very often, living back in a landlocked state. I'm taking my shoes off for the full experience.'

'Me too,' Mori said, tossing her sequined flip flops aside.

Remi also abandoned her tennis shoes.

'Let's walk along the water,' Mori suggested, leading them toward the Atlantic. 'I want to look for shells. Like we did when we were kids.'

The warm sand beneath Avery's feet felt heavenly. Just what the doctor ordered. Walking the beach was something she'd really longed for from the trip to Massachusetts, and suddenly she wished to visit more often. Perhaps she should plan a trip for Jack and the kids soon. The salty air fully cleared her sinuses, and the chorus of waves softly rolling on to shore gifted a glimmer of peace, which she hadn't experienced in the last few hours.

The three were quiet until they almost reached the shoreline and Remi gasped, startling Avery to look up.

'What's wrong?' Avery asked, eyeing her over. 'You step on a seashell or something?'

'No! What's that?' Remi's voice was trembling now, and she sputtered when she added, 'Over there . . . in the water.'

Avery followed Remi's pointing finger toward the shoreline, less than a hundred feet away, where a heap of clothing was being pummeled by an oncoming wave. Avery blinked several times to catch what was in the distance, but came up blurry. She shook her head to recalibrate. 'I can't see what you're referring to. Did we leave our clothes out here the other night when we were skinny dipping?' she asked with a squint. 'I was so drunk that night I honestly can't remember! Whoopsie!'

'I don't think so. I thought Remi brought everything in. Didn't you?' Mori said, looking to Remi who confirmed with a nod. 'Let's go and see what's over there, just in case.'

They picked up pace until things became vividly clear, even for Avery.

It wasn't just rumpled clothing being hit by a wave.

It was a body.

The body of Calista Moore.

TWENTY-TWO

They found her motionless. Her nose smothered in the sand. Her right eye was as vacant as frosted sea glass. Her skin translucent, akin to a jellyfish. The surf had tangled her hair like a mass of unwanted kelp in which the ocean had rudely regurgitated. Despite the sun burning overhead, she was frozen to the touch, her lips as dark as the Atlantic. The waves crashed atop her lifeless body as if she were an abandoned piece of driftwood, smacking her with each additional roll of the tide.

A guttural screech erupted from one of them.

There was no mistaking it.

A friend was dead.

The three recoiled from the body of Calista Moore, tripping back on to the loose sand, as if standing close to their friend's empty shell was far too much for any of them to handle.

Remi collapsed on to the sand first and let out a wail toward the sky. Mori thought the sound erupting from her friend eerily mimicked an injured animal, and she watched as Remi's knees sank deeper into the sand.

'No!' Mori joined in with her cry then, slamming her fists into her thighs. 'This can't be happening!' She looked at Avery, who was as white as a sheet, and asked if she was going to faint, which prompted Avery to speak.

'This is the worst thing I've ever witnessed, and I think it'll be an image locked in my brain for the rest of my life – even when I'll no longer be able to see anything.'

'This is not an image you want to hang on to. Nor do I,' Mori choked out. Her mouth had grown increasingly dry, so much so that she could barely spit the words out. She reached for her water bottle which had been tossed aside on the sand when they had discovered their friend's body.

'We need to call the police,' Avery said, ripping her phone from her shorts pocket.

'I still can't believe this! Avery, what happened? How . . .'

'I don't know, but we need to get the authorities here ASAP.'

'Wait!' Remi hollered. It was clear Remi was so distraught about finding Calista's body that she hadn't overheard the hushed whispers between Mori and Avery.

'For what?' Mori asked incredulously.

'Don't you dare call them!' Remi demanded. Her eyes suddenly blazed with fresh fear.

Avery slipped her phone back into her pocket and weaved her arms protectively across her chest. 'Remi, what's going on? Talk to us. You're not making a hill of beans worth of sense. Why on earth wouldn't we call the police? That's ludicrous!'

Remi was still located a few feet in front of them with her knees deep in the wet sand facing Calista's lifeless body. She had turned at the sound of her name, but her expression looked hollow as she shifted in their direction and rocked back and forth. 'I can't . . . do this. I just can't do this!'

'You can't do what, Rem?' Mori prompted. Her eyes narrowed on her friend, waiting for an explanation.

Remi finally stood on unsteady legs and stumbled a few steps closer to them. 'If Calista was with Gabe at the nature reserve . . . on the other side of the bridge . . . not far from where we are on the Cape . . . did my husband do this? Is he responsible?' Her eyes darted wildly, pleading with them to tell her it couldn't possibly be true. It was as if she needed visible confirmation that she was absolutely, unequivocally wrong. That her thoughts were baseless.

However, Mori couldn't give her that. With Gabe still missing, this new development certainly didn't look good for him. Especially if he had been the last person to see their friend alive. And he still hadn't contacted his wife. *Why?*

'I . . . don't know . . . Remi . . .' Avery stuttered. 'You don't . . . actually . . . think . . .?'

Mori didn't think it could be possible, but Avery's face turned a shade whiter, and she continued, 'Either way, we must call the police, Remi. We have to. This is a private beach; they'll never find Calista out here. The medical examiner needs to be called to find out the cause of her death. This is insane!'

'Yeah! Exactly! And they'll want to know how she got here. Can you explain *that*?' Remi spat. 'Because I certainly can't!'

Mori hadn't thought of that. She was still in shock at finding Calista's lifeless body on the beach, and her brain was initially slow to process. But now her writer's mind was kicking into overdrive, playing with scenarios and details. How the hell did Calista wind up on the shores of Jerome's private beach? Unless her body had been placed there. Or, worse, killed there. Mori could count on one hand the number of people who knew where they were staying this week. But Gabe most likely knew. Would Remi be considered a suspect too? What if the police believed Calista *was* having an affair with Gabe? Wouldn't that make Remi seem like a guilty party as well? Would Detective Reed want to question her further about her husband's behavior?

This line of thought only intensified Mori's feelings.

Had Remi snuck out of the cottage last night while they attempted a few hours of shut-eye? To her knowledge, the police hadn't checked the beach. They had no reason to.

Either way, each possibility was growing increasingly more terrifying. Mori hated that her thoughts took it so far. That she could entertain the fact that one of her friends had done this heinous act. But that's how the brain of a writer operated. Taking things as far as they could go on the page, so as not to lose the reader. Keep them reading long into the night until their eyes were practically bleeding. Mori needed to stop this train of thought, though, and think realistically.

Thankfully, Avery interrupted her musings when she bellowed, 'Well, we can't just leave her here! You have a better option?' Her anger seemed to be escalating to match Remi's.

'OK, ladies, let's take a moment,' Mori said evenly. 'We need a plan.' Someone needed to provide a sense of stability in this mess, and she guessed, for reasons unbeknownst to her, she'd have to be the chosen sane one. 'Let's just all calm down.'

'What we need to do is find out how Calista died,' Avery countered. 'What the cause was, I mean.'

'You want us to look at her dead body again?' Remi hissed. 'Are you crazy?'

'It's either that or we call the police first. Your call,' Avery volleyed with equal intensity.

'She's right, we need to find out what happened to Calista. If we are to keep the police from focusing their investigation on your husband, then we need to do this.' Mori didn't add *the investigation on you, Remi*. She'd keep that horrible thought deep within. Instead, Mori beckoned them to follow. 'Take a deep breath. We're going to have to look closely at her again. This time with fresh eyes.'

When the three reached Calista, a feeling of dread washed over Mori. She couldn't believe Calista had met her fate here on this beautiful beach. Before letting her mind overthink it, she waded in the water and searched both sides of Calista's neck to see if there were any visible marks or bruises. As far as she could see, there weren't any. 'It doesn't look like she was strangled. At least to me, that doesn't appear to be the cause.'

Avery also waded in the water to get a closer view, while Remi watched from the shoreline. 'I'm not seeing any visible bruising either. Or blunt force trauma to her head. Or gunshot wound or anything. Perhaps she drowned?' Avery murmured.

That option was perplexing to Mori. 'Unless the salt water washed away any blood from the wound. It's hard to see without moving Calista's hair, and I'm not going to do that. I'll leave that to the police.' The very last thing Mori wanted to do was physically touch her. It was all so morbid.

'Avery, are you some undercover cop or something? Or are you really a corn farmer as you claim? Because your choice of words is quite interesting, to say the least,' Remi frowned.

'I told you. Jack and I watch a ton of *20/20* and *Dateline*,' Avery defended. 'You learn things. You ought to try it.'

'Oh,' Remi huffed, 'and that makes you an expert, I suppose. Watching a TV show!'

'Ladies, *please*!' Mori pleaded. 'Let's stick to the process, here.'

Avery seemed to ignore Remi completely then, when she leaned into Mori and replied under her breath, 'I think she drowned.'

'How?' Mori asked. 'That doesn't make sense! Why wouldn't she have come to the cottage to greet us after she *knew* how long we'd been waiting for her arrival? She wouldn't be walking out here on the beach alone! Why hadn't she texted any of us? Someone clearly placed her on this beach to send a message. Or, worse, to frame one of us!' Suddenly, Mori realized her own head could be on the chopping block, and that frightened her to the core. She shuddered at the thought of being locked behind cold steel bars and her life as a writer ending abruptly. Could she still write from jail? Did they supply pens and paper? Or was a pen considered a weapon to use on other inmates and therefore against all rules and regulations?

Avery interrupted her musings when she said, 'Good point. How did Calista get here and how did she drown?' Avery paused then while she gnawed on her lip. 'She's wearing a sundress. You're right, Mori, not exactly swimming attire,' she pointed out with a cluck of her tongue. 'The killer must've lured her here and held her head underwater until . . .'

'Exactly,' Mori nodded. 'That actually sounds plausible.'

'We need to look for drag marks across the beach. To see if someone killed her somewhere else or lured her here as you suggested – to drown and dump her. I think we need to investigate further,' Avery added.

'I think I'm going to be sick,' Remi said and then, without further warning, vomited on the shoreline.

Mori returned her attention to Avery and pleaded, 'What are we going to do? Should we scour the beach for more clues? Or what? Honestly, I don't know which way to turn. Her body isn't exactly giving us any insight to what happened out here.'

Avery whispered, 'Well . . . I know it's terribly morbid but – we have her face . . .'

Mori rolled her hand in the air to prompt Avery to continue her words. '*And* . . .'

'*And* . . . we have her phone,' Avery replied solemnly.

'Right. It's the only concrete thing we have,' Mori finished with a nod. She looked to Remi, green as an apple, who was wiping her mouth with the back of her hand.

'Hey, Rem, I think we have a plan.'

TWENTY-THREE

Remi held Calista's phone between trembling fingers and tried to even her breath to stop her hand from shaking wildly. She steeled herself to position the phone in front of Calista's expressionless face, with its blue tinted lips. All the while, straddled over her friend's lifeless body as the tide splashed around her ankles. She couldn't believe it had come to this. Never in her life did she think this was how the reunion would end up.

'You open that phone and you might be opening Pandora's box. Are you sure this is something you're ready to know?' Avery asked, chewing the inside of her lip like cowhide. She was standing beside Remi with her hands on her hips, waiting expectantly.

'Nice time for you to ask,' Remi replied as she eagerly turned the phone in her hand but came back empty. 'It's still locked. Damn it!'

'Maybe her eyes need to be opened more,' Avery suggested. 'You think?'

'And are you volunteering to do that?' Remi asked sarcastically.

'I'll do it,' Mori said, stepping forward like a soldier ready for battle. 'Our friend would want us to do this, right? If it led to finding her killer. I know without a shadow of a doubt that Calista would encourage us to push through this. Besides, we need answers.' Mori kept repeating everything to further convince herself.

Her repetition was driving Remi mad. She wanted to yell at her to shut up, but instead she held back. The stress was building like an oncoming thunderstorm which at a moment's notice could erupt through the clouds.

Mori cranked her shoulders back and took another step forward to stand above Calista's head and instructed Remi to give her the cue when she was ready.

'I'm ready,' Remi said. Though she wasn't ready in the least.
Not now.
Not ever.
How could she be?

The three of them stood over their friend's lifeless body, trying to open Calista's phone. *Literally, over their friend's dead body. Who the hell does this?*

Mori held Calista's eyes open wider and Remi repositioned the phone to her face. She flipped the phone in her hand expectantly; instead, the phone flew from her grasp and plunged into the water, landing beside her foot with a splash. 'Damn it!' she shouted as she snatched it up before the oncoming wave dragged it back out with the tide.

It was already too late.

Remi desperately attempted to dry the phone with the edge of her tank top, to no avail. She grunted before adding, 'Looks like we might need a bag of rice.'

'Will rice work?' Avery asked. 'I know it did with the old phones, but does that still work with the newer ones? I'm not familiar.'

'I dunno! But we've got to try something!'

Remi stumbled away from Calista's body and collapsed in the nearby sand. Fat tears flooded her eyes and then she felt a guttural wail erupt from her belly as she pounded closed fists beside her, before Mori came out of nowhere and folded her into her arms, rocking her back and forth while she openly wept.

'It's going to be OK,' Mori soothed. 'We'll fix it, honey. Not to worry,' she added, moving loose strands of hair away from Remi's face and wiping her tears tenderly.

Meanwhile, Avery snatched the wet phone from her lap. 'I'll be right back with a bag of rice!' she said before abandoning them and kicking up sand in her wake.

Remi couldn't stop the waterworks now. The tears were therapeutic, and a long time coming. Calista, Gabe, Taz . . . it was all too much to handle. All the emotions she'd been holding back came in like a tidal wave. She let them freely fall but tried to even her exaggerated breaths so as not to scare the hell out of Mori, who was now looking at her with such a tender, pained expression that it caused a fresh wave of shame.

'Listen, Remi,' Mori said, turning her chin to fully face her. 'You and I have been through some shit in our lives. And you're going to continue to get through it. *All of it.* I promise you.'

Remi didn't believe her, but she numbly nodded nonetheless. Everything felt so desperately horrible and bleak. She didn't even know where she would begin to pick up the pieces of her life. Even the fleeting thought of Taz no longer gave her mind the escape she often craved.

For a moment, they allowed the sound of the tide to soothe them. Remi attempted to match her own body's rhythm to it, but then a new thought overcame her, giving her a fresh jolt, sending her spine rigid. 'The tide is coming in. Isn't it?' she asked, shifting her gaze toward the shoreline once again, yet trying to avoid her eyes directly meeting Calista's body.

'Yeah, it sure is,' Mori answered quietly. 'Sun's coming up too. It's getting hot out here.'

'Hell, I can't catch a break, can I?' Remi said with a sarcastic chuckle, resting her arms on her knees and kneading her forehead. A fresh headache was about to erupt.

'How do you mean?'

Remi flung her hand in Calista's direction. 'We're going to have to move her body, Mori. Or the sea will take her.'

Mori held back a yawn and then slapped both cheeks as if trying to revive herself. 'Oh, shit! I don't know why, but I didn't think of that.'

The two shifted their gaze back to the lifeless body in the sand that they'd been trying to avoid. It was hard to observe Calista that way.

So lifeless and cold.

And *dead*.

She was so very dead.

'I guess we have no other choice. Let's do it before I lose my cool,' Mori said, rising from her seat and wiping her backside of loose sand. 'Come on, give me a hand.' She reached out to help Remi up off the ground, but Remi remained planted firmly in place.

'Right now?'

'You said it yourself, Rem: the tide is coming in! We can't take a chance that she'll wash out into the Atlantic. That would be *really* bad! We can't allow that to happen, can we?'

'Fine,' Remi complied, scrambling to her feet and following Mori's lead. When she arrived in front of Calista, Mori directed, 'Grab her there, underneath her arm.'

Mori was already positioned on the far side of Calista's body ready for action, but Remi hesitated. She shuddered. She had never touched a cadaver, and this one belonged to the best friend from her youth. Remi danced a little in the sand and waved her hands, frantically trying to work herself up to the task.

'What the hell are you doing over there?' Mori asked. 'This is no time to break out into a dance!'

'Preparing myself,' Remi admitted.

'For what? A fuckin' party!' Mori scoffed. 'Hurry up!'

'How can you touch her. She's *dead*!' Remi wailed. 'Oh God! This is awful!'

'It's either that or we call the police right now before she gets swept into the ocean. Which do you prefer?' Mori challenged, with a laser stare.

'*Fine.*'

Remi reached below Calista's armpit, but before grabbing a firm hold of her, she whispered in her friend's ear, 'I'm so sorry, Cal. I'm sorry for all of this. I was really hoping we could reconnect. I've missed you and now I'll never know why we didn't remain friends all these years.'

'What did you say?' Mori demanded.

'*Nothing.*'

'Really? Because to my ears, it sounded like a confession!'

'Seriously, Mori? I'm just apologizing for what's happened to her in case she's up there listening!' Remi flung a dramatic hand to the sky. Her tone reached hysterics when she added, 'She's probably up there, somewhere in the universe, watching us do all of this to her! Just imagine that if you can! I'm sure this isn't the reunion Calista was hoping for either! What do you suppose she thinks of all this?'

'She doesn't *think* or know anything. She's gone, Remi,' Mori replied.

'How do you know? Maybe when we die—'

'Just stop right there,' Mori halted her with a raised hand. 'This is not the time to get all philosophical or religious. You need to hurry up, please!' Mori's gaze moved toward the Vineyard then. She was either worried about the rushing tide or wishing herself home across the bay; Remi couldn't gauge. 'Come on! Hurry up!' she pushed.

Just as Remi got up the nerve and they were hauling Calista's heavy body toward shore, Avery came back into sight.

'What the heck are you two doing!' Avery yelled at them when she was within earshot.

'The tide,' Mori grunted as they inched Calista's body closer to shore.

After reaching just a few feet away from the shoreline, Remi mumbled, 'Isn't this far enough for now?'

'I guess, but we'll have to keep an eye on her,' Mori replied with a groan. 'If the police don't come soon, we'll have to keep moving her.'

'Did you two honestly think that idea through?' Avery asked bluntly, landing her hands firmly on her hips. And shaking her head at them as if they were her naughty children and not two grown adults who were trying to handle this ordeal.

'We didn't have much of a choice. The tide is coming in,' Remi defended. 'We couldn't let her wash away!'

'Now your DNA is all over her! It's going to look like you two are involved somehow!' Avery spat. 'How on earth will you explain that?'

Remi shared a discouraged look with Mori.

'We had no other choice.' Mori shrugged. 'We'll just have to explain that to the police when they arrive. That we needed to move her or she'd never be found again. They'll believe we were trying to save her body, won't they?'

'Wait! That's a good idea! We can tell the police she drowned out here and we tried to save her!' Remi suggested. 'That could work!'

'Not a chance Rem,' Mori said firmly. 'We will tell them the truth: that we moved her because of the tide. Period. End of story. No more lies!'

Remi replied with a shrug. 'How would you feel if there was a chance your husband might be involved? I'm only trying to protect what's mine!'

'OK, well, regardless . . . what's done is done, I guess. Calista is moved and we'll keep an eye on the tide,' Avery continued with an eye-roll. 'Hey. Side bar – I have good news and bad news.'

'I don't think I can handle any more bad news,' Remi admitted, rushing back to the water to rid the sand from her hands. Returning quickly to her friends, she dried her hands on her shorts and noticed her shoulders ached as if she'd done way too much weightlifting. Yet the only lifting she'd done was that of her dead friend. Which was incredibly hard to wrap her mind around.

When she was within earshot, Mori said, 'Just spill it, Avery. We'll deal with whatever comes. *When* it comes.'

'OK. Well . . . the bad news is Brody arrived while we were down here, and he's already started cooking breakfast, so he might catch on to what we're doing out here if we don't get moving. He just assumed we were still in bed. The good news is he fixed the phone.' Avery handed the iPhone to Remi and for the first time in a very long time her lips lifted in a weak smile.

'How'd he manage that?' Mori asked.

'Dunno, the boy's a miracle worker. I asked him if he wanted to borrow a hair dryer to do it and he said heat would ruin it, but a cold fan might work. He found a cooling fan in the back of the closet and *wa-lah*!'

'You told him to stay in the kitchen, right?' Remi confirmed, taking the phone back into her possession. 'You're right; it would be very bad if he found out what was going on here. And that we didn't immediately call the police.'

Avery nodded. 'Yeah, let's hope he doesn't come down this way, but one of us will have to head him off at the pass if we notice his feet hit the boardwalk. We'll have to keep a lookout.'

Mori signaled them to follow closer to Calista. 'Let's hurry, then! We need to open the phone!'

This time, without a second thought, they all moved into their previous positions.

But despite their efforts, the iPhone remained locked.

'Still not working,' Remi grunted.

'I think there's only one thing to conclude,' Avery said.

'What's that?' Remi asked.

Mori answered, 'It's not Calista's phone.'

'*Then whose phone, is it?*' the three said in unison as they shared a look of fear.

TWENTY-FOUR

Avery was losing patience with her friends. While the clock was ticking, the answers to how Calista's body ended up on the private beach in front of their rented cottage were disappearing with each roll of the rising tide. '*Guys!*' she pleaded. 'We really need to call the police. We can't hold this up a minute longer. Not to mention, Detective Reed is going to wonder why we haven't showed up at the nature reserve yet to join the grid search. Very soon, our absence is going to make it obvious that something is amiss. Don't you think?'

'I vote we look for more clues first. You said it yourself; we need to find out how Calista landed here before the police come and we're kicked off the scene,' Mori stated firmly. 'We won't learn anything once they arrive. We'll be completely pushed out of the investigation – and you know it, Avery.'

'The more I think about it, that would probably be a good thing,' Avery admitted with a wince.

'Why?' Remi challenged. 'You were the brilliant one who suggested investigating in the first place! I thought you were our wannabe expert at this.'

'I know.' Avery held up a hand to cut off the protest. 'But I was wrong. If the police find our footprints scattered all over the beach, it's going to mess with their investigation. And we don't want to take the chance of screwing it up for them. They only have one shot at this. As it is, they're going to follow our trail down here, which might prove misleading.' Avery looked down at the sand and for the first time noticed that the beach beyond them had been raked. 'Wait? Who did this?' She pointed out the rows of rake marks a few yards from where they were standing.

'I'm sure Jerome has a service that comes out with a machine to rake the sand,' Mori said. 'It's not uncommon when you own waterfront properties like this to keep it manicured. After all, the beach is an extension of his lawn. He hosts a ton of parties out here, so he likes to keep it looking nice. No seaweed, that sort of thing.'

'Wait. Did you say we're renting Jerome's house? The guy you . . .' Remi trailed off.

'Yeah, I'm not supposed to say anything,' Mori warned, zipping her lips with her fingers. 'Mum's the word.'

'I'm not sure that will remain a secret with Calista's body found out here. I'm sure the press will have a field day with it as soon as word gets out!' Remi interjected. 'You know I'm right about that!'

'Let's stick to the matter at hand, you two. We have enough problems to deal with, without adding more,' Avery directed. 'I'm not surprised that your friend hires a company to rake the beach. However, I am surprised that the person who raked the sand didn't see Calista's body out here. How could that be? Near impossible, I would think!'

'Maybe she was brought here after?' Mori shrugged. 'Or . . . the tide was up, and the service didn't make it that far down the beach? Good question, though. It might help us with the timeline of Calista's murder.'

'Perhaps she was dumped here via boat. That's a possibility too, right?' Avery suggested. 'It would need to be someone who knew where we are staying this week, though, and that's rather perplexing. Only our family members know our location. None of us shared it on social media or anything. Right? And, Mori, like you just said, you were keeping it on the downlow that Jerome was the person who lent us a place to crash.'

'Do you think *I'm* being framed for this since the killer is making it look like Gabe's involved somehow?' Remi asked nervously. 'If you're suggesting the killer dumped her here on purpose?'

'You're not the only one being framed here, Rem. It could be any one of us,' Mori stated matter-of-factly.

'Which is why we need to call the police!' Avery pressed again.

Finally, the others agreed.

TWENTY-FIVE

They say that time heals old wounds. *It doesn't.* Each day that passes, each hour and minute, only solidifies the infection and molds it into something like concrete within the heart. A hard nugget forms – a rock-solid core which remains there until death unless surgically removed.

Was this a revenge killing? Or a crime of passion?

Mori knew Calista and Gabe hid a sexual relationship back in high school. She knew it because she'd witnessed the two of them with her own eyes. She remembered the day she discovered them together as if it were yesterday. Those once-in-a-lifetime events which hold a special place of memory in the computer file of the mind are often hard to forget. Because it was the day Mori had received her driver's license. So elated was she to have passed the test that she had driven her mom's piece-of-shit pea-green Dodge in search of Calista, to join her for a celebratory Heath Bar Blizzard at the local Dairy Queen. That was the day she discovered their secret. When rounding the corner to Calista's neighborhood, Mori witnessed the two of them tripping out of the woods hand in hand with faces flushed. They had landed at the tree line and kissed for almost a full nauseating minute. Calista's back was pushed against a tall oak, and Gabe intimately moved the hair away from her eyes before both fervently looking around to see if anyone was watching. And then they parted ways.

Mori had confronted Calista to fess up about what she'd witnessed and what was going on between them, knowing that Gabe had recently started dating Remi. She and Calista had been sitting across the table from each other, their spoons dipped into thick ice cream overloaded with Heath Bar when Calista absently held out her spoon, remained mute, and just looked back at her with a blank expression. The same blank expression Mori's father had upon his shame-filled face when he cheated on her mother. For a millisecond, that disgusting, obvious look of guilt had washed across his face and crushed her mother's heart when she had challenged him with the exact same question: *How long have you been cheating?*

That's the moment when Mori knew it wasn't just a one-time thing. This had been going on for some time between Gabe and Calista. Had it continued through adulthood? Mori had held the secret of their clandestine relationship because Calista *never* admitted the truth to her. It was Mori's word against hers. Who would believe her? She knew she would lose her friendship with Calista over it if she pressed harder on the subject or told anyone. In fact, she thought she'd lose all of them. Every single one in her friend group would most likely vanish. And she couldn't take the chance of becoming a loner once again, with only her library books to keep her company on football Friday nights. Instead, she'd tucked the secret away deep and never told a soul.

Did it mean something *now*? After all these years? Or was it a non-issue? Had Remi ever been told? Mori's thoughts were interrupted when Remi alerted them that the detective had arrived on the beach and was swiftly walking in their direction.

'You found her,' Detective Reed said grimly when he came within earshot. His eyes glanced toward the shoreline at Calista's lifeless body and then back to them. 'Did you touch anything?'

'We didn't have much choice. We had to move her; otherwise, we feared she might wash out to sea,' Mori admitted before her gaze dropped to her sand-covered feet where she curled her toes into the warm soft earth. She didn't want to chance another look at Calista. She couldn't handle it – viewing her friend like that, all lifeless and cold. It was too much.

'I see,' replied the detective.

Remi moved closer to Reed, kicking up half the beach in her haste. 'Did you find Gabe?' Her words tripped out breathlessly; she was clearly afraid of what he might say. As if Gabe, too, had met an untimely demise.

Detective Reed didn't utter a word; he only shook his head solemnly. So careful. So calculated with his words. Mori wanted to take him and shake him like bar dice and will him to speak something of value besides a mere nonverbal.

Where the hell was Gabe?

Instead, the detective eyed them carefully, one by one. 'I need to separate you three. And take you down to the local police department for further questioning.'

'*Why?* We didn't do anything!' Remi cried, her fists in balls defiantly by her side. 'Can't we just talk out here on the beach?'

she pleaded, unclenching her tight fists and placing them in praying hands in front of him, begging him to change his mind.

'No, I think it best to have your statements recorded. Don't worry, I won't keep you there any longer than necessary.'

'Are we suspects?' Avery asked tentatively. Her eyes held fresh fear. Then her gaze darted between Mori and Remi before landing back on the detective, looking for absolution.

'I wouldn't take it that far. More like persons of interest.'

'Well, that certainly doesn't make me feel better,' Avery mocked, throwing her hands up in disgust. 'You need to be out there looking for who did this to her! Because you're wasting your time if you're looking at one of us!'

'Why are you separating us? I need my friends!' Remi continued with a squeal. 'This has been one of the worst days of our lives and you're tearing us apart? That's not fair!'

'Don't take it personally,' he replied flatly. 'It's just procedure – standard protocol.'

'Standard protocol, my ass!' Mori blurted. 'She's right: this hasn't exactly been an easy thing for us to digest this morning! Clearly, we're all still in a state of shock. It may be standard for you, Detective, but there's nothing standard about this for us!'

'He doesn't want us swapping details. He's separating us to see if our stories match. He can't officially clear us otherwise,' Avery interjected and then looked to the detective for confirmation. 'Right?' she asked, staring him down intently.

'That's right.'

'But we didn't do *anything!*' Remi shrilled. 'And we don't have time for this! What we *need* to do is to be out there searching for my husband! Not hanging around the local police department!'

Avery put her hand out to console Remi, but the detective stopped her and ordered them to part ways and remain on the beach separated by a few yards minimum before he could decide which officer would accompany whom down to the Falmouth Police Department. Directly behind him, a pack of uniformed officers descended on to the beach like picnic ants and fanned out in all directions.

This frustrated Mori because it didn't give her a chance to press Remi about whether she knew that Gabe and Calista shared a past. Or had Gabe kept that little tidbit from his wife throughout their entire married life? This weighed heavily on Mori's mind as she wasn't sure if she should be transparent with the police about it or not. Was it her place to bring it up *now*? After all these years? Was it even relevant? The last thing she wanted to do was implicate a friend. Her mind was spinning in overdrive.

After reaching her designated spot away from the others, Mori slumped to the sand and leaned her weight against a large boulder adjacent to the dunes, listening as the seagrass whistled eerily in the wind. She then held her head in her hands to think it through. But doing so did little to help alleviate her stress. Mori still couldn't decide if she'd remain mute on the matter. Without coming up with a definitive answer, she lifted her eyes to watch the scene unfold. CSI-type investigators were located by Calista's body taking photos and placing markers all over the beach as if in some kind of movie. She wished that were true and she was merely watching the behind-the-scenes production unfolding. At that moment, nothing seemed real.

Mori wiggled her toes to feel something because her feet were suddenly turning blue, not from the sand being cold but from lack of blood flow. She needed to feel something. Anything. Her body felt numb. Her emotions felt numb. Her mouth felt dry as if she had a hangover. She slapped her cheeks to wake herself from this awful feeling. From this awful dream.

Detective Reed had moved to talk with two uniformed officers and pointed in the direction of the three friends. It seemed as if he was ordering them to divvy up who would be their escort back to the police station. She really needed to get ahold of Jerome before the news hit. So much for anonymity. Mori doubted she'd be able to keep his home address out of the public eye now. And she felt horrible about that too. Hopefully, he'd understand and forgive her; that all this had landed quite literally on his doorstep. What a mess!

Mori moved to stretch her legs, and her eye spotted something gleaming after her foot had disrupted the sand. The sun caught the object, causing it to glimmer further. She reached for it, thinking maybe one of Jerome's house guests had accidentally lost an expensive diamond while attending one of his wild parties. She brushed off the sand and held it in her palm. It was a heart-shaped pendant from a necklace and the attached fixing was broken. The same heart-shaped diamond pendant that Remi had been wearing the day she arrived at the Cape. The necklace Remi had mentioned

Gabe gave to her that she never took off. Mori held it loosely in her hand as her eyes rose in search of Remi.

When did Remi's necklace break?

And why hadn't she mentioned losing it if it was so important to her?

TWENTY-SIX

For the second time in less than three seconds, Remi wiped her sweaty palms upon her shirt but still couldn't relieve the clamminess of her hands. She couldn't stop her heart from racing either, despite her years of yoga training. When Detective Reed approached, she scrambled to her feet and brushed the sand from her legs before greeting him. Remi studied the detective carefully when she asked, '*Where* is my husband? I'm losing my mind here! None of this is making any sense.'

'That's something I was hoping you could tell me,' he prodded with a narrowed brow, studying her warily as he waited for her answer. When she didn't reply, he continued, 'It still seems odd to me that you haven't heard from him.'

'No,' she murmured. 'And if you think I'm trying to cover for him, I assure you I'm not!' she added through clenched teeth. 'I need to find my husband! Believe me, I'm just as frustrated as you are.'

'I'm sure you are.' His eyes examined her a little too intently then, as if checking her body language to verify if she was lying. Which – quite frankly – made her mad. If he wasn't an elected official, she'd clock him one. This was getting ridiculous.

'Is the search team still out looking for him at the nature reserve? Or has that been called off now that we found Calista's body out here on the beach? *Please* tell me someone from your department remained back there to keep looking.' Remi's gaze left his momentarily as she scanned the beach. It seemed as if the slew of officers who had been back at the search site were now combing the beach for fresh clues. In that case, no one would be out looking for Gabe, which sent a fresh wave of frustration that she had to swallow. It took all her inner strength to remain calm at this point.

'We're working with limited resources here on the Cape,' he replied, clearing his throat. 'Falmouth isn't exactly home to a full-on investigation team. I've reached out to gather investigators from other neighboring agencies who might be able to provide assistance.

Please understand, we're all stretched a little thin these days. But we are doing the best we can to assemble a team.'

When he still didn't answer the most important question on Remi's mind, she reached out and clutched him by the arm desperately and met his eyes directly. 'I'm very concerned about my husband – we need to keep searching. He could be out there lying in a ditch somewhere! If no one is out there looking, please release me so I can go and search for Gabe myself! If Calista was murdered, don't you see that he could be in trouble too!'

'Yes, of course we're still looking. There's a BOLO out on him.'

'Bolo?'

'Be on the lookout.'

'But you're not going to release me to go look for him. Are you?'

The detective didn't answer.

Remi breathed deeply, but it did little to calm her erratic heartbeat. She assumed they had different reasons for needing to find her husband anyway. Her reason was love. His was wanting to interrogate him. The thought of Gabe involved in any of this made her blood run cold. 'I suppose you're searching for my husband not because you are worried sick, like I am, but because you think he might be involved somehow,' she voiced finally. 'If you didn't hear me the first time, please listen to me now. Gabe had nothing to do with Calista's murder! I promise you. My husband is a good and gentle man. When you meet him, you'll see that for yourself. It's completely out of the realm of possibility, let me assure you.'

'If we're talking assurances, then let *me* assure *you*, Ms Toussaint, that your husband has not been identified as a suspect, nor has he been officially eliminated from the investigation. Look, I don't jump to conclusions either. I follow the case wherever it leads me. Which is why I can't release you and your friends just yet. We need to talk.'

'I see,' Remi said, despondently. She thought her assumptions about the detective were spot on. Calista was dead. And Gabe was missing. It didn't take a rocket scientist to do the math. Who else was to blame? If not one of them or both of them? She could think of no one else on whom to cast responsibility.

Detective Reed held out his palm. 'That reminds me. Give it here.'

'Give what here?'

'The phone.'

'You want my phone?' Remi asked. 'I'd rather not, in case by some miracle my husband tries to contact me. I need to hold on to it for now,' she explained. 'You understand . . . In case he calls.'

The last thing she wanted was a Snapchat from Taz popping up on her cell phone and the detective witnessing it. She could only imagine the drilling she'd receive from him if that happened. And she was in no mood to explain her life to him. Nor send him down a needless path.

'No, the phone you neglected to tell me you found at the nature reserve.'

Remi hung her head. 'How did you know?'

'It's my job to know. I'd like it now, please.'

'OK.' Remi reached into her pocket, but instead of doing as commanded, she asked. 'Why do you want it if I didn't get it open yet? I could—'

'Hand it over.' The detective was clearly growing impatient as he threw out a hand for her to place it in his palm.

'I didn't mean anything by taking it. I honestly thought it was Gabe's – it was dark outside. I can still try—'

'Not with your friend's body over there, you can't,' the detective scoffed, flinging out a long finger in the direction of the shoreline. He then wagged his finger between them. 'Things have changed a little bit since the last time you and I talked. Now, hand it over.'

'Oh. Sorry. OK, then.' Remi plucked the phone from her pocket and handed it to him. 'I dropped it in the ocean, and then it was dried with a fan. Hopefully, you can get it to work.'

The detective eyed her again. This time his guarded look caused goosebumps to rise upon her flesh. She didn't like his implication one bit. It was as if he believed she was trying to destroy the phone and hide whatever was on it. She wished she had more time to try to open it. Truth was, in her opinion, it might be the only key to finding out the truth. And now he was taking that from her.

'What?' she defended.

Detective Reed didn't respond. He only tucked the phone into an evidence bag he'd pulled from his pocket and then beckoned her to follow.

'Where are we going?'

'Local police station,' he said over his shoulder, dismissing any further protest by spinning on his heel and turning his back to her.

Remi opened her mouth to argue, but it was pointless. A shadow passed above, causing her to flinch, and she realized the darkness coursing over the beach was only the shadow of a seagull flying overhead. The stress made her jumpy at every turn. Out of the corner of her eye, she caught Mori staring at her and she lifted her shoulders in defeat, waiting to understand why her friend was watching her exit the beach with such intent. But Mori only dropped her gaze and shook her head in disapproval. Remi felt the weight of this. It seemed as if she was guilty by association. Just because Gabe was missing, it was now somehow her fault that Calista was dead. The blame was all cast in her direction.

As she followed the detective across the beach, her thoughts wavered between being completely pissed off at her husband for not telling her why he was in Massachusetts in the first place and fearing he too was in dire straits. Either option led to erratic paths of doom in her mind. Her relationship with Gabe might never recover from this. Remi's stomach began to cramp, and she held her belly tight. 'Hold on, little one,' she whispered.

'Did you say something?' The detective stopped mid-stride and turned to face her directly.

'No,' she answered quietly.

It was obvious he didn't believe her; his stare lingered on her for an uncomfortably long moment before he continued his stride toward the boardwalk.

The idea of a ride in Detective Reed's unmarked vehicle felt foreign to Remi. 'What about my friends?' she asked as she ducked her head into the backseat of his vehicle.

'Oh, don't worry. They'll be following on right behind us to the police station.'

He hadn't handcuffed her or anything that drastic, yet the drive was still mildly unnerving. They rode in silence. Remi desperately wanted to say something to break the quiet but held back for fear of saying the wrong thing. Crumbs were scattered on the overworn seat, and an empty potato chip bag littered the floor behind him. It looked as if the car had never seen a vacuum. The smell of fried food hung in the air too as if someone had recently downed a burger and fries.

The smell made Remi's pregnancy gag reflex work in overdrive. She had to hold it in check with the back of her hand on several occasions and was thankful when she noticed them pull into the parking lot of the local police station. In her life, she had never had so much as a speeding ticket and here she was getting out of the car and following a detective into his place of work. This was not the vacation she had planned in her mind when she'd flown to Boston less than a week ago. She wished now she had never made the trip. If she ever made it back to Florida, she vowed this would be her last vacation.

Ever.

'Do you need anything? Would you like a soda or coffee?' Detective Reed asked, holding the door for her to enter.

'May I use the facilities?' Remi asked meekly. 'I probably should've gone back at the cottage before we left.'

'Sure,' he said, escorting her down a long concrete hallway. 'Second door on your right. I'll be right here waiting.'

I bet you will, Remi thought. She already felt like a criminal from that statement alone. At least she'd have a moment of privacy before joining his commanding presence once again. His stature and attitude unnerved her. It was as if he already found her guilty.

After using the toilet, she stopped at the sink to wash her hands and was struck by her appearance in the mirror. The loose hair which had escaped her ponytail was standing on end, wildly askew. Her earlier sun-kissed face now looked sallow, and her typically lively eyes were surrounded in clouds of deep charcoal where her eyeliner had smudged.

After drying her hands, she removed her ponytail and quickly smoothed her hair using fingers dipped in water to flatten it back down before setting it back in place. She figured if she was going to have her mugshot taken and plastered all over the nightly news, she could at least look *somewhat* presentable. She hoped she was being overdramatic and it wouldn't come to that. She needed to lose that train of thought completely and put on an air of confidence. She willed herself to do this through gritted teeth as she gripped the porcelain sink, wondering what the next hour would bring.

'Everything all right?' the detective asked when she greeted him back in the hallway.

'Yes,' Remi replied meekly. Which was the opposite of what she felt. Everything was not all right. In fact, it was *all wrong*. Calista was dead. Gabe was missing. And she was wasting critical time in which she could be looking for her husband with this charade. She realized, though, that any further protest to the detective would fall on deaf ears, so why bother? The sooner she got this over with, she hoped, the sooner he would release her.

They entered a cold-looking room which instantly made Remi's skin crawl. Sure, she had seen this type of interrogation room on television. But to mindfully step foot into a space where hardened criminals had once been questioned, most probably *guilty* of the crime, was jarring to the core.

The seaworthy grey room, which looked as if it belonged in the belly of a submarine, had a large glass one-way mirrored window on one wall and a flat painted cement wall facing it. An oversized metal table with a bar along the top of it centered the room. Remi assumed the metal bar was for those who were cuffed and needed to be secured to the table. A fleeting thought of Taz crossed her mind, and whether an act of bondage could be performed there, before shame coursed through her body and jolted her back to the present moment. A moment of weakness. Taz was always the diversion she fled to in her mind when under stress. Her escape. But there was no escaping this, she thought, as she looked at the table set between four folding metal chairs. And that was the extent of it.

The detective gestured for her to take a seat.

The metal from the chair legs scratching across the cement floor echoed in the room when Remi moved it to get comfortable. However, there was nothing comfortable about it. The chair was hard and cold. She swallowed the bile that suddenly rose in her throat, as she realized the depth of the predicament she found herself in.

'I'm just going to ask you a few questions. Nothing to worry about,' Reed said casually, leaning back in his chair.

Remi noted the detective was good at sensing things; nothing seemed to escape his gaze, even though he was attempting to make her more comfortable. 'Easy for you to say. This is all very intimidating,' Remi replied meekly, folding her hands upon the table between them.

The cramping in her stomach seemed to grow with each word out of his mouth. And she tried not to wince in pain. This was not the time to explain her pregnancy. Would he somehow misconstrue that as motive?

Detective Reed pointed to the corner of the room. 'As we discussed, before we begin, you are being videotaped.'

Remi interrupted, 'Are you going to read me my Miranda rights?' Her heart nearly beat out of her chest. 'Am I being arrested for Calista's murder?'

'No, this is just standard procedure. We're only here to talk. But your reaction is leading me to believe that maybe I should. You do have the right to counsel if you so choose.'

But nothing about this was standard procedure in Remi's world. Nothing at all. She gripped her stomach tighter and moaned when warm fluid gushed between her legs.

TWENTY-SEVEN

'What is your relationship to the victim?'
Avery stared blankly across the table at the investigator from the Falmouth Police Department. His name was Warren Fletch, and he didn't look old enough for the police academy, never mind promoted to detective. A full head of curly blond hair covered Warren's head, yet no five o'clock shadow appeared on his clean-shaven baby face. She wondered why he would ask a question he clearly already knew the answer to. Didn't he and Detective John Reed exchange notes? Could he really be that ignorant of why they were here?

'Ms Williams?'

'Avery. Please call me Avery. The only people who call me Ms Williams are the parents of the kids who attended my Sunday school class back in Iowa. And right now, I'm so far from the farm it isn't even funny,' she added with a nervous chuckle.

'OK, Avery.' Warren shifted in his seat, leaned forward, and steepled his stubby fingers atop the table. 'How do you know Calista Moore?'

'I'm sorry, I don't understand. I'm quite certain you already know the answer to that question.' Avery laced her arms protectively across her chest and sank further into the chair to distance herself as far as humanly possible from the officer. If she could leap from the room and remove herself completely from this investigation, she would. She was beginning to feel like a caged animal, demanding to run free.

'I need to hear it from you.' Detective Fletch then pointed out the video camera in the corner of the room that was beaming an uncomfortable shade of red. A red that notified her that they were being recorded at this very moment.

'Calista is a friend of mine. I mean *was*.' She winced. 'Sorry. It's hard to think of her in the past tense.'

'Understandable,' he replied, devoid of emotion and rolling his hand for her to continue.

The fact that this line of questioning seemed redundant to the detective sent a fresh wave of sadness to Avery's heart. Nothing about Calista's murder should be matter of fact. Especially when discussing someone she knew. Someone she grew up with and went to the movies with. Someone with whom she spent Friday night football games, pizza nights, and sleepovers, and made smores around campfires at the beach. Their friend group had been inseparable back then. And now one of them was gone. It all held an uncomfortable sting that felt way too close to home. Avery swallowed the lump in her throat and forced herself to continue.

'Calista was part of the group I hung out with at Hopkinton High School. We reconnected on social media and thought it would be fun to host a reunion somewhere on Cape Cod where we spent a lot of time together, back in the day. Especially since Calista had recently turned forty, and we're all nearing that milestone birthday.' She didn't add that Detective Warren was too far from that age to be able to understand how hard forty was to accept. Looking at the boy who sat across from her, she doubted he'd be able to empathize.

'Who planned it?'

'Pardon?'

'Whose idea was it to host the reunion?'

'I think it started with Remi. Wait. No. That's not right. Maybe Mori?' Avery kneaded her forehead to force out the correct answer. 'Honestly, I can't remember how it all came together. It just did.' She shrugged. 'I'm not as active on social media as the rest of the group, so you'll have to ask one of them.' For some reason, she felt hesitant to mention that it was potentially Calista or Kirk's idea, and she didn't know why.

'Ah.'

'*Ah* what? What is that supposed to imply?'

The detective ignored her line of rhetorical questioning and instead asked, 'During this reunion, was there ever a time when you were separated from the rest of the group for an extended period? In other words, were you ever alone?' His eyes studied her intently.

Avery's mouth went dry, and she had to swallow hard before she could speak again. 'You mean besides sleeping?'

'Yes.'

'No, I was never alone. I mean, Mori, Remi, and I have been pretty much joined at the hip since my arrival. Why do you ask?'

'You're absolutely, unequivocally sure of this?' he repeated, rubbing his chin thoughtfully.

Avery wasn't sure which angle the detective was pursuing with this train of thought and wanted to head it off at the pass.

Did she need to protect one of them? Or all of them? Was he thinking the three of them were in on this?

Anxiety was rising in her chest, causing her airways to constrict. *Was Mori or Remi involved in this?*

No.

Neither one of them could lift a finger against Calista. Never mind kill her!

'Avery?'

'Yes.' She cleared her throat and faced him directly. 'Yes, I'm sure.'

'Because Mori mentioned that you both were drunk one night, and Remi had escorted you to your bedrooms. And neither of you knew where Remi went after that. Is this true?'

Avery chewed the inside of her cheek while her eyes darted around the room like a bull in a bull pen looking for an escape. Was he asking her to pin this on Remi?

'Avery?'

'Yes, Mori and I had too much to drink one night. But the answer is no, I don't recall if Remi brought me upstairs. The last thing I remember is hanging around the campfire on the beach. I don't remember anything after that,' she admitted sheepishly. 'I don't know what time I went to bed. You must understand, I rarely drink – and I can't . . .' she trailed off.

'So, you're saying that Remi *did* have time alone. Without you and Mori present? Is that right?'

Avery rose from her seat and, with both palms set firmly on the table, leaned forward and said, 'Are you trying to hang this on Remi? Because I can promise you, she didn't have anything to do with what happened to Calista. I wouldn't be friends with her if she did.'

'How can you promise that?'

'Because I know her!' Her tone rose a little too harshly, and she sat back down and tried to cool her jets. She wrung her hands beneath the table where he could not witness her further distress.

'You mentioned earlier that you don't really know them at all anymore, that you're not on social media much. Isn't that true? Are you changing your statement?'

'You're trying to trick me with words, and it's not going to work,' Avery uttered. 'That's not fair.'

'No, I'm not, I'm merely asking you to state what happened,' he said matter-of-factly. 'Are you aware that Calista and Gabe were seen together leaving a hotel room this week? Here in Massachusetts?'

'*Excuse me?*'

'Yes. We received a tip from a hotel worker and followed up on the video feed from the Holiday Inn. We confirmed it was them. Calista's SUV's license plate was registered to the room.' He studied her. 'Just a few blocks from the nature reserve. Can you explain that? To your knowledge, were the two involved?'

Seeds of doubt began to creep into Avery's mind. She shook her head. 'Does Remi know?'

'That's not important. What *is* important is that you tell me what was going on between Gabe and Calista. To your knowledge, were they having an affair?'

'But it is important! You're basically implying Remi found out about this and killed Calista over it!'

The detective remained poker-faced.

Avery blinked back at the sudden blurry lines that filled her vision, and she attempted to even her tone. 'Look, you're right. I don't know anything about these people anymore! I live on a farm, back in Iowa. The only thing I know *for sure* is how to till a field and plant corn! And make one helluva strawberry shortcake. I came out here to reconnect with some friends that I haven't heard from or seen in decades. Yeah, *seriously*! It's been at least twenty years since we've spent time together! How would I know? I don't have much else to say. At this point, I'm asking for a lawyer to be present. I'm not saying another word.' Avery closed her lips tightly together as if they were bonded with superglue.

'Why? Do you think one of your friends is guilty? Or do you have something to hide, Ms Williams?'

'No! I've just watched enough crime shows to know that I don't like the way this conversation is headed. I'm done talking.' She zipped her lips again before adding, 'That's my right. Correct?'

'Yes, that's your right.' After glancing out the two-sided window and offering a curt nod, the detective rose from his seat. 'You're free to leave.'

But Avery didn't think any of them was free from this.

At least not yet.

TWENTY-EIGHT

As soon as she noticed Avery step over the threshold and exit the interrogation room, Mori rushed quickly to her side. 'We need to go to the hospital,' she said breathlessly, linking her friend by the arm and giving her a strong tug in the direction of the door that led to freedom. Freedom from interrogating questions, uncomfortable stares, and innuendos. This departure could not come soon enough.

Avery shook her head as if coming out of a cloud of smoke and then muttered, 'Huh? What? Why? Did they find Gabe? Is he hurt?'

'No. It's Remi. They took her by ambulance.' Mori's answers were coming out in short pants now as if adding additional words might cause things to sound audibly worse. As if things could get any worse. 'We need to follow her over to Falmouth Hospital, right away.'

'Oh no.' Avery stopped mid-stride and gripped her heart with both hands. 'Did she?'

Mori didn't wait for Avery to finish her line of thought before rushing down the narrow hallway. 'I don't know. But please, we need to hurry,' she replied, beckoning Avery to follow.

Mori was never so happy to be exiting a police department in her life and hoped this was the last time she'd be questioned regarding Calista's murder. If she never saw the detective again, she'd be elated. Something deep in her soul, though, knew this wasn't over. It was only the beginning, and she may as well come to peace with that fact.

'Is Remi going to be all right?' Avery asked again, as if she was slowly coming out of her daze.

'I sure hope so and that this was just the paramedics taking extra precautions and getting her checked out. You know, on second thought, we probably need to stop by the cottage first and pick up a change of clothes for her before we head to the hospital. The patrol officer mentioned she bled through hers.'

'Oh no, that's not good. Not good at all,' Avery replied.

After exiting the dark hallway, the bright sun blinded Mori the minute she stepped outside. She turned and noticed Avery blinking rapidly too as if trying to catch her bearings. 'Can you see?'

'Yeah, just take my hand,' Avery pleaded. 'I'm struggling a bit with changes in brightness.'

'You bet!' Mori took Avery by the hand and led her across the parking lot to the passenger seat of her SUV and then helped her get situated inside, before running around the front of the car.

'I'm glad they let you drive your own vehicle over here. Otherwise, we would've been stuck grabbing an Uber or something,' Avery said as soon as Mori joined her, behind the wheel.

'I know. They took a little convincing, but I told the patrol officer to follow me to the station because we needed a way to get home, and he allowed it. How did the interrogation go on your end?'

'Not great,' Avery said, clicking on her seatbelt. 'You?'

'Yeah, it wasn't the most pleasant experience for me either.'

Avery shifted in her seat to face her. 'Did they mention to you that they saw Gabe and Calista leaving the Holiday Inn not far from the nature reserve? What was that about? That caught me totally off guard, that's for sure! You?'

'I think the investigators are trying to gauge if this is about an affair or something. And maybe we know more than we're sharing.'

'That's ridiculous!' Avery exclaimed. 'What on earth would make them think that? I really hate being in the middle of this!'

'Yeah, me too.'

Mori pulled on to the main road and turned in the direction of Jerome's. 'Besides the hotel, did you learn anything else? To me, it certainly doesn't look good for Gabe that they were seen leaving a hotel together and he's the last person to see her alive. And he's ignoring his wife's phone calls! Does it?'

'I know . . . but . . . They're just friends. We're all *friends*. As far as I know, Gabe and Calista were close neighbors and have been good friends for a long time. Nothing more. For crying out loud, Gabe lives in Florida and runs a gym; it's not even geographically possible for them to carry on an affair all these years!'

It seemed to Mori that Avery didn't know about Gabe and Calista's history back in high school. Mori wondered if she should say something now. And what about Remi's pendant which she had found on the beach? When had she lost it, and why hadn't she mentioned anything?

The air between them grew uncomfortably silent.

'Why are you so quiet all of a sudden?'

'Just thinking things through.'

'What things? Please, Moriah, don't shut me out. We need to get to the bottom of this.'

Mori reached for her purse behind the seat and held it on her lap while she simultaneously drove the SUV with her knee and dug out the pendant she had found on the beach. She then handed it to Avery.

'What's this?' Avery held the diamond heart in her palm and then tilted her head in question.

'I found it on the beach.'

'So?'

'So . . . it belongs to Remi. Why didn't she mention anything about losing it? Gabe gave it to her, and she *never* takes it off! That's what she told me the day she arrived.'

'Where did you find it? By the campfire? Maybe it broke while we were sitting around having quahogs the other night? It's possible—'

'No, it was nowhere near the campfire. That's what's perplexing. Because I found it out by the dunes when the officers split us apart.'

'What are you implying, Moriah?'

'I'm not implying anything. I'm merely following a clue. Remi not saying anything about the loss of her necklace is bothersome. I mean, what if an altercation led to it breaking? We were both drunk that night. She had plenty of time alone . . . What if Calista showed up at the beach house? Or Gabe? Heck, what if both showed up? We really don't know each other like we thought we did. Not anymore—'

Avery interrupted, 'Mori . . . you don't think—'

'I don't know what to think!' Mori slammed her hand on the steering wheel. 'And to be honest, I never thought I'd be forced to question my friends like this! I hate being put in this position! This is awful!'

'Well, let's back up a bit and think through this logically. If you're going to commit murder, you must have a motive to do so. And there's just no motive, in my opinion.'

'An affair isn't motive enough?'

Avery chuckled. 'I don't see how they could have pulled off an affair. That's just dumb. Tell me, how?'

'You wanna know how? They certainly hid it back in high school!' Mori blurted.

'What did you say?'

'*Shit.*'

'Mori.' Avery's tone was direct and expectant; there was no avoiding it now. 'Look at me. What. Did. You. Say?'

Mori blew out a breath of frustration.

'You need to tell me. If there are things going on that I'm unaware of, now's the time to spill. I'm getting dragged into this too. I ought to know everything.'

Mori pulled the vehicle into the garage, jammed the gear in park, and faced her.

'Avery, I caught them back in high school coming out of the woods, kissing. I pressed Calista about it, but she would never budge. She never admitted that they were sleeping together, but I knew they were. Hell, I smelt his cologne on her all the time. I can't tell you when it ended, but I know without a shadow of a doubt that this went on for a long time. I'm sure of it.'

'*When?*'

'About the time Remi and Gabe started dating.'

'Why didn't you say anything!'

'Seriously? It wasn't my place!'

Avery held the heart-shaped diamond pendant between them. 'And you think this all came out now? And maybe Remi stopped trusting Gabe, and the anger got the better of her? Huh? Is that really what you think?'

Mori shrugged. 'I honestly don't know. And as I said, I don't like being in a position to have to question my friends. Do you? In a perfect world, Calista would still be alive, and we wouldn't be having this discussion. We'd be sitting around the campfire eating smores, but that isn't gonna happen now, is it?'

'Did you tell the police?'

'Tell the police what?'

'That you found Remi's necklace?'

'No. I couldn't. Not without knowing for sure.'

'Who *else* would have a motive to hurt Calista?' Avery asked. The frustration in her tone was evident. 'We need to figure this out.'

'I wish I knew. We don't even *know* Calista anymore. Seriously! I haven't a clue as to what's gone on in her life over the last decade. Except for what she's posted on social media! And come on, is any of that real? Are those posts her true self? Her true life? Does anyone post their true self, *really*? Or is it all just for show? How are we supposed to know? No one airs their dirty laundry online!'

'You think her life was just a façade? Yeah, I don't know,' Avery huffed, throwing her hands up in frustration.

'Right now, we need to go inside, pack some clothes for Remi, and pretend we never had this conversation. We need to support our friend. And find out who did this.'

'Do you think our phones are being tapped?' Avery asked.

'What do you mean?'

'Do you think the police split us up to tell us about Calista and Gabe leaving the hotel together to see what we'd say? See how we'd react?'

'I don't know. If they did, it would be smart policing on their part.' Mori wrapped her purse strap around her shoulder before adding, 'You do watch a lot of crime TV to even come up with that idea. I never would've thought of it.'

Avery rolled her eyes and shrugged before exiting the vehicle.

'You think we can do it? Support Remi through this? Even if you think she had the capability to kill one of our friends. You can pull that off, you think?'

'I didn't say that. Again, I'm just following breadcrumbs here! What choice do we have? We're only making assumptions at this point. We need to find out the truth. And we *need* to find Gabe.'

Mori and Avery stepped into the garage, and Mori was just about to close the garage door behind them when she heard someone step inside and say, 'You looking for me?'

TWENTY-NINE

Remi's eyes fluttered open. Her lids felt sticky and wet, as if she'd cried herself to sleep. She blinked several times before trusting the cloudy vision in front of her. She knew she was in the hospital; she recalled the ride over in the ambulance. She remembered the rush of paramedics at the police station too. And talk of dehydration. And finally landing in a private room in which to grieve. But maybe that wasn't why she had been placed in a private room as she felt the squeeze around her wrist: one arm was handcuffed to the bed. And what confused her now was who was standing at her bedside.

'*Gabe?* Is that you?' Remi blinked again and rubbed her eyes vigorously with one fist before trying to adjust her vision once again. 'Am . . . I . . . dreaming? Is . . . it . . . you?'

She felt a warm hand squeeze hers. 'Shh,' he whispered. 'Try and relax, honey.'

'The baby . . .' she stuttered and then attempted to swallow. Her mouth felt parched as if she'd been sucking on cotton balls. She licked her lips with what saliva she had left, and Gabe must've understood as he reached for a nearby cup of water and helped her sit upright in the bed. He moved the IV aside so as not to accidentally pull it out before she took a sip, which dribbled down her hospital gown. Remi then looked her husband over with fresh eyes. 'Why are you wearing hospital scrubs? And your hair? When did you shave your head? How did you get here?' She blinked, trying to unmask the confusion coursing through her.

'Shh,' he whispered. 'I'm trying to blend in. The police are looking all over the state of Massachusetts for me, and I need to find a way to clear my name before I turn myself in. I had to wait until the officer who was stationed outside your door knocked off for a cup of coffee before sneaking in here. If both of us are in jail, no one will be able to clear us of this. But I needed to see you and make sure you're OK. I was worried sick about you.'

'Turn yourself in?' Remi attempted to adjust her position to sit higher in the bed, but the handcuff held her back from doing so.

'Did you do this? Did you kill Calista?' she whispered in a dreary haze.

'No! Of course not, don't be ridiculous!' He smoothed Remi's hair away from her face and kissed her forehead before encouraging her to lean back on to the pillows. 'Just relax, now,' he cooed. 'We need to take care of you and get you healthy again. Don't stress, my love.'

Remi was at a loss for words; the medication she was given was affecting her brain's ability to put things together. It was a supreme effort just to find the words to form a sentence. 'The baby!' she cried. 'I lost . . . the baby, didn't I?'

'I don't know that for sure. If I talk to the doctors, they'll turn me in. I can't stay . . . I just wanted you to know I'm all right. And make sure you are too. I love you, Remi! Where is your necklace?'

Remi reached for her neck in search of it, but her collarbone was oddly bare. 'The paramedics must have it. I . . . don't . . .'

'It's OK, not to worry about that. We can replace it. It's only jewelry.' He laid his hand on her chest and added, 'Know my heart is right here with you.'

'How did you . . . how did you . . . find me?'

'I followed you. I've been following you all over Cape Cod. We've always shared locations on Snap Map. Remember?'

Remi had completely forgotten when she set up Snapchat on her phone that Gabe had enabled this feature. It meant he possibly knew all the times she'd visited Taz without him. Her cheeks suddenly burned with shame. She wondered if Gabe had known all along and never said anything. In that moment, she realized that she was just as deceitful as he was. And that they had more in common in their unscrupulous behavior than either of them had ever known. She hated the thought and quickly changed the subject.

'They think I hurt Calista.' She locked eyes on the handcuffs and then returned her gaze to Gabe. 'What would make them think that?'

'Don't worry. I'll fix this. I'll fix everything, honey,' he soothed.

'You didn't . . . call me . . . or text.'

'I'm sorry. Please let me explain. I didn't want anything to trace back to you. I was trying to keep you safe.'

'But why? Why . . . are you here? I don't understand.' Remi winced then, a sudden pain in her abdomen coursing through her. 'In Massachusetts?'

Gabe's attention turned at the sound of commotion, and Remi followed his gaze. A nurse stood just outside the doorway talking to a doctor who was flipping a chart. And seemingly discussing Remi's prognosis.

Before the nurse or doctor stepped fully into the room, Gabe whispered in her ear, 'Look, I gotta run. I'll explain everything later. I just need a little more time. I love you.' He kissed her on the cheek and bolted from the room before she even had a chance to say goodbye.

The nurse entered with a wide smile and greeted her. 'Who was that? I didn't think we had another nurse on the floor tonight. I didn't recognize him.'

'Oh, I don't know . . . he may have said something about being a med student. Honestly, I'm not sure. I wasn't paying much attention when he checked my IV.'

'Ah, not to worry, I'll look into it. Good to see you're up! How are you feeling? Any pain?'

'I'm OK.' Remi returned her smile weakly and asked hesitantly, 'I lost the baby, didn't I?'

The nurse's smile faded, and she didn't mince words when she said, 'Yes. I'm so sorry.'

THIRTY

By the time they reached the hospital, Avery's stomach was in a complete knot, and her head was pounding to the beat of its own drum. She reached into her purse and popped two ibuprofen, swallowing them dry while en route to the elevator. She hated the smell of hospitals: like antiseptic and germs mixed in a blender fighting for real estate. It made her want to gag. And the building stress of the investigation into Calista's murder didn't help either.

Learning that Calista and Gabe shared a past caused Avery's loyalty to waver. Did Remi know? And would she and Mori bring it up? She absolutely hated confrontation. Since she was a child, she would go along with the flow, fearful of interrupting anything. But now . . . this was so much bigger than anything she'd ever been involved with. They needed answers. And yet now was not the time or the place to be poking the bear. Not when Remi was lying in a hospital bed.

They rode the elevator to the second floor, and while they waited privately behind closed doors, Mori stated firmly, 'We're not going to talk about what happened back at the police department or anything to do with the ongoing investigation. We can deal with all of that later. This is only about her health. Are we in agreement on that?'

'Yes, complete agreement. Bad timing to bring it up,' Avery nodded. 'By the way, your friend Jerome was a lot more understanding than you gave him credit for, despite his house and beachfront becoming a crime scene. It was nice to meet him. I can see why you two are kindred spirits.'

'Seriously, when he stepped into the garage, I almost shit my pants!' Mori admitted with a laugh. 'Yeah, he's a sweetheart of a man. A lifeline, if I'm to be honest. I don't know what I would do without him.'

'Nice of him to let us stay at his place indefinitely while we work through all of this. I don't know how many people would do that and choose to be inconvenienced in that way. He's a good friend, Moriah.'

'Yeah, he really is. One of the only people that has my back, time and time again. He's a rare gift,' Mori said with a sigh. 'Now that he's checked in on me and gathered up a few of his things, I'm sure he'll remain in New York until this all blows over. He really doesn't need that kind of publicity.'

'Nor do you,' Avery chuckled.

'That is a true statement!' Mori agreed with a laugh. 'But it looks like we have no other choice than to face the music alone.'

The elevator door popped open and the two remained quiet as they searched for their friend's room. Avery was surprised to find Remi sitting up in bed and nibbling on a piece of toast when they entered. Her face was flushed, but other than that, if Avery didn't know any better, her friend looked more rested than she had since the whole ordeal began – in spite of the elephant in the room: Remi was cuffed to the hospital bed.

'Hey,' Avery said, moving to take her free hand. 'How are you feeling, Rem?'

'I'm doing much better, thanks. The bleeding finally stopped. The nurse just came in and said I can leave as soon as I have a ride somewhere and a place to rest for the afternoon. Do I? Or will it be a jail cell to rest?' She snorted then, looking back at her handcuffed arm.

'Of course you do!' Mori gushed, rushing to Remi at the other side of the bed.

'I'm afraid to ask,' Avery said hesitantly, moving closer, 'about the baby . . .'

Remi's expression sobered, and Avery didn't even have to hear what words would be coming next. 'I'm so sorry.'

'Oh, Rem, I'm sorry too,' Mori added with a pinched expression.

They each took one of her hands and held it. The three connected to give Remi the emotional and physical strength she needed.

'You know what? I'm surprisingly OK,' Remi admitted. 'I was really starting to struggle with Taz being this baby's biological father, and all of that. And add Calista's death on top of it? It's just too much.' Her gaze dropped to the bed sheets. 'I don't think I'm meant to be a mother. I'm not exactly sure why I pushed the issue now when I'm nearing forty. And seemingly going to jail,' she added with a huff.

Avery and Mori shared a look of sadness before returning their attention to their hurting friend.

A Falmouth officer whom Avery recognized from the beach suddenly made an appearance and fully entered the room. 'Looks like it's your lucky day,' he stated matter-of-factly as he reached for a set of keys from his uniform. He then moved to Remi's bedside to unlock the cuffs from the bed. Remi rubbed her wrist the second her arm was freed. 'Not enough evidence to charge you,' he said flatly. 'But if I were you, I wouldn't leave the Cape just yet,' he warned with a raised brow.

'I'm innocent!' Remi cried. 'And guess what? When we find out who did this to our friend, you are going to owe me the biggest apology of your life! Mister!'

The officer didn't respond. He only frowned and shook his head before abandoning the room with a click of his heels.

'Can one of you go and find the nurse to see if I can get outta here?' Remi pleaded. 'I wanna go home. *Wherever* home is at this point,' she added with a chuckle. 'I have no idea where I'll live after this whole ordeal is over.'

'I'll do it,' Mori offered, hastily rushing from the room.

Avery was at a loss for words. She didn't know what to think or whom to blame, or even if she was in the presence of Calista's killer. So many times she'd witnessed people on *Dateline* or *48 Hours* doing heinous things to people they supposedly loved. Was this one of those times?

Remi plucked at her IV line. 'Ugh. I can't wait to get out of here.'

Avery managed to respond with, 'I bet.'

'I have to tell you something,' said Remi as she glanced over her shoulder and then toward the hallway. 'But I can't share it here,' she whispered.

'I don't think this is a time when we should keep any more secrets,' Avery said firmly. 'I think we need to be completely honest. Don't you? It's the only way, I think, that we can all move forward.'

'What are you saying?' Remi asked.

The nurse stepped into the room and Mori followed. 'Looks like I can discharge you now,' the nurse said happily, bustling around the room.

Avery wondered how a nurse could be so cordial to a woman who had recently been handcuffed to a bed. Kudos to her for her professionalism. She didn't think she could ever be so understanding. Especially with the most recent events.

Because those seeds of doubt about Remi were now becoming full-on weeds.

THIRTY-ONE

Despite the whirlwind drama of the last forty-eight hours, the pure exhaustion of it all had allowed at least a few hours of shut-eye for Mori. The three of them had had quite literally collapsed as soon as they'd arrived safely back at the cottage. And it was warranted. A full-body boost underneath the rain shower head helped ease her aching shoulder muscles too.

Attempting the fresh attitude of a brand-new day, Mori made her way down the staircase toward the kitchen, but she was saddened to think Brody wouldn't be standing beside the stove cooking breakfast. The previous night, she had phoned him on the way home from the hospital and told him it would probably be in his best interests if he did not return to the cottage. The last thing she wanted was a college kid to be wrapped up in the investigation too. She reminded him she would pay his full wages, though. It wasn't Brody's fault he was hired to work at what was quickly morphing into an official crime scene.

Avery was standing by the window with a mug of coffee cradled between her hands and turned toward Mori as soon as she entered the room. 'Hey,' she greeted.

'Hey, yourself. You get some rest?' Mori asked.

'A little. You?'

'Yeah, I think I'm still drained, though. It's going to take a while to catch up, I'm afraid.' Mori opened the refrigerator and pulled out the orange juice and poured herself a glass. This time minus the champagne.

'Same. I can't remember a time I've been this exhausted. Even after a full day's physical labor on the farm, I usually feel better than this,' Avery chuckled. 'I guess emotional trauma can do that to a person.'

'Yeah, we're all running out of adrenaline and starting to crash, I think.'

'Yup.'

'Speaking of crashing, is Remi up?'

'No, I haven't seen her yet.' Avery set the coffee mug down and reached for a piece of coffee cake, cut herself a slice, and placed it on a nearby plate.

Meanwhile, Mori kneaded her shoulders with her fingers, attempting to relieve some of the lingering tension that the shower hadn't fixed. 'Where did that thing of beauty come from?'

'You just missed Brody. He stopped by and dropped off some food. Said he'd already bought the groceries anticipating he'd be cooking for us, so he baked a few things to hold us over for a few days. I haven't gone through it all, but the scent when he came through the door was utterly amazing! That kid has quite a gift in the cooking department.'

'Oh, I didn't hear the Ring doorbell. He must've stopped in while I was in the shower. What a lifesaver he is!' Mori joined her by the cake and cut herself a hefty slice, while Avery handed her a fork. To hell with the diet at this point. She took a huge bite and instantly tasted buttery cinnamon which melted in her mouth.

'Hey.' Avery bumped her with her hip. 'Can we talk? Just between us chickens?'

The sound of Avery's tone alerted Mori to lean in even closer. 'Sure. What's on your mind?'

Avery eyed Mori and then her gaze traveled beyond the staircase before she lowered her voice as if they were co-conspirators. 'I'm having seeds of doubt,' she whispered, and then took another bite of cake and licked the crumbs before following up with a napkin.

'How do you mean? With Remi?'

'Yeah. I completely understand why we didn't mention anything to her at the hospital because of what she was going through with the miscarriage. But if the police suspect Remi – and they had her cuffed to a bed – how do we go about handling all this? I can't just go along and pretend that none of this is happening. It seems the police are just attempting to solidify their case before taking her away.'

Mori evened her breath, 'I know. I've been struggling too. Lying seems to come so naturally to Remi.'

'Exactly!' Avery illustrated by ticking off her fingers. 'First she lies about Taz to her husband, then she lies to the police about finding the phone. What else is she lying about?'

'Yeah, I know. I hear you. I need some answers regarding the necklace too. That's still nagging at me. Because if the pendant was that important to her, and she lost it, why didn't she say anything?

Why didn't she ask if we'd seen it somewhere?' The acid of the orange juice seemed to tickle Mori's throat, causing her to cough momentarily. Perhaps she needed the champagne after all. She took another gulp of juice to force it down.

'You don't actually think she had any part in Calista's death, do you?'

'Of course not.' Mori grimaced as if it was complete and utter nonsense. Yet, to be honest, something was nagging at her in the center of her gut. 'I just wish she'd clear up a few questions in my mind, is all.'

'So, should we confront her? The hospital sent her home to recover. In my opinion, if she's well enough to be here at the beach house, she's well enough to talk to us. We need to clear the air around here. I feel like I'm walking on eggshells. All of this is so stressful,' Avery said, setting her mug on the counter and kneading her temples as if to ward off a headache.

'OK, we can talk to her. But let's handle this gently, and then maybe she'll trust us enough to open up about everything. I'm not going to hit her with accusations. I don't think that's fair. Just because the police suspect her doesn't mean we should. That's just plain wrong.'

'No, I totally agree,' Avery nodded. 'We won't go in there guns a-blazing!'

'Did you get the impression that the detective suspects that one of us is involved too? Or just leaning toward Remi?'

'I didn't get that impression. More like they just wanted to see if our stories matched.'

Mori nodded, 'Yeah, me too.'

'What's next, then?'

'I think I have an idea.'

'You do? Are you going to record the conversation with your phone or something? See if she'll confess to anything? Then we can share the evidence with the police?'

'No,' Mori said with a wave of dismissal. 'I wasn't thinking that drastic.' She wagged a finger between them. 'If it really came to that, there would be two witnesses giving statements against her. I don't think we need to record anything. Besides, I think if she ever found out we had doubts about her, our friendship would be over.'

'Yeah, I suppose that's true.'

'Perhaps we could load a tray of food and bring it to her bedroom to check on her. If it seems like she's feeling OK, we go for it. But if she's ill and not up for it, we wait. Remi's been through a lot already. She might need more rest before we confront her. Deal?'

'If you think so. I guess that seems fair.' Avery finished her cake and rinsed her plate in the sink while she asked over her shoulder, 'You know this kitchen better than I do. Where would Jerome store a food tray?'

'I'll find the tray; you snag some food from the refrigerator. And maybe a cup of tea.'

The two scrambled around the kitchen to assemble the snacks and beverages, and then marched up the stairs as if heading into battle.

As soon as they reached her bedroom door, Avery gave a hard knock. 'Rem, you up?'

They heard a grunt from the other side of the door, and after exchanging a glance, they hesitantly let themselves inside. Remi was propped up on the bed with pillows, scrolling her phone. She dropped the phone to her side to greet them.

'Hey, guys.'

'How are you feeling?' Mori asked gently, setting the tray of food on the bedside table.

'Just sad,' Remi replied with a groan and then covered her face momentarily with a pillow. 'So incredibly sad,' she muffled through the pillow. 'I think I've run out of tears.'

'I'm sure,' Mori said sorrowfully, taking a seat beside Remi on the bed and patting her hand gently.

'Do you have an appetite? Brody dropped off some food.' Avery gestured to the tray and eyed it like she herself was growing hungry for a second slice of cake.

'Thanks, but since I no longer have another mouth to feed, I can wait,' Remi replied sadly. 'That was nice of Brody, though. He's a good kid.'

Avery pointed to the iPhone beside her on the bed. 'Speaking of good . . . Any good news? Have you heard from Gabe? Or has the detective phoned you with any updates?'

Remi noticeably stiffened but didn't answer. Her glance dropped to the bed sheets, visibly avoiding them.

Mori looked at Avery as if to say *Tread lightly* with her eyes, but Avery pushed on.

'We need to talk to you, Rem. About a few things that are not adding up.' Avery cleared her throat and acknowledged Mori with a wave of her hand as if she wished her to take over the conversation and continue.

Mori took the cue and reached into her pocket and fished out the heart-shaped diamond pendant. She held it in her palm for Remi to view and waited with bated breath for her reaction.

'My necklace!' Remi's eyes lit with gratitude. 'Did the paramedic give that to you? Or someone at the police department? I assumed I'd lost it forever when I dropped it at the hospital.'

Mori and Avery exchanged a look.

'What?' Remi asked innocently. 'What did I miss?'

'I found it on the beach,' Mori replied, studying her. She thought she noticed Remi flinch, but it happened so quickly she couldn't be sure. She looked at Avery to see if she'd noticed it too, but Avery gave no sign.

'I'm so glad you found it!' Remi gushed, reaching into Mori's palm and taking it into her own. She held it then before tightening her hand around it into a fist, until her fingers turned white. 'Thank you so much.'

'How did your necklace end up on the beach?' Avery demanded. Her eyes lasered in on Remi as if she could see right through her. Like she was now under a visible lie detector test and insisted she speak up.

This time, Remi cowered into the pillows under the accusation.

'Stop messing around and tell us the truth!' Avery exclaimed.

Fat tears sprang into Remi's eyes, and she said between sniffles, 'This is not my fault; I didn't start any of this.'

'Start what exactly?' Mori asked calmly. Her writer's feelers were exploding all over, forcing her to go deeper. There was more. She had felt it. Mori could sense they were on the precipice of something big, and she was hoping that their good cop/bad cop routine might just be the ticket to get Remi to spill her guts.

'Nothing,' Remi uttered.

Avery wouldn't back down. 'Why. Was. It. On. The. Beach? We are not letting you leave this room until you give us an explanation!'

'Because I ripped it off my neck and threw it at her!' Remi spat. 'When she stole my heart from me!'

Mori's pulse quickened and thundered in her ears. So much for playing good cop: a wave of fresh adrenaline caused her to leap up off the bed. 'What did you do, Remi?'

'I didn't do anything!' Remi choked out.

Avery stood as stiff as a board with fists clenched by her sides when she said through gritted teeth, 'You saw her! You saw Calista! And you didn't tell us! You owe us something right now, Remi! You owe us the truth!'

'I owe you nothing,' Remi said, turning her face into the pillow and sobbing.

THIRTY-TWO

The energy in the room was palpable. Avery was pacing a hole in the floor trying to maintain her composure, while Mori stood and stared at Remi, willing her to stop crying long enough to speak. Avery wanted to shake the truth out of Remi, but thankfully Mori beat her to it.

'You need to calm down,' Mori said finally, handing Remi a tissue. 'And talk to us.'

'Exactly. This is so not fair,' Avery added. 'You hid this very important detail from us. How could you?'

Remi blew her nose, took a sip of tea, and set the cup down on the bedside table before returning their gaze with a blank stare.

'Say something!' Avery exclaimed, causing a seagull that had landed on the balcony railing to squawk and flap away. It reminded her that they were supposed to be having a lovely reunion on Cape Cod. Instead, the three left were trying to solve their friend's untimely murder.

Remi visibly flinched before she sat up higher in the bed and said calmly, 'OK, fine. I suppose it's time I tell you what happened on the beach.'

'You think?' Avery replied.

Mori reached out a hand to attempt to calm Avery down, but it did little to soothe the electricity that was traveling through her body as she waited for Remi's explanation. Though, in her mind, no explanation would be enough.

'I haven't exactly been forthcoming,' Remi started.

Avery opened her mouth to spew out another accusation in response to this, but Mori physically placed her body between them to block her, seemingly to allow Remi to have the floor.

'I saw Calista on the beach,' Remi said quietly.

Avery threw her hands up in frustration before landing them firmly on her hips. 'I knew it!' She then looked to Mori who appeared visibly shaken to the core. 'I knew it!' she repeated. 'I felt it in my soul!'

'When?' Mori wanted to know.

'The night you guys were drunk and went to bed, and I was left to retrieve the clothes you left scattered all over the beach. Calista must've smelt the smoke from the campfire and came out to the beachside instead of knocking on the front door. I'm guessing she assumed we were all out there.'

Mori nodded slowly and said through what seemed like a calculated breath, 'OK.'

'You need to tell us everything from the very beginning,' Avery warned. 'And don't skip one little detail. Or I swear—'

'Or you swear what?' Remi cried. 'Stop threatening me!'

'Seriously? Remi! You haven't stopped lying since you've been here! You lied about Taz, you lied about the phone, you lied about the necklace! And now we learn that you saw Calista! I'm wondering at this point if Mori or I can believe a word that comes out of your mouth!' There. Avery said it, and it felt so good to finally unload what had been plaguing her ever since she had been interrogated at the police station.

'Really?' Remi charged.

'Yeah, really,' Avery volleyed.

'You think you're so perfect? Little miss Iowa farmgirl. Oh, so innocent. What about *your* lies?'

Avery felt her defenses kicking in and she wanted to jump across the bed and physically shake Remi, but she held back, instead straightening her spine, cementing her feet to the floor, and giving Remi a laser stare down. 'Excuse me? What are you talking about?'

'You're going blind, Avery! And your family has no idea. None whatsoever! What do you call that?'

'That's not the same thing,' Avery replied. 'It's not even in the same ballpark. You're only trying to downplay the damage you've caused here.'

'Oh. It isn't?'

'Remi, don't,' Mori warned.

'Oh, and you? *You* should talk,' Remi said flippantly. 'Little miss author girl. Mori, I believe you have a few lies up your sleeve as well! What about your feelings for Jerome instead of Adam – your *husband*? Where are we staying this week, huh? In your lover's house? And what about the truth of what you *really* want to write for a living – not that smut. You're not even living your truest self!'

'He's not my lover,' Mori stated evenly.

'OK. You only *wish* him to be.' Remi shrugged and then threw up her hands in disgust. 'You want us to believe that, so I guess it's OK for you to lie. We believe you, right, Avery?'

'It's not the same . . .' Mori trailed off. 'We're all damaged people, Remi, it's about leaving as little carnage behind as possible.'

'Look around you. Both of you. We're *all* liars here,' Remi said squarely, looping them in with her imaginary lasso. 'I'm probably the most transparent one out of all of us and yet I'm the one being crucified! Who do you think you are to cast stones?'

'OK, maybe that's true, Rem. We're all just a stinkin' bunch of liars. But our lies didn't end in someone getting murdered!' Avery challenged with a pointed finger.

'Well, neither did mine.'

Mori's sad gaze traveled between her and Remi, and then she said in a begging tone, 'Please. Let's stop this right now. This isn't helping.'

A moment of silence hung between the three of them, and the only thing to be heard was the rolling tide outside the open doorway leading to the balcony. It all seemed so peaceful.

Until it wasn't.

'I'll tell you what happened if you stop the accusations and just listen. If you can't do that, then I'm not sharing another thing,' Remi said, pulling the covers tightly over her legs protectively and then wrapping the blankets up under her chin.

'Before you tell us the details, I just have to know . . .' Mori started.

'What?'

'Did you kill her?'

Avery leaned in closer to be sure she would be able to hear.

'Yeah. Did *you* kill Calista?'

THIRTY-THREE

Remi couldn't believe her friends could accuse her of such a thing. Obviously, they really didn't know her at all. And clearly, they were never her friends in the first place, or they would've understood her loyalty. They would've *known* her. They would've *trusted* her. But that's why she never told them that she saw Calista on the beach in the first place. Because, deep down, she knew it would come to this. She knew they wouldn't believe her. And it would all fall in her lap.

'Answer the question,' Avery pressed. 'Is Calista gone because of something that happened that night, something you did. Look.' She squared her body to face the bed. 'Even if it was an accident—'

'I didn't kill her! When are you going to get that through your thick skull?' Remi interrupted, screaming in defense. 'But I highly doubt you'll believe me at this point, so why bother?' she added sarcastically with an eye-roll. 'Maybe you should just call the police and have them escort me back to the police station if you're that uncomfortable with me being here with you!' she added, flinging her wrists out from the covers dramatically as if Avery had the ability to handcuff her and take her away.

'Stop! We're trying to find the answers,' Mori said in an equally raised voice. 'We're trying to find your husband and someone – anyone – who is responsible for this! You need to be forthcoming, Rem! Calista is dead! And we have no idea why!'

'Yeah,' Avery chimed in. 'Because *someone* is responsible. And we're going to get to the bottom of it and find out who. If it's the last thing I see in my God-given life, it will be justice for Calista.'

'I didn't hurt her,' Remi stated calmly. 'In fact, I didn't even lay a hand on her, except for welcoming her with a hug, if you count that,' she added with another eye-roll. 'Is that acceptable to you two? That I shared a hug with my *old friend Cal*.'

'We believe you. Now, go on,' Avery said, her tone dropping a few notches. Calmer than she'd been since she'd first stepped inside the bedroom throwing out accusations like a slingshot.

But Remi didn't buy it. She didn't think Avery believed anything. Avery just wanted her to tell her what happened – it was so obviously plastered across her face. Which is why Remi decided to tell them *everything* that transpired that night, not caring what they may or may not judge. At this point, she had nothing to lose, except their friendship.

The two continued their unnerving stare in anticipation, as if they absolutely hated her.

Remi tucked her hair behind her ear and began, 'As I mentioned earlier, I needed to assist you two drunks to bed and then I headed back to the beach to clean up the mess left behind. Calista was standing by the campfire and ran toward me as soon as I stepped off the boardwalk. She asked about both of you, but I explained you were both intoxicated and already in bed for the night and she'd have to catch up with you two in the morning. She seemed happy about that. Maybe not happy,' Remi paused. 'More like relieved. Because she said she needed to speak to me alone. She had something important on her mind and she wanted to unload.'

'What would Calista need to speak to you alone about?' Mori asked, her tone growing gentle. 'After all these years?'

'You really want to know? Because it was so wildly inappropriate and so "all about her,"' Remi added, throwing up air quotes. 'Honestly, I'd forgotten that about Calista. How calculated she could be and how the world had to revolve around her wants, desires, and plans. Completely out of left field, she shows up after twenty years with a bombshell to blow up my world.'

'Now, isn't that the pot calling the kettle black,' Avery said under her breath.

It looked as if Mori was desperate to hold back a smile, but couldn't, as her expression seemed to crack under the pressure. Remi wanted to slap the two of them. So smug, so arrogant. Neither of them capable of seeing their own flaws and failings. So quick to point fingers. It was so easy for them to judge.

Instead, Remi continued, 'Calista didn't waste any time in telling me that she was in love with my husband and had been in love with him her entire life. She confessed she slept with him back in high school while we were dating. Even now, she was *still* wondering if she had a chance with him. So I put an end to it right then and there! I was tired of hearing all about her needs, wants, and desires!'

Avery covered her mouth with her hand and then exclaimed, 'Wow.'

'Darn right wow,' Remi replied through a whistle in her teeth. 'That's when I ripped the necklace off my neck, threw it at her, and yelled at her for stealing my heart. What is wrong with her? How could she do that to me? Now? After all these years. And me being pregnant!'

The way Mori was searching her face led Remi to believe that she knew something more, but she let it slide. Until she noticed that Mori and Avery shared a private look and another knowing smile. That changed everything. That's when Remi realized they'd always known that Gabe and Calista had been together and had shared a past. She was the only one in the dark.

Liars.

They were all liars!

'What?' Remi asked finally. She wanted them to come clean and say they were liars too. Even though she knew they would not. This was confirmed when Avery spoke again.

'Please continue,' Avery said with a roll of her hand. 'Don't let us stop you now.'

Remi wanted to halt this conversation right here and now. But she knew from the interrogation required by her so-called friends that she couldn't stop now. She cleared her throat and took another sip of tepid tea before continuing, 'Calista also told me that Kirk was divorcing her. And I wondered if this was why she wanted Gabe back in the first place, because Calista never could be alone. She always had to have a guy on her arm ever since we were in high school. I doubt she's ever spent a night by herself in her own house. She's very *needy* that way. I mean, she used to be,' Remi swallowed. 'Before she died.'

'And then what happened?' Mori asked.

'Then I told her to get the fuck off the beach, and I covered my hands over my ears and told her I didn't want to hear one more word. I needed time to cool off before she could return and face the music . . . in front of all of us. Otherwise, I would've strangled her.'

Avery took a few steps closer to the bed, leaned in, and asked, 'And did you?'

'No, you idiot! Stop trying to catch me in something I didn't do! Calista ran off the beach at that point. And I never saw her again! Until—'

Avery looked at her warily.

Remi covered herself with the sign of the cross and then exclaimed, 'I swear!'

'What about Gabe? Did Calista say if he was sharing the same feelings in wanting to reconnect with her?' Avery wanted to know. 'Or if they were having an affair?'

'Yeah,' Mori added. 'And did she say where Gabe was? Or why he didn't join her to dump this on you? Or why he was in Massachusetts in the first place?'

'No. She never mentioned that he was in Massachusetts. She just said that they collectively decided that she should be the one to talk to me. Woman to woman. I just figured she was the one to deliver the message because she was geographically here. I didn't get far enough into the conversation to determine if this affair was ongoing because, as I said, as per usual, it was all about *her* and *her* needs.'

'Gabe used to run away from everything,' Avery said under her breath. 'Even when he played baseball with my brother, and they lost a game, he would run off the field before congratulating the other team. The coach would get mad at him, and he'd always use the excuse that he needed to use the bathroom. He's a runner. Always has been. I bet he was too scared to man up and talk to you first, Rem.'

'Yikes,' Mori voiced with a grimace.

'I'm not in the mood to defend my husband to you two. Especially when it's all one-sided at this point,' Remi replied. 'That's not what this is about. It's about clearing my name and finding out who murdered our friend.'

'How do you feel about all of this? Hearing that from Calista must make you want to confront Gabe even more! No?' Mori asked. 'Maybe that's why he hasn't been responding to you. He wants to talk to you face to face. Because it seems their plan quite literally blew up in his face? And perhaps now he's worried about what you might think?'

'My take? I think this was all in Calista's head,' Remi replied, gesturing to suggest that Calista was crazy. 'Gabe and I are completely transparent with each other. We share everything. I mean, come on! We shared Taz, for Pete's sake! If my husband had been carrying on an affair all these years, I would've known. A woman knows these things!'

'Do you think your husband knows that *you're* carrying on an affair with Taz, then?' Avery asked with a raised brow.

Remi's face burned.

'Not helping, Avery,' Mori said firmly, and Avery cowered as if she realized she had taken it a little too far.

Remi was no longer conflicted about telling them that Gabe had stopped at the hospital to see her. Because she knew if she did, she would lose her footing with them. They'd never believe her. Or him for that matter. Therefore, she held her tongue and kept that one safely inside the vault.

'Was she wearing the same outfit?' Mori wanted to know. 'It could help with the timeline.'

Remi nodded. 'Yes, when I saw her, she was wearing that same sundress. The one we found her in.'

'And Gabe?' Avery asked.

'I told you! She never mentioned that Gabe was in Massachusetts. I had no idea at that point. None whatsoever. Otherwise, do you think I would've let her go?' Remi then put her hands over her face and began to sob.

THIRTY-FOUR

'What we need is irrefutable proof that you didn't do this,' Mori said as she paced across the bedroom floor, searching for answers on how to solve Calista's murder. Uncanny how she was suddenly thrust into writing the suspense novel that she'd always dreamed of. She had to refrain from fleeing from them and running to her keyboard. She could see it now: *#1 Bestselling Author Mori Hart*. Photos of her book cover plastered on billboards in Times Square and across the country. Options for movie rights—

Mori's thoughts were interrupted when Avery said, 'She's right, you know. Or you're going to jail for a very long time. You must see how this is all going to come back to haunt you!'

Remi's face tightened. 'I can't believe it's come to this.'

Avery moved toward the balcony and beckoned them to follow her outdoors.

As soon as the three stepped outside, they felt the hot sun beat down on them. Mori tented her eyes, then fanned herself with one hand and asked, 'What are we doing out here, Avery? It's friggin' hot.'

'Looking at the crime scene,' Avery replied as she scanned the backyard seemingly in search of a big break in the case.

Mori wondered if Avery was almost getting some kind of charge out of this. Meaning. Purpose. *Something*. But all Mori was getting was clenched muscle spasms in her shoulders due to the stress of it all. And darn good research. Jerome had been right about that.

Remi turned away from the scene and crossed her arms protectively across her chest as if she couldn't bear to look anymore.

'Where were you standing, Remi, when you and Calista had the altercation? Before she ran off,' Avery asked in her official 'detective' voice.

Remi pointed to an area close to the boardwalk, tucked within the dunes.

Avery then turned to Mori and asked, 'Is that where you found the necklace?'

'Yeah,' Mori nodded. 'Over there by that rock.'

'What are you doing, Avery? It feels like you're still trying to trip me up. Playing detective again? I told you I didn't murder Calista! I don't understand the need to stand out here and do this!' Remi grunted. 'It's not helpful.'

'I'm trying to gauge the scene,' Avery said with a hint of frustration in her tone. 'And help your case, because if the police discover that you saw Calista . . . I'm guessing you didn't share that little tidbit with the detective when you were being questioned?' she added with a raised brow.

'No,' Remi replied flatly. 'No, I did not.'

'Actually, it's a good idea to figure this all out,' Mori chimed in. 'Which way did Calista go after you guys argued? Did she run further down the beach? In that direction?' She pointed beyond the dunes where a neighboring property was hidden, beyond a tall fence and seagrass.

'Yeah. Or did you happen to hear a car pull away, like she drove off?' Avery asked. 'Anything?'

Remi frowned. 'It was dark. I don't know which way she went because I was crying and then I was trying to reach Gabe to see if what she told me was true. And then I phoned Taz to talk me off the wall.' She shrugged and then shook her head. 'I dunno. It was a rough night.'

Mori breathed deeply. 'Look, Remi, you need to give us something to help you here. The police are building a case against you. It's only a matter of time—'

Remi's eyes widened. 'A matter of time until what?'

'A matter of time before they arrest you. Don't be so naïve, girl!' Avery exclaimed.

'She's right. If you're innocent, as you claim, we need to find a way to exonerate you,' Mori said matter-of-factly.

Maybe too matter-of-factly because Remi pleaded, 'They can't do that! They can't arrest an innocent person for a crime they didn't commit! That's ridiculous!'

'It happens all the time, Remi! Get your head out of your ass and help us find your husband!' Mori exclaimed. 'Otherwise, you might go away for a very long time for the murder of Calista Moore.'

'No!' Remi cried, causing her teeth to whistle again.

'Then help us. How are we going to find Gabe?' Avery asked.

'I think that's our best move to get more answers, don't you two? It's our only move, really.'

'I think I might have an idea. I just thought about it before you guys came upstairs,' Remi said between sniffles.

Mori prompted Remi with a shoulder bump to spill it. 'What's that?'

'I don't know why I didn't think of it before, but Gabe and I are on Snap Map.'

'What's Snap Map?' Avery wanted to know.

'No shit,' Mori murmured.

'What is it?' Avery pressed.

'It means that Remi can find out exactly where Gabe is at this very moment!' Mori said with a grin.

THIRTY-FIVE

Despite the fact that it was eating away at her, Remi didn't dare tell them that she only learned how to locate Gabe when she was in the hospital. She instead decided to play dumb about the whole thing in the hope they'd buy it. If they knew that Gabe had come to see her, and that she was hiding that information too, they'd have her locked up for sure. And she'd do anything to prevent that from happening. She clicked on to Snapchat as the others watched over her shoulder. When she opened the map portion of the app, an address on the Cape popped up after she followed the Gabe avatar icon to his location.

'Oh, no way! How cool is that!' Avery exclaimed. 'Is that showing where Gabe is in real time? I know that street!'

The address was Beechwood Lane in Sandwich. *What is he doing there?* Remi wondered. She didn't know anyone who owned a cottage in Sandwich. So how would Gabe? Were there more secrets in their relationship of which she was unaware?

'Hand me the phone,' Avery said eagerly, taking it from her grasp.

Remi had no choice but to give in.

Mori looked on and asked, 'Why would Gabe be in Sandwich and not call or text? That doesn't make any sense to me.'

'I don't know why he's not responding to my calls and texts. Maybe the battery is low because he left his charger back in Florida. Or, like you said, he wants to see me when facing the music. Who the hell knows!' Remi said with a grunt. No way would she share with them that her husband had mentioned that he was protecting her and that's why he wasn't communicating. That he didn't want any connection leading the police to believe (if they subpoena phone records) that she might be involved somehow. Mori and Avery would halt the search right then and there if they knew!

'The name of that street is familiar to me. I think that's where the Blackwells own a summer place,' Avery said, her eyes not leaving the phone. 'My brother used to go there sometimes in the summer for softball parties, and Gabe probably did too. Yeah, I remember it clearly now: Jay Blackwell's parents have a weekend getaway cottage. It's small, but perhaps Gabe is couch-diving there!'

'You sound like Brody,' Mori chuckled.

Finally, Avery looked up from the phone and joined in with a smile.

It was the first hint of happiness Remi heard between them since they entered her bedroom. She needed to tread lightly if she wanted them to stay on board with finding her husband. 'Well, what do we do?' she asked innocently.

'We get dressed and go over there! Will that map follow him wherever he goes?' Avery wanted to know.

'I'm not sure, I've never really used it,' Remi replied. 'But I think so.'

Mori tapped Remi on the backside. 'Hurry up! You're the only one not dressed! We have a mission to accomplish! Toot sweet!'

'Fine! Don't worry, I'm going!' Remi pulled the nightshirt off her head en route to the bathroom and secured a bra before donning a clean t-shirt. She then carefully slipped into a pair of workout shorts, still feeling a hint of soreness from the miscarriage. She couldn't care less at this point if the others looked on. It wasn't the first time they'd seen her naked. And besides, she was proud of her body and secretly relieved her baby bump would never actually develop and change her figure. She'd inwardly decided that getting pregnant with Taz's baby had been a huge error in judgment. A mistake that she wouldn't make again. She wondered if a part of her instinctively understood this and that's why her body miscarried in the first place. She couldn't help but catch the shame washing across her face as she brushed her teeth and looked in the mirror. But she needed to cast all this aside and move on with fixing the mess she was currently in. 'Do you think the police will follow us?' she asked, abandoning the bathroom.

Mori and Avery shared a look of concern and then both blurted, 'Why?'

'Wouldn't you *want* the police to find Gabe?' Avery continued. 'Unless you have a reason to suspect that might be problematic?' She studied her a little too intently then.

Remi wondered if either of them believed that she hadn't had phone contact with her husband. To her, no matter which way she turned, all the guilt pointed in her direction, and she didn't like that feeling. Not one little bit.

THIRTY-SIX

A crack of thunder shook the SUV, and Mori struggled to maneuver the vehicle on the road, despite the wipers running at full speed. Remi was seated beside her in the passenger seat and visibly jumped when a bolt of lightning hit a nearby tree and bark shot off just a few feet from them. The storm was only adding to Mori's stress level. When they found Gabe, would it fix things? Or would it only add more questions?

Remi gripped a hand to her heart and cried out, 'That strike was wicked close!' She then reached for a sweatshirt by her feet and attempted to wipe the fogged-up passenger window with the sleeve. After which, she rested her sneakers on the dashboard and grunted, 'We certainly didn't dress for this! I think we need rubber boots and a raincoat!'

'Sorry. Not turning around for a change of clothes. We're just going to have to fight through it,' Mori replied, gripping the steering wheel tightly. 'But that humidity sure hit its peak,' she added, leaning toward the windshield in search of funnel clouds. It wasn't exactly common for Cape Cod to be hit with a tornado, but it wasn't out of the realm of possibility either. The sky exhibited an eerie shade of pea-green, leading her to believe that anything could happen. She guessed she would have to let the story unfold where Gabe was concerned too and take one moment at a time.

'Hopefully, the storm will pass quickly, and we'll cool off a bit,' Avery joined in from the backseat.

'You don't know the half of it,' Remi snorted, shifting in her seat. 'Try living in Florida in the summertime. It can get downright brutal.'

'I bet,' Mori replied with a nod.

'OK, Moriah, turn right up here,' Avery directed from the backseat. She was handling the route via the Waze app, and Mori hoped her friend wouldn't lose cell service before their arrival in Sandwich. In her view, how the cell towers could even work under these stormy conditions was nothing less than miraculous.

'Slow down; it's up here on your right. I think it's the one with the dark blue shutters,' Avery continued, unclicking her seatbelt and squeezing her body between the two front seats. She nudged Mori on the arm to pull over.

The cedar siding cottage with blue shutters was obviously weathered from the sea. And it was *tiny*, but not unlike a typical summer home found on the Cape. From Mori's perspective, the home was smaller than her garage on the Vineyard. It was tucked into the shade of a few maple trees along with towering pines behind it, and a gravel driveway wound along the side.

'Did anyone follow us here?' Remi asked in a hesitant tone. Her gaze then darted in all directions as if afraid the police had tailed them.

'Is there something more you want to tell us, Remi?' Avery prompted. 'I would think if the police found Gabe, it would be in his best interest, but you're making me think otherwise. Is there something more you're still not sharing? Because—'

'No! I'm merely suggesting that Calista could've gotten herself involved with some unsavory characters and we could be in danger! I mean, what if she started smoking pot again? It certainly wouldn't be out of character. Heck, we all did it in high school. Maybe weed wasn't enough for her and she explored other drugs? Huh? Did you ever think of that? You keep acting like Calista's delusions were shared by my husband. Or that this is all his fault! Or mine!' Remi growled. 'When this has nothing to do with either of us. You don't even know Calista anymore or what she was involved in! She's a teacher, right? Maybe she was inappropriately involved with one of her students. Don't you recall how she used to love being the center of attention?'

'Now that's just absurd!' Avery cried. 'Stop coming up with baseless allegations. Calista isn't here to defend herself. She's gone and you're spitting on her grave!'

'Can't you two just get along?' Mori interjected, unclicking her seatbelt. She was tired of hearing the bantering going on between the two of them as it did nothing to fix the situation. 'We are three imperfect . . . let me repeat that . . . *imperfect* grown women who will continue to support each other. Can we please act like it? Quit the nitpicking, and let's help each other get to the bottom of this, shall we?'

She turned and glared at Avery then, willing her to stop. If Gabe *did* have something to do with Calista's murder, forcing him into further hiding was not exactly the answer to their problem. The sooner they found him, the better.

'I wish the rain would slow before we get out of the car. Can't we wait a little bit?' Remi asked.

Mori wondered then if Avery was on to something and Remi just wanted to be sure that they hadn't been followed before getting out of the car, on the off chance her husband was a sitting duck at this residence. 'How about I go? And you two hang tight and wait here?' she suggested.

'Nope. I vote we all go,' Avery said, not waiting for a reply and opening the door before either could protest further. The roar of heavy rain grew louder before Avery closed the door behind her.

'Let's make a run for it!' Mori said. She followed Avery's lead and flung her arms overhead in a pathetic attempt to not get wet, all the way to the front door of the cottage. Rain showered heavily above just as Mori reached to ring the doorbell.

By the time Remi had joined their side, Mori's t-shirt, its slogan reading *Write On Girlfriend*, was already soaked through. She plucked it away from her body, but it returned to stick to her like an unwanted hug.

After a few moments of heavy rain, no one came to answer the door. 'Now what?' Avery asked.

'Check your phone, Rem, and see if Gabe moved somewhere else on your Snap Map,' Mori suggested, flinging the drops of rain from her arms.

Remi pulled out her phone as directed and frowned. 'It's still showing that he's here,' she shrugged, and then held up the screen for the others to view it. A crack of thunder caused her to jump, and she fumbled her phone, very nearly dropping it into a puddle before she could tuck it safely back inside her pocket.

Avery pounded on the door with both fists. 'Maybe the power went out and the doorbell isn't working?' she said over a whoosh of heavy rain shooting from the rain gutters.

Mori beckoned her friends to follow. 'Let's return to the car and regroup before we get struck by lightning! That last one was too close for comfort.' She led them by navigating around a large puddle in the driveway before reaching the safety of her SUV. The chill from the air conditioning caused her arms to erupt in fresh goosebumps, and she rubbed them vigorously in a failed attempt to warm up. She then wiped the wet strands of hair off her face and waited.

As soon as Remi was tucked safely back in the vehicle, she said, 'If my husband is in there, I need to wait! What if he's injured and can't get to the door? Something's wrong!' she wailed. 'Why isn't he answering? Snap Map doesn't lie!'

'I have a thought,' Mori replied, returning her gaze toward the front door of the Blackwells' cottage, wishing it would open and Gabe would be on the other side to welcome them.

'Do you have a better idea?' Avery wanted to know.

'Most people who own a second home at the Cape keep a key hidden on the property in case they need it. There must be a key somewhere around here.'

'That's right,' said Avery. 'In case they forget and leave their key at home, or a friend wants to use the place or something like that. Good thinking.'

'Where would you keep a key, then?' Remi asked. 'Better question is, how do you plan on finding a needle in a haystack in the middle of a thunderstorm?' she added dryly.

'I'm calling Billy,' Avery replied, scrolling her phone.

Mori hoped for all their sakes that Avery could get hold of her brother, and he would have a reliable memory and would be able to provide insight. It didn't take long before Avery was grinning ear to ear and said excitedly. 'He said they used to keep a spare key inside the shed!'

'Wow!' Remi exclaimed. 'No offense, but I didn't think your brother would be any help at all.'

'Uh, yeah,' Avery scoffed. 'I knew he would. He has a memory of an elephant.'

'I'll go look for it,' said Mori. 'You two stay here and see if anyone comes to the front door. It'll be much easier for me to explain why I'm digging into the Blackwells' shed if we get caught. I'll chalk it up to research and hopefully ask forgiveness over permission!'

Leaving her friends alone in the car for a few more minutes would give Mori a breather from the constant strife lobbing between them. She spent so many hours alone working in her writing cave that she wasn't accustomed to the constant drama and noise.

'I doubt you'll get caught,' Avery pointed out. 'There're no cars parked in the driveway, and they don't have a garage that goes with the cottage, so it looks like we should be in the clear. Remi and I will wait here as a lookout, as you suggested.'

'How did Gabe get here?' Remi asked softly. So softly that Mori almost didn't catch her words.

'That's something we all want to find out, isn't it!' Avery replied.

Mori opened the door, letting the storm hit inside the vehicle full-on once again. Before ducking outside, she said, 'Just cross your fingers they don't have nosy neighbors.' She chuckled. 'If it looks like I'm going to get caught, honk the horn and I'll make a beeline outta there!'

Remi gave Mori a thumbs-up. 'You got it!'

Mori scrambled around the side of the Blackwells' cottage in search of the elusive tool shed. Overgrown shrubs sided the house, blocking her view. Heavy raindrops blocked her vision too, and she wiped them away with the back of her arm before her eyes landed on a rickety metal garden shed located along the tree line in the backyard.

Great, she thought. *Just the place I want to be when the next wave of lightning strikes – in a metal object!*

Mori gritted her teeth before darting closer, but then noticed the shed was locked with a padlock. She wanted to scream out an expletive from the depths of her soul. She ran back to the safety of the SUV, splashing muddy water around her ankles along the way.

'Any luck?' Remi asked as soon as Mori closed the door behind her.

'It has a padlock on it,' Mori sighed, wiping her brow, flinging the wet droplets from her forehead, and then shaking out her hair with her hands. 'I don't see how we're going to get in. This is becoming impossible.'

'My guess is they have another key hidden somewhere around this yard. It's pretty common to do that,' Remi said. 'Maybe a flowerpot or something, but I didn't see one on the porch.'

'Yeah, but good luck finding it. You got a set of bolt cutters in the trunk?' Avery asked Mori, squeezing between the seats and meeting her eyes.

'Yeah, Avery. I'm a writer who drives around with a set of bolt cutters in my trunk. You know – for research,' Mori replied incredulously. 'You're more likely to find a pen and notebook back there than a fuckin' tool!'

'Don't you have anything in the trunk in case you get a flat tire or something?' Avery pressed.

'Do I look like the type of person who would change a tire? It's called AAA, my friend! You should invest in it!'

'There's gotta be something back there I can use? It wouldn't be the first time I've had to break a padlock.'

'Excuse me?' Remi asked, finally joining the conversation as she sat shivering and nuzzled up to the front seat as if desperate for warmth.

'What?' Avery frowned and then sank into the backseat. 'Hey, I work on a farm. I can't tell you how many times Jack or the kids locked one of our barns and then lost the key and I had to pry it open. You do what you gotta do.'

'I suppose,' Remi continued with an eye-roll. 'The more we hang out together, the more I realize how drastically differently we live our lives.'

Mori searched for Avery in the rearview mirror until she caught her gaze. 'Looks like we need to go to a hardware store. Any chance you can find the closest one on Google Maps?'

Her answer came in a loud clap of thunder.

THIRTY-SEVEN

By the time they had returned to the cottage with a brand-new set of bolt cutters, which dangled a shiny price tag, the storm had eased some. Avery couldn't help but wonder how she could finagle bringing this tool home on the plane with her, because she could certainly find use for it back in Iowa.

It was still raining, but the electricity in the sky seemed to have waned. Avery looked out the passenger window. 'At least I won't get struck by lightning when I go and do this,' she chuckled.

'Are you sure you want to add breaking and entering to the list of offenses they are collecting on us down at the police department?' Remi asked hesitantly. 'Especially if, as you say, they're already building a case against me?'

'Not exactly!' Mori grunted. 'The idea of sitting in a jail cell doesn't really thrill me, but what choice do we have? We need to find answers.'

'What if we get caught by one of the neighbors?' Remi pleaded. 'I'm starting to think maybe this isn't such a great idea after all.'

'Yeah, three middle-aged women breaking into a cottage. A neighbor would just assume we're stupid renters who forgot the key and move on with their day,' Avery replied.

'Why don't you go knock on the door again and see if Gabe will answer this time. If not, Avery and I will go and break out the key,' Mori suggested.

'OK, I'll try knocking again.' Remi didn't wait for the others to follow and left them alone in the car.

'I don't know how to gauge her reactions,' Avery admitted. 'Does she want to find her husband or not? I feel like she's still hiding something! Don't you?'

'I hear you. The only way we're going to get to the bottom of this, though, is to get Gabe out in the open. If he happened to have played some part in Calista's murder, we can't force him further into hiding.'

'Good point. Hopefully, he left a clue behind inside the Blackwells' cottage.'

Avery then regarded Remi who was still standing at the door waiting for it to open. She turned away from the cottage, shook her head, and shrugged. 'Look, Remi's not getting anywhere. It's go time!'

The two abandoned the vehicle once again, and Mori directed Avery toward the shed with shiny new bolt cutters in hand. Avery quickened her pace. It took a few attempts before she was finally able to pop the lock. 'Yes!' she squealed and then shared a fist bump with Mori as if they were fifteen again and breaking into someone's locker. But this was so much bigger than that. And the stakes even higher.

Mori acknowledged with a smile, 'Nice job.'

They stepped inside the metal shed, thick with cracks, and rust along the edges.

'I for one have had my tetanus shot. The kind of work I do . . . it's a no-brainer. I'm guessing you're not up to date?' Avery lifted a brow in Mori's direction who replied with a shake of her head.

'I'm not exactly sure if I'm up to date with my immunizations or not,' Mori teased. 'But looking at this shed, I'm guessing I ought to be,' she added dryly.

Avery handed Mori the set of bolt cutters. 'Here. You just hold on to these; I'll go look for the key.'

'Fine by me,' Mori said, taking the tool from her and grimacing at the sight of a spiderweb overhead.

Avery stepped deeper into the shed and navigated around a snow-blower, a push mower, and an old garbage can that looked as if it'd seen better days. Her eyes peered into the dark corners of the space, and for a second, she had to recalibrate her brain to see. The thought of going blind suddenly overwhelmed her, sending a fresh jolt of fear down her spine. She blinked several moments and willed the shiny key to make an appearance, to no avail. Her eyes explored the walls, the ceiling, *everywhere*, and she was beginning to grow frustrated.

'Hey!' Mori said excitedly, grabbing her attention. 'Look what I just found.'

Avery turned and saw Mori grinning ear to ear, dangling a key in front of her like a pendulum.

'Where?'

'Right here behind the door, on a shelf.' Mori smiled and then blew the dust from her fingers.

'Excellent! Let's hurry!' Avery swooped the key from Mori's hand and ran in front of her, taking the lead to the front door. She was breathless with excitement when she reached Remi's side.

'You got it?' Remi's eyes widened and then she clapped her hands and rocked on the balls of her feet as if she was on the precipice of breaking out in a cheer.

Avery slipped the key into the lock and held the door for Remi to take the lead.

'Gabe? Honey? You in here?' Remi called hesitantly before they huddled together and followed her inside.

There was nothing but silence for a reply.

The three momentarily remained close to the entryway, wondering if they were going to get caught. When no one responded, they took a step deeper into the room, and Avery closed the door behind them.

The blinds were shut tight inside the small cottage, making the room feel dark and damp as if the humidity trapped inside was desperate to escape. To Avery, the stuffiness of the space led her to believe that the windows hadn't been opened in a very long time. She wasn't sure how long anyone could survive in this uncomfortable temperature as she herself was already growing hot. She fanned her shirt away from her.

It was obvious no one was joining them inside. The doors to all the rooms were ajar, and the space, less than a thousand square feet, led Avery to conclude that they were alone.

The pine paneling in the main living room beyond looked as if it could use a fresh coat of white paint to bring it up to date and current with Cape Cod decor. They stepped further into the room, following each other like a train of cars through the narrow entryway until they reached the living room.

Remi squealed, causing Avery to jump.

'Gabe has been here! There's his phone!' Remi pointed to a dark oak table on the side of a sheet-covered sofa where an iPhone lay face down.

'How do you know for sure?' Mori asked. 'It's a black case, which to me means it could belong to anyone!'

'Because,' Remi replied, shaking her own phone in front of their faces, 'it's still showing he's in here on Snap. That's why we're getting a signal! And that's why he's not responding to me!'

Avery and Mori moved closer to the table to retrieve Gabe's

iPhone while Remi moved from room to room, calling out her husband's name at every turn.

A small, folded sheet of paper was tucked beneath the phone, and Avery moved to retrieve the note. Her eyes darted across the page, reading the chicken scratch ferociously, and her hands began to tremble. She then let out a guttural screech and dropped to her knees, causing Remi to rush back into the living room, while Mori stood like a deer in the headlights.

'What?' Remi cried.

Avery looked up then and gave her friend the most encouraging expression she could muster.

'It's a suicide note – from Gabe.'

THIRTY-EIGHT

'No. No! NO!' The sound of Remi's voice echoed in her own ears like a fresh bolt of thunder as she fought to remain composed. The news of this horror sent her reeling into a whole new wave of utter shock. Mori had to hold Remi up by the arm to keep her from joining Avery on the dusty hardwood floor. Mori then led her by the elbow to sink into a nearby chair and Avery rose to follow.

'Here.' Avery's hand visibly trembled when she handed Remi the unfolded torn sheet of paper. A sad look in her eyes, which swiftly flickered to deep sympathy, crossed her face too when she added, 'You need to read it for yourself.'

Remi's eyes were hesitant and cautious. Afraid to read the words that would change her life forever. She wanted to run from the room and scream. She wanted to shield herself from further pain! But she forged on. She regarded her friends one more time before she forced herself to look. The note was composed of a half-sheet of paper, which had been torn from a notebook. It was handwritten in blue ink which read:

> Remi,
> I'm deeply sorry that I cheated on you with your best friend. I don't deserve you. Nor do I deserve to share the seed I planted inside of you. I hope our baby takes after you and not the likes of me. It's better now that I go and be with Calista on the other side. I hope you find peace in your heart to carry on and a husband who is worthy of fatherhood.
> I wish I could've loved you the way you deserved,
> Gabe

The cottage was silent, save for the rain beating heavily on the rooftop. Neither Mori nor Avery seemed to have any words left for her.

Remi re-read the note to herself three times before returning her gaze to her friends. Her mouth turned sour.

'You OK?' Mori asked hesitantly, putting a gentle hand on her shoulder.

'No,' Remi croaked. 'I—'

'Where do you think he went?' Avery asked, her eyes darting around the room as if she wished him to appear in front of them and confirm this all was a big mistake. 'Did you check all the rooms?'

'Yeah, he's not here,' Remi managed to get out.

'Then where is he?' Mori wanted to know.

Remi shook her head and fat tears began to form. 'I don't *know*.' She pressed her mouth to hold back a sob. 'I can't believe he left this.'

'Can I see it?' Mori asked gently.

Remi handed her the note.

After a few moments, Mori's brow rose and she met Remi's eyes when she asked, 'Are you sure this is from Gabe?'

'How could you even ask a thing like that?' Avery replied incredulously.

'The choice of words, here.' Mori tapped the paper thoughtfully. 'Something doesn't fit.'

'What do you mean?' Remi sniffed and looked over Mori's shoulder to re-read the passage she was pointing to.

'He says here, "the seed *I planted* inside of you,"' Mori replied. 'But we all know—'

Avery's face turned ashen, and she interrupted excitedly, 'But Gabe didn't plant the seed; Taz did!'

Remi ripped the note from Mori's hand and read it again. 'Now that you mention it . . . At second glance, I'm not sure this is even my husband's handwriting!'

'Seriously?' Avery asked, searching her excitedly.

Remi leapt from the chair and waved the note in their face. 'Yeah, and the other problem is that this is written in the present tense! He says I'm pregnant in this note! But he *knows* I lost the baby, so why would he write this?' she added eagerly.

'How would he know you lost the baby. That doesn't make sense,' Avery asked with a frown.

'Because I saw him at the hospital!' Remi exclaimed.

Avery and Mori responded with dropped jaws and reproachful eyes once again.

THIRTY-NINE

A moment of silence hovered over the group of three. Mori wanted to take Remi and shake her for not telling them about Gabe's visit to the hospital, but she refrained. Pushing Remi's husband further into hiding was only going to create more havoc. As it was, this investigation seemed to go on a continuous loop, and she was running at her last straw.

She had a book deadline looming, and the longer this took, the longer she could feel her career slipping away from her. She needed to return to the Vineyard and get her words in! Avery had remained mute about the matter too. Mori wondered if their little pep talk in the car had helped, and she realized being flippant was getting them nowhere.

'If we determined that your husband didn't write the note, then what's our next move? Because he could be in danger. Grave danger!' Mori asked finally as she paced in front of her friends who were now sitting side by side on the sheet-covered sofa. She stopped pacing when the sound of an iPhone ringing startled the three of them.

'It's mine!' Remi reached into her pocket and her eyes glanced at the screen. 'Oh *no*! Not *now*!' she said, slamming a fist to her thigh. 'It's the detective calling me! What should I do?'

'Answer it!' Mori and Avery screamed in unison.

'Yeah,' Mori continued with a grimace, 'he might have news.'

Remi clicked the phone on to speaker so her friends could help walk her through the conversation.

'Hello,' Remi said hesitantly. Her eyes darted from Mori to Avery.

'Ms Toussaint?'

'Yes, this is she.'

'This is Detective Reed. I'm standing in front of your summer rental. Can one of you let me in?'

'Oh,' Remi said with a hint of surprise, clearing her throat. 'We're not at the cottage; we're out on an errand.' She winced then and shared a look of shame with her friends.

'An errand?'

'Yes, we're just on our way back now.'

'All right, I'll wait for you here then. I need to speak with you, and I'd rather not do it over the phone.'

'We'll be there just as soon as we can,' Remi replied and then she heard the detective click off.

'Good job,' Avery said. 'I don't think he's aware we are in the process of breaking and entering. Otherwise, he would have shown up at this door and we'd be in a cow heap of trouble. No?'

Beads of sweat lined Remi's forehead. 'What if he's there? What if whoever is responsible found Gabe – and killed him? Because if he didn't write this note, someone did. And that person is attempting to cover up a double homicide.'

'Let's go. You deserve to find the answers. We *all* do,' Mori replied. She just held back that there was an itch in the back of her neck that made her feel as though Remi and Gabe might not be completely innocent. Because it seemed to her as if Remi's lies flowed like the ever-changing tide.

FORTY-ONE

Despite the evidence the three friends had produced and his obvious disappointment that Remi hadn't been completely forthcoming with the police department, the detective still didn't seem to waiver on his analysis that Gabe had attempted to end his own life. In Reed's humble opinion, he and Calista were having an affair. To hide the truth from Remi, Gabe had killed her before she could join their reunion, and then, unable to handle the guilt of what he'd done, he attempted suicide.

Mori felt bad for Remi. Learning that the detective was pretty much shutting down the case was a harsh new reality. She understood why Remi had held back the important detail that the baby was not biologically Gabe's, leading to inconsistencies in the suicide note. She knew Remi feared it would only muddy the investigation and add confusion to the detective's mind. And if Remi had brought it up, he might have found a way to include Taz in the mix. Instead, with Mori's promptings, Remi had focused on the handwriting and the fact that the note wasn't *worded* the way she expected her husband would write.

Detective Reed had stood firm in his decision. The discovery of a suicide note seemed to have the opposite effect and most likely sealed the deal for him. The detective had left them then, in a state of confusion as to which way to turn next. Mori had to physically cement her feet to the ground to stop herself from running down the driveway after him with arms flailing to share the rest of the story, regarding Taz. But she was stuck between trying to remain loyal to Remi and the nagging feelings of doubt that still plagued her.

The three were now standing in Remi's bedroom, watching as she packed an overnight bag. The rain had finally subsided, and a cool breeze entered the room from the open balcony, briefly catching Mori's attention. Night was upon them, and Mori couldn't understand when it had become dark outside; the day had been such a long, awful haze. But the darkness seeped into her consciousness too, as she wondered who was right and who was wrong. And if all the pieces added up as easily as the detective understood regarding Calista's murder.

'Do you need us to spend the night with you at the hospital?' Mori asked, interrupting their silence as she watched Remi zip the bag shut. Part of her wanted a break from all of this and hoped Remi would decline the offer. She needed time alone to process. It was rare for her to spend this much time with people. She missed being alone, shut away in her writing cave for days, poking away at the keyboard. And she longed for that escape from reality almost as much as she longed for Jerome. Maybe she would phone Jerome before bedtime so his voice could soothe her like a lullaby and whisk her off to sleep.

A sense of honest relief came when Remi replied wearily, 'No, it's OK. It doesn't sound like Gabe will be allowed to have visitors, so I'll just go. You guys stay here and get some much-needed rest. We'll regroup tomorrow.'

'Let me at least drop you off at the hospital,' Mori encouraged, pulling Remi in for a hug.

'Now, that I'll take,' Remi replied with a thin smile. 'I was really hoping you'd offer, and I wouldn't have to call an Uber.'

Mori scoffed, 'Don't be ridiculous! Of course I'll take you.'

'Don't forget, *you* need rest too; you really need to take care of yourself,' Avery said, meeting on the other side of Remi as the three huddled closer together. 'After all you have been through, I don't even know how you are still standing!'

Remi shared a weak smile. 'Maybe I can rent a cot over there. Or they'll put me in a room and bring me back to health with an IV,' she added with a snort. 'I am officially hitting the wall.'

'How do you feel about Detective Reed at this point?' Mori asked, pulling away from them. She didn't dare ask Remi if she thought her husband would be capable of any or all of this. She couldn't go there – at least not yet.

'I think he's an ass,' Remi replied dryly, lifting her overnight bag off the bed and lugging the thick strap over her shoulder. 'It seems to me he just wants to wrap this up and blame it all on Gabe.'

Mori didn't know what to think at this point. She was so tired herself that her brain couldn't compute any longer. 'You ready to go, then?'

'Yeah, thanks,' Remi said, closing the balcony door before leading them out of the bedroom.

When Mori returned to the cottage, she found Avery in the kitchen polishing off a slice of coffee cake. 'Did you leave any for me?' she asked hopefully. Cake sounded like the perfect ending to a horrible day.

'Yep, I'll cut you a slice.'

'Thanks,' Mori said wearily, sinking on to a nearby stool.

'Everything OK with Remi? Did you guys talk about anything on your way to the hospital?' Avery prodded, handing her a plate with a fork sticking out of a hefty slice of cake.

Mori sighed. She was so very weary. And she wasn't sure she was up for more co-conspiring with Avery and her theories. What she needed was to rest first and clear her mind. 'No. She was pretty quiet on the drive over,' she said finally, hoping that would appease Avery.

But it didn't because Avery continued with her musings. 'If Calista told Remi that she was in love with Gabe, and she wanted him back after all these years, it just seems weird it would be so one-sided. From my memory of her, Calista wasn't so off-tilt that she'd pine away for something that may never come to fruition. Like a relationship with Gabe. The feelings must've been mutual. Don't you think?'

'Avery, I'm sorry. I just can't anymore. Can we talk about this in the morning?' Mori then shoved a very large piece of cake into her mouth to prevent herself from sharing another word and taking the conversation any further.

'Sure,' Avery chuckled. 'I'm going to head upstairs then.' She then turned away from her.

Mori swallowed the lump of cake and then choked out, 'Get some rest.'

'Yeah, you too.'

Avery started to walk away and then turned back to face her. 'Oh, and one more thing.'

Mori didn't think she could handle one more thing, but she looked toward Avery expectantly, giving her friend all the energy she could muster.

'There's lasagna in the refrigerator, along with a few other creations Brody had packed up for us. And might I say, it hit the spot! Have a bite before bed.'

'Now that's the best news I think you shared all day,' Mori said, her mood lifting.

'G'night, Moriah.'

'Night,' Mori said wearily, raising herself from the stool and heading to the refrigerator. Her mouth watered at the mere thought of something cooked by their sweet, hot chef.

FORTY-TWO

Bright sunlight flooded the kitchen from every angle when Avery entered in search of her morning brew. She had already taken a shower, phoned Iowa, and been brought up to date on everything she had missed back home on the farm. Iowa felt like miles and years away from her now. So much had happened since her arrival in Boston that it was good to catch up with her kids and Jack too. She was really starting to miss them.

Her new favorite sound of visiting the Cape, though, had become the hiss that came along with an instant cup of coffee, and she reached for her morning gift reverently. She decided to step outside and sit on the patio and take in some pure vitamin D from the sun, and was surprised to find Mori was already seated there. She had just assumed her friend was still in bed.

'Mornin',' Mori greeted, tipping the flute of her orange juice. The juice which Avery assumed was splashed heavily with champagne as her friend's eyes held a glaze.

Avery took a seat beside her, beneath the umbrella. 'How'd you sleep?'

'All right, I guess. You?'

'Same.' Avery cradled the warm mug in her hands. Despite the growing sunshine and the heat that abounded, it was still comforting to hold. 'You hear from Remi this morning?'

'Yeah, she just texted. Gabe made it through surgery and, as Detective Reed suggested, he's in ICU. She said Gabe hasn't spoken to her yet. Or woken up, for that matter. She said she might come back this afternoon and sleep for a while and then return to the hospital tonight. She's not sure if his family is going to fly in from Georgia yet. Things are certainly up in the air for her.'

'Ah, I can't imagine how physically and emotionally exhausted she must be at this point. It's not even happening to me, and I feel like I've been hit by a Mack truck,' Avery added and then took a sip.

'I know, right? I think Calista's death is about all I can handle,' Mori said sadly.

'It's a blow, for sure,' Avery agreed, closing her eyes momentarily and seeing Calista's lifeless body washed up on the shore. She wasn't sure she'd ever be able to erase that image from her mind. It already haunted her.

'It's nice to see the sun again,' Mori said, seemingly trying to shift the conversation and lift their moods.

Avery tented her eyes and gazed out to the Atlantic. Sunlight speckled like diamonds and bounced across the sea in a path leading directly toward them. The haze overhead didn't seem to prevent the sparkles from lighting up the ocean.

'Indeed. A beautiful morning.'

'You want to take a walk on the beach?' Mori asked, pushing away from the table, and rising a bit unsteadily to her feet. Avery noticed she almost missed the table when setting down her champagne flute.

She addressed Mori's lack of equilibrium by grabbing on to her elbow and steadying her before replying, 'Sure. If you're OK with it.'

Neither of them seemed to want to bring up the fact that the last time they had walked the beach merely two days prior they'd found Calista's lifeless body washed up in the tide.

Avery drained her mug and set it down on the table before following Mori to the boardwalk. A soft breeze filled her lungs with salty sea air, clearing her sinuses from the stuffiness she'd experienced the night before. A fitful night of sobbing into her pillow. She didn't share this with Mori, though; each had to grieve on their own.

'You mind if we walk the other direction from where we found her? I'm not ready . . .' Mori trailed off.

'I was hoping you would say that.' Avery linked Mori by the arm and headed in the opposite direction to where they had found Calista. They made their way to the shoreline and walked in silence, both deep in their own thoughts.

Mori leaned over and picked up a moon shell and showed it to Avery before putting it in her pocket. The tide was low, exposing the tide pools, a place not unlike the ones they often explored when they were kids.

'Calista would've loved this,' Avery said sadly. 'I can almost see her jumping in the tide pools and excited to go on another treasure hunt. I remember spending hours looking for starfish and sand dollars with her. Can't you?'

'Mmm,' Mori answered.

It was clear to Avery that Mori needed a break from talking, so she allowed that time, wondering if Mori was silently grieving too. Instead, she focused on the sights and sounds of the rolling tide as they walked. The soft sand beneath her toes and the cool water splashing around her ankles felt soothing. She thought about collecting shells along with Mori, but then realized the stench that would cause if she tucked them inside her suitcase. She decided to admire the seashells but leave them behind. A sailboat far off in the distance leaned dangerously to one side before the captain righted it. Her gaze dropped to the pool of water around her feet when a crab scurried by, stealing her attention.

Avery looked up and noticed a large white mooring buoy with a blue stripe hung up in a tide pool, and she watched as it rocked back and forth with each oncoming wave. 'Someone lost a buoy,' she said, breaking their silence.

'Yeah, and those things aren't cheap,' Mori chuckled.

'Really?'

'Yup, some of them can run up at a hundred bucks or more, if you can believe it!'

Avery moved to retrieve it from the water. 'I don't want any wildlife to get caught up,' she said, making a splashing run for it before it washed back out to sea. The buoy was stamped with *FV* and an IMO number. 'Looks like it came from a fishing boat!' she hollered back to Mori.

Mori smiled and gave a thumbs-up.

After navigating the rising tide and moving toward her friend, Avery said, 'I watched this documentary once where sea turtles were getting stuck in fishing nets by the thousands. It was so sad!'

'That's horrible. I certainly have heard how plastic is affecting our marine life in a negative way; it's often on the news down here. The fish and birds either get entangled in plastic or they're eating it. One of the sea turtles they showed had a bucket's worth of plastic in its stomach. It was so gross!' Mori replied, reaching for her phone that was suddenly pinging a message in her pocket. She held the phone up and said, 'It's Remi. She's wondering if we can pick her up at the hospital in an hour so she can come home and take a nap. She wants to wait and see what the doctor has to say first before she leaves, though, and he's not in yet.'

'Any word on Gabe?' Avery asked, moving to Mori's side.

Mori shook her head. 'Not yet. I'll wait until we get to the hospital. She mentioned she has little phone service inside the building, so she stepped outside to see if a text would go through.'

'Oh,' Avery said, gripping the buoy tighter. 'You mind if we go now? I need to make a stop.'

'Stop where?'

'I'd like to stop by the marina and see if we can find the owner of this thing.'

'Why bother?' Mori chuckled. 'Let's just throw it out!'

'Look, my friend, please don't take this the wrong way . . . I mean no harm by it. But I think you've forgotten what it's like to need to be frugal; nickel-and-diming your way through life. I mean, look at where we are?' She gestured a wide hand behind them where the cottage, which looked more like a mansion, was far off in the distance from the tide pools where they lingered.

Mori smirked.

'If these buoys are as expensive as you say, I think the local fisherman would want it back. They don't make a lot of money, Moriah. Trust me, I'm a farmer. They need every penny they can get. It won't take long to drop it off at the marina.'

'I guess.' Mori shrugged. 'If you insist.'

'I insist.' Avery grinned then, before sprinting toward the boardwalk before Mori had a chance to change her mind.

FORTY-THREE

Part of Mori didn't understand the need for it, but she acquiesced just the same. Had she become so frivolous with money that chasing down the owner of a buoy which fell from a fishing boat seemed like a complete waste of time? Heck, a couple of hundred dollars could be spent on one dinner alone back at the Vineyard. She realized that she had become awfully spoiled because it was true: it wasn't very often that Mori even gave money a second thought. Her bank account was so stuffed with cash that she didn't think twice when purchasing something. For the first time during the trip, the chasm between the lives they each led became glaringly evident.

Mori pulled into the marina and parked in the only available spot.

'You coming with me?' Avery asked.

Mori drummed her fingers on the steering wheel. 'Do you need me to?'

'No. But it would be good research for your next novel,' Avery grinned. 'You can add a hardworking fisherman into your writing. Come see if you can remember how the other half lives,' she teased.

It was as if Avery had read her mind, and Mori suddenly felt ashamed. She opened the door as her nonverbal answer before popping the trunk and gesturing Avery to remove the buoy. She did not want to pick up that stinky thing with her manicured fingernails that had most likely cost more than the buoy itself.

Mori held the door to the marina, and they were greeted by a wave of air conditioning which immediately chilled her to the bone.

An older gentleman was standing behind a polished wood counter which looked as if it belonged on the belly of the *Mayflower*. His eyes looked away from the computer in front of him to greet them.

'Mornin', ladies. What can I help you with?'

Mori looked to Avery expectantly in the hope that she would be the one to explain.

'We found this on the beach this morning,' Avery began. And then explained to the man all the reasons she needed to return it to its rightful owner. Mori found herself tuning Avery out as she scanned one wall of the marina which was filled with nautical attire for sale. Her focus only returned when the man said, 'What did you say the IMO number is?'

Avery read the number stamped on the buoy as the man clicked the keyboard with his sausage-puffed fingers.

'Ah,' he said, looking up from the computer. 'You're in luck. That belongs to *Moore Than Enough*. The owner rents a slip here, and I noticed sometimes he sleeps on the boat. I can probably take it for you and return it.'

'See,' Avery grinned at Mori, her expression gleaming with satisfaction. 'I'm glad we took the time to drop it off.'

'Yeah, he'll definitely appreciate it. That guy's had some wicked hardships,' he continued, sharing a nod and then slapping his hand on the countertop to the point it made a thud.

'Oh, no? I imagine being a fisherman is tough. I own a farm back in Iowa, and it's hard work – you have to love the lifestyle or opt out. Everything OK?' Avery wanted to know.

Mori couldn't help but wonder if Avery was just trying to prove her point further that Mori was rich and everyone else was poor. And that they had made the right decision to return it.

'Yup, he recently lost his wife and has decided he has no use for it anymore. It's wicked sad . . . he just bought the boat like a month ago.'

'Oh, that is sad,' Avery mimicked.

Meanwhile, Mori's writer senses prickled with interest. Maybe her friend was on to something, and this was a good avenue for researching her next novel. She should pay more attention.

'Thanks again, ladies,' he said, dismissing them, taking the buoy from Avery's grasp, and laying it in a corner on the floor behind him. 'I'm sure Kirk will appreciate this kind gesture,' he added over his shoulder.

A sudden chill shot down Mori's spine, and this time it wasn't from the air conditioning. She cuffed a hand beside her ear, 'Come again?'

The marina attendant turned and smiled. 'Kirk Moore – the owner of the fishing vessel, *Moore Than Enough*. He'll be wicked glad you stopped in.' He saluted them and added, 'Wicked glad indeed.'

'I bet he will,' Mori said, looping Avery by the arm in a hasty exit.

FORTY-FOUR

Remi's eyes were crusty and heavy as she leaned forward in the chair, resting her arms on her legs. One wrong movement and she would topple to the floor from pure exhaustion. She looked up at the beeping equipment beside Gabe's bed, trying to make sense of it all. Wires and tubes fanned in and out of her husband's body in a mass of tangled webbing, leaving Remi's nerves to feel just as messy. The doctor entered then, catching her attention, and she stood to greet him.

'Well?' she asked expectantly.

Dr Carrington flicked on a nearby computer screen and, with his back to her, said, 'His numbers are stable.' The doctor continued to scan the screen before turning to face her directly. 'It's a wait-and-see. You probably should go home and rest. I can call you if there's any change,' he said finally, folding his hands together and holding her gaze sympathetically.

'OK.' Remi sighed. 'I was hoping to be in the room when he wakes up.'

'I understand.' He moved a step closer and tapped her lightly on the shoulder encouragingly. 'It could be a while yet. Go on home; otherwise, you're going to end up in a bed down the hall, and we don't want that,' he said gently. 'Can I have the nurse call someone for you?' His eyes were the color of Taz's, kind and reassuring. The realization almost sent her reeling in a whole other direction.

'No, I'm OK,' she finally stumbled out. 'I've got a ride. Thanks.' She folded her arms protectively around her chest and then shifted from his gaze.

'Get some rest and take care of yourself,' he replied with a thin smile. 'This could be a long haul, and we're just at the beginning,' he added before turning on his heel and leaving her alone to the cadence of beeps.

Remi moved to Gabe's bedside and regarded the stillness of his form. So different from his constant energy and enthusiasm at the gym, he seemed almost unrecognizable to her. Careful not to disrupt any tubes, she leaned in to kiss him on the cheek and gently brushed her hand along his forehead. 'I love you,' she murmured. 'You need to pull out of this and wake up soon. Do you hear me? I need you.'

Her husband's face was expressionless. And his usual tan Florida complexion remained as pallid as the sheet that covered him.

She was talking to a ghost. An empty shell. She almost wanted to shake Gabe's arm to see if he would react, but she refrained. It would be futile.

Remi left him then and headed down the long hallway until she hit the double doors leaving the ICU. She blew a kiss over her shoulder and said a silent prayer for her husband all before reaching the elevator. When she stopped to press the button, the elevator doors opened to reveal Mori and Avery, each with a Dunkin' Donuts coffee in hand. The scent of coffee bean wafting in her direction and her friends in front of her brought a fresh wave of tears to land just behind her eyes.

Avery and Mori stepped out of the elevator, and Avery handed her a coffee. 'Looks like you can use this more than I can. Sorry, it's a large regular, but I think today you can handle the sugar and cream. You think?'

The elevator door had closed after their greeting, so they had to wait for another to make their descent.

'Thank you,' Remi replied appreciatively with a yawn and then took a sip. The coffee was still warm and, with the added sugar, tasted like coffee ice cream. She couldn't remember the last time she added sugar to her coffee. It almost made her crave a French cruller to go with it. Now that she was no longer pregnant, her splurges would return to a minimum, though, and she would work hard to get her abs back in shape. After everything she'd been through in the last few days, the idea of motherhood slid briskly to the back burner.

While they waited, Mori asked hesitantly, 'How you holding up? How's Gabe?' Her worried eyes searched Remi's face nervously, as if afraid of the answer.

'He's stable,' Remi replied. 'The doctor says it's a wait-and-see at this point. I'm praying he pulls out of this.' She sighed deeply. 'One minute at a time – that's about all we've got. I have to admit, it's really hard to see him this way.'

Mori and Avery huddled her in a hug that was reminiscent of

their high school days, and then took it a step further when they covered her with a prayer and words of encouragement.

When they parted, Remi asked, 'What have you two been up to while I've been here? Did I miss anything, or did you catch up on sleep the entire time?' She laughed wearily.

Mori and Avery exchanged a glance that made Remi's skin crawl. Despite her fatigue, she had to know. 'Oh God. What *now*?'

As soon as the elevator door closed and shielded the three of them in private conversation, Avery said, 'Remember how Mori mentioned we need to find irrefutable evidence to exonerate you?'

'Yeah?' Remi was hesitant. She knew she'd lost all credibility with her friends, and she wanted desperately to win it back. For the life of her, she didn't know how she'd ever accomplish that.

'We think we found something important,' Mori continued eagerly.

The elevator opened, and a couple stepped inside while they made their way out. Remi couldn't wait to leave the building and feel the fresh air on her face. And return to the cottage for a piece of toast or a banana. It had been hours since she had last eaten a bite, and the coffee was turning her stomach.

The three walked out of the hospital before any of them said another word. As soon as her foot hit the pavement and they were back out of earshot, Remi asked, 'Please tell me, what did you discover?'

'We think we know how Calista ended up on our beach, and it wasn't only because she was arguing with you. There's more,' Avery said, wrapping her arm around her shoulder.

'Yeah,' Mori continued. 'We found out that Kirk owns a fishing boat that he bought less than a month ago and he's already selling it.' Mori was a few steps ahead and turned back to face her. 'During the planning stages of our visit, Calista never mentioned anything about her husband buying a boat. And since he knew we were all gathering on the Cape for our reunion, Avery and I found it a bit suspicious that he had one mooring at a nearby marina. Don't you? I mean, wouldn't he have offered us a boat ride if that were the case?'

'That's not the only thing we found suspicious,' Avery added. 'According to the guy we talked to at the marina, Kirk sometimes sleeps aboard the boat, and something belonging to his vessel washed up on our shoreline.'

Remi gasped. 'Which means Kirk has been boating somewhere around the beach house! Is that what you're implying? But *why*?'

'Exactly!' Mori said, hitting the fob to unlock the SUV so they could all climb inside.

'Did you see him?' Remi asked expectantly. 'Does Kirk know you discovered any of this?'

'No, we didn't go anywhere near the boardwalk leading to the boat slips in case he was there. We didn't want to tip him off or take the chance until we had a little more time to work on our theory,' Mori replied.

'Anyhoo, it's our humble opinion that Kirk Moore had the means to kill his wife,' Avery said triumphantly. 'Now, we just need to find the motive,' she added with a click of her tongue.

'Why would Kirk want to kill Calista? Do you think he believed that she was having an affair with my husband? Or that they had slept together over twenty years ago? That seems a bit weak if you ask me,' Remi pondered. 'I seriously don't see how they were carrying on an affair if Gabe has been by my side at the gym in Florida. We're practically joined at the hip!'

Mori looked at her resolutely as soon as she clicked on her seatbelt. 'I don't know, girlfriend, but stick with me because we're going to find out.'

FORTY-FIVE

'Yup, we're going to nail him,' Avery said determinedly as she leaned against the railing of the boardwalk staring out to sea. Ever since she'd found Kirk's buoy, she'd realized Remi was innocent.

'I'm so sorry, Remi. I'm sorry I ever doubted you,' Avery said woefully.

'It's OK, I understand,' Remi replied sadly. 'I wasn't exactly forthcoming when I should've been. I was just afraid if I told you both the truth, you'd never keep searching for Calista's killer.'

Avery allowed her eyes to travel to the place where Calista's lifeless body was found and then back to her friends, before removing her shoes, rolling up the bottom of her jeans, and stepping on to the sand. She then reached to take the picnic basket filled with wine and smores supplies out of Remi's sluggish grasp.

'How are we going to prove *anything*? I don't think finding a buoy is enough. Kirk would be able to weasel out of that one.' Remi's voice sounded defeated. Although their friend had received sustenance the minute she had arrived back at the cottage and had taken a four-hour nap, she still appeared extremely discouraged. Remi had shared that as soon as she woke, she had phoned the hospital to learn there was no improvement in Gabe's condition. She then asked to stay back with them for a little bit longer before they took her back to remain at Gabe's bedside for the nightshift.

The three headed toward the campfire to discuss their next move. When they arrived, Avery dropped the picnic basket at her feet and took a matchbox from her pocket. She started the fire, silently appreciating Brody who had cleaned up their last bonfire and already set new logs in the shape of a teepee.

After settling around the roaring blaze, Remi turned to Avery and asked, 'Seriously. How are we going to go about doing this? We have no *motive* where Kirk is concerned. I don't even know where we'd begin.'

'I think we should try to get a confession out of him, because I get the impression the detective is thinking this case is closed, and clearly it's not. Don't you think we need to at least *try* to reveal the truth?' Avery replied, digging her heels into the sand. After the storm had blown through, a cold front had landed, which gave a coolness to the earth that felt good on her feet.

Mori agreed with a nod. 'We don't have much of a choice. It's probably the only way to clear your name.'

'That would be great, if only it were that easy,' Remi said wryly and then moved to warm her hands in front of the fire. Avery handed her a marshmallow at the end of a stick, causing her to smile back at her after she'd declined with a wave of her hand.

'Mori? You want a smore?' Avery asked.

Mori shook her head, and her gaze dropped to her lap where her hands were neatly folded. She then looked up abruptly. 'Wait. You have any wine in that basket?'

'Of course. I figured it would be warranted for you two,' Avery grinned.

'That's right!' Remi said impatiently, leaning in to investigate. 'Now that I'm no longer pregnant, I can have a glass! Pour one for me, please. And take it to the very top!' She grinned.

Mori smiled and reached to grab the basket from Avery's side. 'You bet!'

As Mori was pouring the wine, Remi received a phone call.

'It's the hospital!' Remi said, looking up at them with hope-filled eyes.

Avery and Mori watched with anticipation as they waited for Remi to finish the call.

The color drained from her face.

'What happened?' Avery asked.

'Gabe's taken a turn for the worse. I need to get to the hospital.'

FORTY-SIX

Remi rushed through the ICU doors, her friends close at her heels. They weren't allowed to follow her past the line, though, into the hallway of doom. The ICU had strict rules for family members only. Mori and Avery had no other choice than to wait on the plastic chairs located along the wall in front of the elevator for her to return with news.

A nurse was pushing a patient on a gurney, and Remi had to tuck against the wall for them to be able to roll past. The horror of the ICU, where people were on the verge of death, sent a sudden wave of bile to her throat and she held it back with her hand. In their entire married life, neither she nor Gabe had suffered any major health issues. The last time she had sat by Gabe's bedside in a hospital was when he'd had the bike accident decades prior. They had been lucky. They also worked tirelessly at maintaining a healthy lifestyle, so it wasn't all luck. Which made it all so unfair that he was lying in a hospital bed close to his last breath.

Remi rushed into Gabe's room where a nurse was fiddling with an IV. 'Is he OK?' she cried. Her words came out hoarse, as her mouth was growing increasingly dry. She moved her tongue over her teeth in a sad attempt to salivate.

The nurse turned and smiled encouragingly, 'We stabilized him again. At one point, we thought he might go into a coma. But your husband is a strong man. He pushed through.' The nurse then flicked the IV and took a step closer. 'You can visit with him, but only for a bit, OK? We need him to get some rest. You should probably sleep at home tonight. It would be healing for both of you.' The nurse's gaze traveled to her clothing and she must've realized Remi was still wearing the same attire as on her last visit. 'But I can give you a few minutes if you'd like.'

'I'd like that,' Remi choked out.

The nurse gave an encouraging nod before leaving her alone with her husband and the now familiar beeps which were constantly tracking Gabe's fragile grasp on life. Remi took a hesitant step closer and moved by his ear and said firmly, 'You need to get better;

I need you. You hear me? Not to worry, I'm going to fix this, Gabe. I'm gonna get that son of a bitch Kirk for you! I don't know why Calista involved you in all of this, but I'm going to get to the bottom of it and get you out of this mess. I promise you!' Fat tears tumbled from her eyes and landed on his face. Gabe flinched.

He flinched!

Remi grabbed his hand and gave an encouraging squeeze. 'Can you hear me? Gabe!'

He grunted an inaudible word in a gravelly voice. His parched lips barely parted when she heard a second attempt, which also came out as a grumble.

'*Gabe!*' Remi begged again, willing him to open his eyes and tell her. 'What did you say, honey? I'm right here!' She leaned on to his chest, her ear to his mouth, hoping for him to speak. Yet he only coughed out one word.

'*Devon.*'

FORTY-SEVEN

Mori and Avery were talking among themselves when Remi rushed through the double doors of the ICU, causing the two of them to sprint to their feet and greet her with concern-riddled expressions.

'Is he OK?' Mori asked, reaching out for her hand, giving it a comforting squeeze, and then releasing it.

'He's stable,' Remi replied hastily, rushing to press the elevator button. 'We need to hurry and get out of here! I need to talk to you guys. It's wicked important.'

Mori wondered if Remi was on the verge of a panic attack and she should alert a passing nurse. Her face was flushed and her high energy so palpable that Mori's own heart skipped a beat. Instead, the doors of the elevator closed them in, and Remi pressed the button to make their descent.

As soon as the door was completely shut and they were heading down, Remi turned to them and said excitedly, 'Gabe spoke! He spoke to me!' She held up a finger. 'One little word! But it might mean something.'

Mori and Avery blurted in unison, 'What word?' and then shared a wide grin.

'He said *Devon*.' Remi explored their expressions then in anticipation of a reply, but they hit the ground floor and the doors slid open before either could speak.

'Devon?' Mori repeated under her breath when they were rushing down the long corridor toward the exit. 'Why would Gabe bring up Calista's son, of all things?'

The three left the fluorescent lighting of the hospital and entered the dark of night as they moved across the parking lot. Mori noticed Avery was blinking her eyes rapidly to make the adjustment. 'You need a hand over there?' she asked.

'Yeah,' Avery replied as she reached out to lock arms with Remi. 'The sudden change in light just did a number on me. I'll be fine in a minute. No worries!'

'OK, then!'

A cool breeze along with low humidity caused Mori to rub a fresh eruption of goosebumps from her bare arms. When they reached the warmth of the SUV, Remi repeated what had happened at Gabe's bedside and shared that this occurred when she told her husband she'd handle Kirk and pursue justice for Calista. That was the exact point when he'd uttered Devon's name.

'Wow. That might be hard to decipher,' Mori pondered. 'When I'm writing a story, I tend to get into my character's head and try to understand their motives, to create a feel for authenticity on the page. His saying Devon's name could mean so many things if I spent any amount of time thinking about it.'

'So many things?' Remi asked. 'What do you mean?'

Mori continued, 'Well, it could mean that Gabe is concerned about Devon's welfare, that the young man will have to endure more if we pursue justice and his father is arrested. He'd lose both parents then. I'm sorry, but either way, we *will* pursue justice for Calista!' she added, banging her open palm on the steering wheel. 'Do you think he's concerned that Devon losing both parents would be too much?' She turned right out of the parking lot in the direction of the beach house.

'Or it could mean Devon's in danger? Like his mother?' Avery resumed. 'Didn't she say she had an appointment with him the morning she was due to leave for the Cape. What if Devon was involved in something? And the text, the morning she went missing, meant something else?'

'Then why involve my husband?' Remi murmured. 'That doesn't make sense to me.'

Neither Mori nor Avery had an answer to that one.

'I vote that we go to Natick first thing tomorrow morning,' Remi said eagerly. 'We need to try to find out more.'

'Do you think Kirk will even talk to us? Or will he throw us out again the minute we arrive?' Mori asked, stopping at a red light and turning to face Remi, seated next to her.

'We still need to try,' Avery said from the backseat. 'Maybe his guilt is why he was acting like a dick the last time we saw him!'

'So that's it, then? We're going on a road trip to Natick tomorrow?' Mori confirmed. Both replied with nonverbal nods.

'We have to get to the bottom of this mess,' Remi said.

'I hate to even say it aloud, but something else is kinda nagging me,' Avery said.

Mori met Avery in the rearview mirror but could barely make out her expression due to the darkness. 'What's nagging you?'

'What if Gabe said Devon's name because he knows something we don't?'

'Such as?' Remi wanted to know.

'What if it means Devon had something to do with his mother's murder? He was eerily calm the day we met him.'

'You think Devon killed his mother?'

'We can't eliminate anyone at this point. Can we?'

'Either way, we're going to find out the truth!' Mori said with conviction. Though if she was honest, she wasn't quite sure if she was ready to uncover the lie.

FORTY-EIGHT

Anticipation inside the vehicle was high and electric when the three arrived in front of 15 Oak Circle, in Natick, Massachusetts. This time, the yard was not peppered with police presence, nosy neighbors, or the press. It was seven a.m., and an early-morning mist hung over the manicured lawns like an eerie ghost, as if an uncomfortably humid day was en route. Avery wondered if Calista's spirit was among them and would help bring her killer to justice.

The three had decided to leave the Cape early in the hope of catching Kirk completely off guard, and when they pulled up against the curb in the quiet cul-de-sac, it looked as if they had succeeded. Because it was so disturbingly quiet, it seemed as if the entire neighborhood was fast asleep.

Avery held up her Android, waved it in the air, and confirmed, 'We all have our phones ready? Yes?' She hoped one would provide backup as her outdated phone wasn't the latest model.

'Check!' Remi said from the backseat.

'I have mine ready,' Mori added with a hint of apprehension to her tone.

'At least if two of us are recording, we'll have a better shot at getting something on tape,' Avery said firmly. 'Hopefully, we'll discover something that might help us pursue the next lead. Or which way to turn in this investigation. Who wants to record and who wants to keep Detective Reed on speed dial?'

'I'll take Reed; you two handle the recording,' Mori said quietly.

'Good. We're ready to move according to plan, then.'

'I really hope Devon had nothing to do with it. That's the worst-case scenario,' Remi said sadly. 'When we met him, I was struck by what a nice young man he was and how proud Calista must've been of her son. I just can't accept that possibility; it's too hard for me.'

'I agree,' Avery said, trying to remain calm and ready for the task at hand. 'But we need to solve her murder, and that's what we must focus on right now. Discovering the next step and keeping an open mind.'

'OK,' Remi said quietly. 'I guess whatever we learn today, we'll have to make peace with it.'

'Are we planning to ring the doorbell? Or do you want me to block the driveway so he can't get his car out to go to work, and he'll have no other choice than to face us?' Mori asked.

'That sounds a little dramatic. Let's go to the door,' Remi suggested. 'I'm not sure I want his neighbors witnessing this conversation if things get loud. And he wasn't exactly cordial the last time we were in his company.'

Avery nodded assent. 'I say we do both. Block the driveway too, so he can't try to run away from us when we corner him.'

'OK.' Mori maneuvered the vehicle away from the curb to park horizontally across the driveway, preventing Kirk or anyone else for that matter from passing.

'Well, that took a weird turn. Suddenly, we're the SWAT team too now?' Remi uttered from the backseat.

'Let's just do this before we overthink it or lose our cool.' Avery opened the door before either of them could protest further. Her hands were clammy with anticipation and almost slipped off the handle. She really hoped this plan would work. Otherwise, Remi and Gabe would most certainly be on the chopping block, and she wasn't sure how she'd handle that and go on with her life back in Iowa.

The three moved quickly up the pathway leading to the front door, which was flanked with vibrant blue summer blooms. A lump rose in Avery's throat at the thought that their friend had most likely planted those gorgeous perennial bushes. She watched in what seemed like slow motion as Mori rang the doorbell and Kirk opened the door wide. A perplexing look washed across his face as soon as he caught wind of them. He didn't greet them with a smile; instead, he asked, 'What are you three doing here? Haven't you done enough damage?'

'Kirk, can we come in?' Avery pushed past him, not giving him the chance to say no. He looked utterly shocked at her brazen behavior, but Avery didn't care. She needed answers so she could get back to Iowa to her family and face her own new blind reality.

'Is Devon here?' Remi asked, stepping in behind Avery with Mori close on her heels.

'He's still asleep after working the late shift. Why are you looking for my son?'

Neither of them answered his question. The three of them just found themselves looking around for a place to land as Kirk wasn't exactly welcoming them inside.

'What's this about?' Kirk asked, raking his hand through his hair. 'Why are you here?'

'You mind if we visit with you in your living room or around the kitchen table?' Avery asked. 'My back is hurting me,' she fibbed. And then instantly a wave of her conversation with Remi washed over her in shame, and how Remi vehemently maintained that they all were liars. Avery's face momentarily burned. She shook her head to recalibrate and then glanced into the living room where gleaming hardwood floors looked so polished that she wondered if anyone had ever stepped inside the room. Had Calista cleaned them with her own hand? Or did they hire a housekeeper?

'Fine.' Kirk seemed to understand they weren't going anywhere until they had a chance to talk. 'If we must,' he said resignedly. 'Follow me.' He led them into a spacious kitchen which looked as if it had recently been remodeled to the nines with gleaming granite countertops and shiny stainless-steel appliances. It made Avery's farmhouse kitchen back home look like something resurrected from a rummage sale. She wondered if Calista had made the selections, or if it had been Kirk who had chosen the flawless design.

When the four of them settled around the oversized kitchen table, Avery became aware of the scent of coffee in the air. She almost wanted to ask for a cup but dared not break the spell. Solemness hung in the air like a storm cloud hovering over them, waiting to burst forth at a moment's notice.

'I don't know why you're here and, to be frank, I'm not sure it's wise.' Kirk flicked a look of disgust in Remi's direction and added, 'Especially since it seems your husband was responsible for my wife's death.'

Remi did as she was told and acted according to plan. She did not object to Kirk's musings. They had discussed this at length en route from the Cape; that Remi would remain submissive and say very little, if anything at all. They thought if they could get Kirk to think they also believed Gabe responsible, he might be more forthcoming.

'You can't blame Remi for her husband's choices,' Mori interjected.

Remi's gaze dropped shamefully, and her neck turned a deep shade of red. Avery could tell her friend wanted to pounce across the table and grab Kirk by the jugular. She held back, though, and took silent breaths. Avery was impressed with her friend's ability to maintain her composure.

'Kirk, did Detective Reed tell you that?' Avery asked, blinking back at him, and then leaning on to the table to stop her vision from playing tricks on her once again. It was horrible timing for her eyes to fail her now.

Mori must've sensed Avery struggling and repeated the sentence on her behalf, 'Did the police tell you that Gabe was responsible?'

Kirk nodded. He then turned his attention back to Remi. 'How is your husband, by the way? I heard there was a chance he wouldn't make it after the suicide attempt. Do you think he'll pull through?'

Avery caught his hesitant demeanor – almost as if he didn't want his old friend to make it. Besides that, taking a cue from Mori's playbook, he chose one little word that seemed off-putting.

The.

For some reason, it made her mind whirl. Kirk had stated after *the* suicide attempt, not after *his* suicide attempt.

Did that mean something? Or was she reaching?

Avery looked to Mori to confirm. Instead, Remi interrupted her thoughts when she shrugged and murmured, 'Even if he does pull through, it looks like he'll be going to jail. And I'll be heading for divorce court.'

Avery nudged Remi's foot beneath the table to let her know she was doing a good job. She didn't flinch at all at this. *Man,* she was a good liar!

'I'm sorry, Remi. I guess I'm not the only victim here,' Kirk said, turning his tone sympathetic then and meeting her gaze. 'Have you spoken to him? Or is he still in a coma?'

'He was never in a coma.'

A look of shock? Or was it disappointment that clearly washed across Kirk's face. A heady pause ensued before he spoke again. 'He wasn't?'

'No. And to answer your question' – Remi met him squarely – 'he only talked to me about one thing. Which is why we're here.'

Kirk's brow rose in question. 'Oh? And what was that?'

'Your son, Devon.'

It felt to Avery as if all the air had left the room as she waited in anticipation. She discreetly reached into her pocket and glanced below the table to be sure her phone was recording. This propelled her to return her attention to Mori then, who gave a nondescript nod of her head. Mori had understood the nonverbal.

Avery knew that Mori had phoned the detective, and Reed, too, would hopefully catch every word.

Kirk's demeanor instantly shifted to uncomfortable when his leg bounced so hard it caused the entire table to vibrate. 'Gabe told you that Devon is his?' he asked, his face stricken. His shoulders then slumped in defeat.

Remi gasped. '*What?*'

Kirk's eyes shot up to meet Remi's and then doubled in size. 'You mean, you didn't know? That Gabe is Devon's father?'

Remi's jaw was rigid, and her expression tightened. 'No. Not until right now, I didn't.'

You could hear a pin drop between them, and Avery fought for composure at hearing this shocking news. Mori had mentioned that Gabe and Calista had shared a past; now she understood why Gabe was involved. He had learned about his son. Things were quickly rolling forward in her mind. *A motive.*

Mori coughed into her fist, breaking the silence, and said, 'Now that we know about Devon and Gabe being biologically linked, it makes sense why Gabe made the trip to Massachusetts, but what isn't clear, and I still don't understand, is why you would involve your son in your wife's murder? Why would you do that to Devon when he has his whole life in front of him? Are you taking this out on him? It's not his fault!'

'What are you talking about?' Kirk spat.

'You led your son to slaughter. You led Devon to kill her,' Avery said sadly. 'He has motive, means, but when did he take the opportunity to do this? The police will subpoena his work records; they'll see he wasn't where he was supposed to be . . .'

'Absolutely not!' Kirk's leg suddenly stopped bouncing and he leaned his weight on the table. 'You don't know what you're talking about! My son is not involved. He doesn't know that Gabe is his biological father. And now that Gabe will be found responsible for Calista's death, I don't think it would be wise to tell him. It would be devastating, and Devon has been through enough. You must understand, he's still my son. I raised him!' he added vehemently. 'Don't you dare involve yourselves in this!'

'I finally understand. You set Calista up. You never planned on her reaching Remi to tell her Gabe was Devon's father. Did you? You planned to kill Calista so Devon would never find out the truth! And then Gabe ruined things by showing up in Massachusetts,' Avery said, putting all the pieces together in her mind. She heard a gasp and then looked up. The horror on her face must've led them all to do the same.

Because Devon stepped into the room. His eyes lasered in on Kirk. 'No . . . no . . .' he whispered, shaking his head in disillusionment and gazing at his father in utter shock. The sheer lack of volume in his tone caused the room to go silent.

'Devon!' Kirk leapt from his seat and reached to greet his son, but it was too late.

Devon stood motionless, as motionless as his mother had been when they'd found her washed ashore and lying in the tide.

'You did this. You killed my mother.'

FORTY-NINE

'Devon, you have it all wrong,' Kirk pleaded. 'That's not what happened!'

'I can't believe you did this! No! No! No!' Devon put his hands over his ears and cowered as if he wanted to put a halt to Kirk's words.

'Listen to me!' Kirk reached for Devon, but his son shook him off in disgust.

'Don't touch me!'

Mori looked at her friends and their expressions mirrored her own. Pure sadness. She didn't know what to say. Nor what to do. Happy they'd finally come to a resolution, sad that it came to this.

'The police are on their way, Kirk. You may as well just give it up,' Avery said quietly.

A look of sheer terror met Kirk's eyes before he pinched the bridge of his nose and stuttered, 'Don't listen to them, Devon. Gabe did this, Gabe killed Calista!'

'Say it all you want, Kirk. We know you're lying!' Remi spat.

'Remi's right, Kirk. I'm just sad that Calista's death was in vain,' Mori murmured aloud, causing everyone seated at the table to look in her direction.

'Huh?' Kirk asked. 'What the hell do you mean by that?'

Remi's sentiment had reminded Mori once again about the conversation with her about lies, and how dangerous those lies could be.

And how lies could lead to murder.

She took the opportunity that presented itself and continued, 'Avery's right. You killed Calista so that Devon would never learn you're not his real father. There must have been so much rage inside of you when you discovered your best friend had shared a past with your wife. That they'd *lied* to you. That for years they kept this secret hidden from you,' Mori said empathetically. 'You didn't know! But Calista knew and she hid it from you. Didn't she?'

'You're right. That bitch lied to me all those years,' Kirk said through gritted teeth. 'Our entire marriage was a lie!' he added, his eyes growing wild as he pounded the table with both fists. 'And she deserved everything she got!'

'You killed her because of it,' Avery said calmly.

'Damn right I did!' he spewed before realizing what he'd said. His face was riddled with fear. He attempted to backtrack, but it was too late. The damage was done. 'No, that's not what happened.' He shook his head wildly. 'She did this. *Calista* did this to us!' He looked at Devon who sadly hung his head while fat tears began to fall from the young man's eyes.

'She ruined us!' Kirk continued. But his pathetic words now fell on deaf ears.

'Yeah, you murdered Calista and then framed my husband for it, you son of a bitch!' Remi spat.

Mori couldn't believe Kirk had actually confessed before the pounding on the door began. 'Police! Open up!'

Devon turned on his heel and, with shoulders hunched, wordlessly abandoned the kitchen to greet them.

'Kirk, you have no way out of this; we have your confession on tape.' Avery held up her phone for him to see and was met with an expression of shock. 'But I have one last question. Why didn't you try to kill Gabe at the Blackwells' cottage? Why bring him back to the woods?'

'I never planned it . . . I didn't.' Kirk sighed and dragged his hand across his face wearily.

'You panicked? That's why you shot my husband?' Remi asked.

'No. Gabe escaped from the cottage, and the idiot returned to the nature reserve to search for Calista's phone, but I fought him for it. He said he was going to prove his innocence, but I couldn't let that happen. This is his fault. Gabe left me no choice.'

Mori could tell Remi was growing tired of this line of questioning regarding her husband and shot Avery a look to let it drop.

After Devon had let them inside, a team of officers flocked upon them and rushed to handcuff Kirk and read his Miranda rights.

Mori was never so glad to see the authorities in her entire life.

FIFTY

Remi could hardly wait to enter the hospital to check on Gabe and share her findings. She was desperate to talk with him when the nurse called to inform her that he was alert. As soon as she stepped inside the hospital room, Gabe turned in her direction.

'Gabe! Oh! My baby! You're awake!' Tears streamed down Remi's cheeks as she ran to greet him. She threw her arms around his neck and held him tight before meeting him nose to nose.

'Ouch,' Gabe grunted. 'Easy there!'

'Oh dear! I'm sorry! Too tight?'

'It's OK,' Gabe replied, shifting in the bed as if trying to get comfortable yet still harboring a ton of pain. He winced and held his chest for a moment before sharing a wobbly smile. 'I'll survive.'

Remi took a seat beside him on the bed, reached for his hand, and held it tight. She searched his eyes when she said, 'We got him, Gabe! We got him! You need to get better because Kirk is going to jail for the rest of his God-given life over this! And you and I need to get back to our lives in Florida. I swear, I'm never taking another trip again!' she added before releasing his hand.

Gabe's brow rose then and wrinkled in question. 'Honey, I think I have some explaining to do,' he said sadly.

'No,' Remi shook her head. 'I already know. That Devon is your son, and Calista hid it from you all these years. What I don't understand, though, is why you are here in Massachusetts? Why did you come? And why the hell didn't you respond to my texts?' she said with an undercurrent of teasing tone and a poke of her finger.

'I'm sorry,' he replied, sending her puppy-dog eyes. 'Can you forgive me?'

'Yeah, but please tell me what happened. That's where I'd like an explanation.'

'Calista flew me out here,' he began. 'She talked me into coming. When she told me at the airport that Devon was my son, Remi, I lost it. The shock! I couldn't make sense of anything. We left Logan Airport and started to drive to the Cape to tell you everything, and

I about freaked. I had a massive panic attack. Worst one ever! Calista wanted to take me to the hospital, but I convinced her I just needed some strong liquor and time to rest and gather my thoughts before I saw you. She brought me to a hotel where we spent the night – in separate beds, I promise!'

At this point, that was the least of Remi's concerns. After sharing a weak smile, she rolled her hand for him to continue. 'I get it. Go on.'

'While I was resting back at the hotel, Calista left to pick up food and a bottle of bourbon for me. She said she discovered that Kirk was following us, because when she got back, she swore she saw his car exiting the hotel parking lot.'

'Ah . . .' Remi interjected. 'I'm guessing after picking up your bourbon, that's when she must've stopped over to talk to me on the beach. Either way, I guess it doesn't really matter now . . . Because that's the last conversation Calista and I will ever have.' Her eyes misted and her gaze turned downcast.

'I know,' he whispered. 'I still can't believe she's gone.'

'Me either. This entire trip is so unreal.'

Gabe sighed heavily and then the two locked eyes once again. He wiped a tear before it fully dropped from her eye.

Remi collected herself and said, 'I'm sorry, I disrupted your train of thought – we need to push through this and get it off your chest. You mentioned Kirk was following you?'

'Yeah, the next morning, we decided to confront him, so we pulled into a nature reserve, hoping we could talk it out. Kirk had a gun, Remi. He was waving it around, saying he couldn't believe we stopped at a hotel instead of driving straight to the Cape to talk to you. He just assumed we were picking up where we left off in high school. Kirk was so pissed. He was wild!'

Remi reached for his hand again and gave it a comforting squeeze. 'I hear you, honey. You poor thing. I can't believe you had to go through all of this without me. I should've been with you.'

'No! I'm glad you weren't a part of it. It was awful!' A fresh look of fear washed across Gabe's face, as if he didn't want to relive the entire ordeal, but he needed to unload all that had happened just the same and looked to her eagerly. 'I begged Calista to run, but Kirk grabbed her before she got a chance. I warned him that if he shot her, there'd be evidence. I tried everything to talk him out of killing her, but it only angered him further!' he croaked.

'I understand honey. Shhh, it's OK. If this is upsetting you . . . Maybe we ought to talk about it later, when you're on the mend.' Remi hoped to soothe him, but it only riled Gabe up even more.

'No, it's not OK. You need to hear the truth! I'm sick of all the lies!'

'I can see that,' she said softly. She hoped lowering her tone would help mellow the situation, but Gabe was clearly on a roll when more explanations fell from his tongue.

'Kirk aimed the gun at me and a shot rang off and I fell to the ground. I knew I'd been hit because I had blood running down my arm. Honestly, the bullet barely nicked my shoulder. Remi, that's when he got the upper hand! When I looked down at my wound, he stunned me by hitting me over the head with the butt of the gun. He was so manic! Screaming and cursing and rambling to himself what to do next! That's when he ripped the lanyard off my neck, and he used it to strangle Calista. Right in front of me! Kirk said if they found the lanyard, it would link her murder to me. I tried to grab the gun, Remi, I did! Instead, he shot it in the air again like a deranged man. All I could think about was our baby . . . and protecting you. I panicked and tried to run! All the while, he kept screaming at me, "You did this! You did this!"'

Gabe's eyes were as wide as saucers as he recounted the memory. Remi couldn't believe what she was hearing but needed to learn the awful truth leading to her friend's demise.

'Oh my God . . . Gabe . . .' Remi held her heart and asked, 'What about Calista? How?'

'Kirk caught up with me because I was dizzy from my head injury and running while holding my wounded shoulder. He held the gun to my head. He forced me to put Calista's lifeless body in the trunk of his car. I didn't have a choice, Remi! He didn't give me a choice!' Tears began to form in Gabe's eyes, and he scrubbed his hand over his face, as if he wanted to erase the memory.

'I'm so sorry you had to go through this. It's gut-wrenching to hear this . . . so I can't imagine living through it.'

'When I convinced him that if the police found me, they'd find him too, he decided to hide me away at the Blackwells' old place over in Sandwich until he decided what to do with me. That's when I escaped and came to see you in the hospital. Remi! I tried to find Calista's phone to prove everything, I really tried! But he was following me the entire time.'

'It's OK, sweetheart,' she soothed. 'You're with me now.'

'No! It's not OK! It'll never be OK! That's when he found me back at the nature reserve and tried to kill me. I ran, but he shot me! The son of a bitch shot me!'

Gabe began to tremble then, as if suffering from PTSD, and Remi realized she might have taken it too far, as a nurse rushed into the room with a worried expression.

'What's going on in here?' she scolded. 'He needs to rest. You need to stop this right now!' The nurse then ordered her out of the room, and she called the girls to immediately pick her up.

Remi had a great deal to share with them.

It was their last night on the Cape, and the three had decided to enjoy one last evening at the beach and host a mini fortieth birthday party in Calista's honor. They were sitting around the campfire, eating chocolate cake, while the stars twinkled above. When the nostalgic sound of Coldplay came out of the boombox, Mori turned the volume up. The boombox, which she'd resurrected from her basement and packed for the trip as a fun flashback of memorabilia from their youth, was now tuning into a host of memories. She stood to dance to the music, and Remi joined her, while Avery looked on with a wide smile. When the song ended, Mori, out of breath, reached to turn down the volume and Remi stopped her with an outstretched hand. 'Hang on . . . wait!'

Charges were filed today against the husband of Calista Moore . . .

They stopped momentarily to listen intently to the local news floating across the radio waves.

'We did it. We nailed him!' Mori said with sweet satisfaction that quickly turned to sadness as the true weight of loss washed over their group again. Blinking back tears, Mori raised her wineglass in a toast and added, 'To Calista. Happy birthday, my friend. We've always got your back' – she looked to the girls – 'and each other's,' then took a hefty sip of Chardonnay.

'To Calista!' Remi and Avery chimed in, clinking glasses.

'I feel so much better that Detective Reed wasn't too upset with me that I found and stole Kirk's phone from the nature reserve,' Remi grimaced. 'I'm glad he's not pressing charges.'

'Nah, he wouldn't. That was just one more thing to help solidify his case. It'll help him prove that Kirk was following Gabe and Calista everywhere they went. *Before* Kirk had kidnapped Gabe and brought him to the Blackwells' cottage and left that fake suicide note. And then following him back to the nature reserve to make it look like he'd been hiding out there all along.'

'Speaking of the investigation, did they ever find out why Jerome's beachcomber didn't see Calista lying there?' Avery asked.

Mori shrugged. 'Sounds like they think Kirk dumped our friend in the water and she washed up to shore after they had already combed the beach.'

'I'm just glad we were able to prove Gabe wasn't involved, and you can get your life back on track,' Avery said with a tilt of her glass toward Remi.

Remi's phone pinged a text interrupting them. 'Speak of the devil. Gabe says I should stay here with you guys tonight. He wants to watch the Red Sox while we're still in town. *Boring!*' she laughed.

'He's getting back on his feet, then?' Avery asked cautiously.

'Are you kidding me? He has those nurses over at the hospital wrapped around his little finger!' Remi laughed again easily.

It was the first time in a long while she'd heard an ease to Remi's laughter, and it warmed Mori from the inside out. 'Did you guys want to tape a note to your sky lanterns?'

'I don't think so; I think I'll just say a prayer for her,' Remi replied, reaching for the box and handing each of them a lantern and then Mori a long-handled BIC lighter.

'Same,' Avery nodded after digging her wineglass down into the sand in front of her to hold it still while she fiddled with her lantern.

They moved away from the campfire and walked to the place where Calista had lain. The place they had found her motionless in the sand. The place where their lives had changed forever.

'I love you, Cal. Save a spot for us up there, will ya?' Mori said silently in her heart as she flicked a flame to light inside her lantern. And then she handed Remi the lighter to do the same.

The three watched as the lanterns floated to the sky and into the twinkling stars above.

Somewhere.

Out there.

In the heavens.

Where their friend, Calista, was watching over them.

EPILOGUE

Mori Hart chanced a peek from the far side of the auditorium curtain. From her vantage point, she couldn't locate even *one* empty seat. The place was packed tighter than Gillette Stadium on a New England Patriots game day. After reaching into her purse and digging out a Xanax, she chased the pill down with the last drop of water left in her Evian bottle. Rumbles of conversation reverberated from the other side of the curtain in anticipation of her introduction, causing her stomach to erupt in fresh butterflies. She wiped sweaty palms on her silk skirt, hoping it wouldn't leave a stain, and tried but failed to even her breath before toying with her two-carat diamond necklace. The celebratory necklace Jerome had purchased when her latest book was optioned for film rights.

'There you are! I've been looking for you. You ready for this?' The sound of her agent's voice caused her to spin on her high heels and paste a smile. Riley Chase was top in the publishing industry, and she was his most valuable client. He was wearing a sharp dark suit with a hot-pink pocket square. The suit matched his equally dark slicked hair, which was held in place perfectly with hair gel. And his smile radiated as if he'd just won the lottery. And he had. When she had dropped her previous agent, he'd won her.

If Mori had been honest, she'd reply with a *Hell, no, Riley . . . I'm not ready! Nor will I ever be!* But she couldn't be that honest; she had to exude confidence. Instead, she squared her shoulders, expecting the diazepam to do its job by the time she had to speak to the crowd, and replied, 'Of course, Riley. I've been waiting my entire life for this moment.' And then gave him her most winning smile.

'The table is set up for the book signing after your talk, and your assistant is ready with a slew of brand-new pens. A quick restroom break and then right to the table. OK? Prepare your fingers, I'm sure you'll be signing for hours; we have a full crowd here tonight. So don't disappear on me,' he warned with a raised brow and a smile.

Her agent knew her well. She'd be jonesing for a flask of wine the minute her feet left the stage. But that wouldn't be possible. She would have to wait.

'I wouldn't think of it,' Mori said, and she meant it. She had waited a long time to have a bestseller under her belt that she could be proud of. One that wasn't filled with raunchy sex scenes from the opening paragraph. *Killer Beach* had performed exactly the way she'd hoped and currently held number one for the eighteenth week on the *New York Times* Bestseller list.

Before long, introductions were made and Mori found herself abandoning Riley with a peck to his cheek and a long walk across the stage, her high heels announcing her every movement. When she reached the microphone, she looked out into the sea of faces and caught Jerome's wide smile. Jerome was seated front and center in the first row, which is exactly where she had placed him, knowing that his encouragement would help overcome her nerves. She sent him a mirrored smile before clearing her throat and beginning her speech.

'Thank you all for coming tonight. What a crowd!' Mori took a half step backward to take the scene in and then lifted praying hands together in gratitude. The gesture made those in attendance clap more loudly. Her eyes were blinded by the bright light shining on her face, but she could still make out an auditorium full of people that was way beyond anything she could count. The crowd erupted in applause and whistles. 'Truly, I'm humbled!' she said again, which only caused the applause to roar louder still. So strange to her that readers expected writers to excel at public speaking. The two went no more together than ice cream and tight jeans. Mori had to remind herself that these people had called her here. They wanted to hear her story. They wanted to hear her speak.

She could do this.

When the hush of the auditorium finally ensued, Mori said, 'The number-one question I'm always asked by readers is: where did *Killer Beach* originate? Or what was the inspiration behind the novel? Well, in all honesty, my inspiration is sitting among you tonight.' It was then Mori looked beyond Jerome to the real Calista, the real Remi, and the real Avery, and shared an inconspicuous wink. The world knew them by these chosen names. But Mori knew them as something else. She knew them as her friends. Friends that flung her a life raft and helped save her career with a week-long trip to the Cape.

'Three special guests flew halfway across the US and are joining us here tonight.' Mori paused, smiled at them, and continued, 'Each one of them has had a profound impact on this work. Please allow me to explain. It all began when I organized a reunion between lifelong friends that was twenty years overdue. When my plan finally came to fruition, the four of us were sitting around a campfire on the shores of Cape Cod discussing my tanking career and how I was desperate to make a change. All I can say is truth is stranger than fiction.'

The room erupted in laughter.

'In all honesty, what led me to write this was a candid conversation about transparency.' Mori held her fingers in air quotes. 'I wanted to explore the impact of those "little white lies." You know the ones – those little fibs we all brush off as being no big deal. And the carnage left behind because of them. Because truth is, there is no "little" lie. Is there? Lies are as dark and deep as the blackened ocean at midnight. And the longer a lie has to sit and fester, the bigger it gets. When we lie to ourselves or lie to the people around us, it shames us. Lies sabotage our relationships and blow a bomb through trust. It can cause us to want to hide. It can cause us to be fake on social media. No one really knows us – not really. I'm not here to preach. All I'm saying is, if you find a friend with whom you can be your true self, you've found a rare gift – a treasure. There is no greater gift than being transparently seen. And I was lucky enough to find three of them with whom I share this story.'

Mori couldn't help but seek Calista in the crowd then, whose hand was tightly woven with Gabe's, their son seated next to them. And Remi and Taz sat directly beside them. And Avery too, with her eyes closed but listening as she leaned her head on Jack's shoulder.

Was it truth or fiction? The audience in front of her would never know.

Acknowledgments

This is one of those rare books that haunted me for years. I was working on juggling other manuscripts, and this story just kept begging to be told and bothered me at every turn. So much so that I had to sneak it in whenever possible. I'm hoping now that the work is finally on paper, I can move on to the next book in the series. Thank you, Laurie, for taking this under your wing and bringing your extraordinary talent along with it. And my team at Severn House – over fifty years of publishing and you chose me. I'm humbled to collaborate with you. Thank you, Jem, the cover is flawless and exactly what Laurie and I envisioned!

There are so many friends who cheered me on during the writing of this book and I so appreciate you! Including but not limited to: Amy, Jean, Tracy, Jill, Tanya, Kel, Julie, Darci H, and Darci R, Linda . . . thanks especially for my beta readers and authors Paige, Liz, Darci, and Tracy, willing to take precious time to read for me. Your notes helped me sharpen my pencil! To all the bookstagrammers, reviewers, librarians, booksellers (whom I now call friends) and who share the love of books with me, I humbly thank you from the bottom of my heart. Sandy, thank you for giving me the chance to try. (I know the crystal ball thing, but I still had to attempt it. Haha.) And yet here we are . . . all because of your efforts! This book is dedicated to YOU!! Mark, I don't know how many other ways I can say it. Your support is endless and your love as limitless as you believe I can soar. Thank you seems inadequate; I'm blessed to have you by my side.